Praise for the Five Realms series

'Will entertain everyone: *Podkin One-Ear* already feels like **a classic**.'
BookTrust

'The **best book** I have ever read.'
Mariyya, age 9, Lovereading4kids

'Jolly good fun.'
SFX

'I just couldn't put it down.'
Sam, age 11, Lovereading4kids

'Five stars.'
Dylan, age 12, Lovereading4kids

'Great stuff and definitely **one to watch**.'
Carabas

'An original fantasy with . . . **riveting adventure**, and genuine storytelling.'
Kirkus

'**A joy to read** and absolutely **world-class**.'
Alex, age 10, Lovereading4kids

'A **great** bit of storytelling.'
Andrea Reece, Lovereading4kids

'Rich with custom, myth, and a little touch of **magic**.'
Carousel

'A story for children who enjoy fantasy, quests (and of course rabbits).'
The School Li

FABER AND FABER has published children's books since 1929. Some of our very first publications included *Old Possum's Book of Practical Cats* by T. S. Eliot starring the now world-famous Macavity, and *The Iron Man* by Ted Hughes. Our catalogue at the time said that 'it is by reading such books that children learn the difference between the shoddy and the genuine'. We still believe in the power of reading to transform children's lives.

About the Author

Kieran Larwood has loved fantasy stories since reading *The Hobbit* as a boy. He graduated from Southampton University with a degree in English Literature and then worked as a Reception class teacher for fifteen years. He has just about recovered. He now writes full-time although, if anybody was watching, they might think he just daydreams a lot and drinks too much coffee.

About the Illustrator

David Wyatt lives in Devon. He has illustrated many novels but is also much admired for his concept and character work. He has illustrated tales by a number of high-profile fantasy authors such as Diana Wynne Jones, Terry Pratchett, Philip Pullman and J. R. R. Tolkien.

The Five Realms Series

The Legend of Podkin One-Ear

The Gift of Dark Hollow

The Beasts of Grimheart

Uki and the Outcasts

Kieran Larwood

Illustrated by David Wyatt

First published in 2019
by Faber & Faber Limited
Bloomsbury House,
74–77 Great Russell Street,
London WC1B 3DA

Typeset in Times by M Rules
Printed by CPI Group (UK) Ltd, Croydon CR0 4YY

A CIP record for this book
is available from the British Library

ISBN 978–0–571–34279–2

2 4 6 8 10 9 7 5 3 1

For Ethan

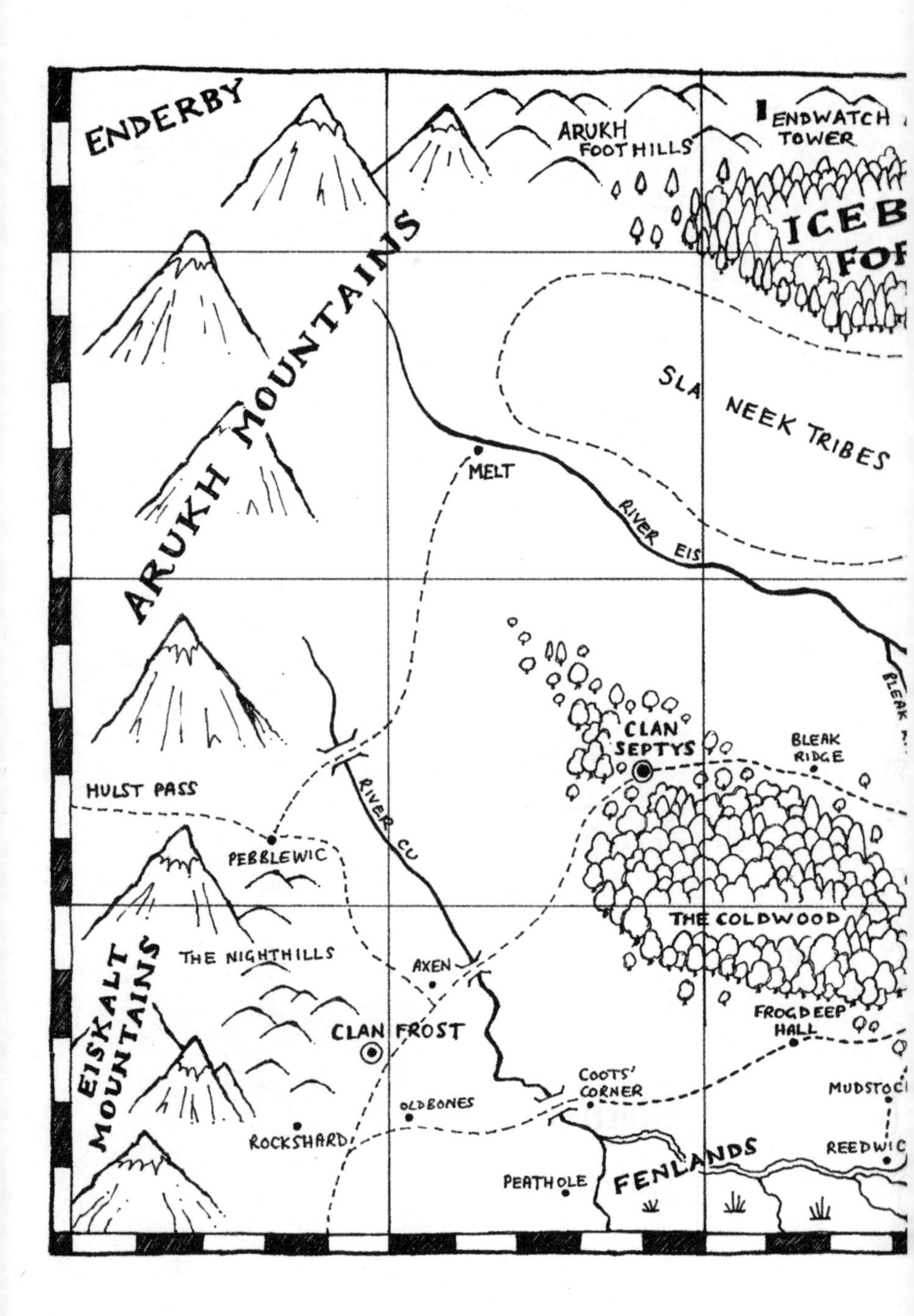

ENDERBY
ARUKH MOUNTAINS
ARUKH FOOTHILLS
ENDWATCH TOWER
ICEB
FOR
SLA NEEK TRIBES
MELT
RIVER EIS
BLEAK
CLAN SEPTYS
BLEAK RIDGE
HULST PASS
RIVER CU
PEBBLEWIC
THE COLDWOOD
THE NIGHTHILLS
AXEN
EISKALT MOUNTAINS
CLAN FROST
FROGDEEP HALL
COOTS' CORNER
OLDBONES
MUDSTOC
ROCKSHARD
FENLANDS
REEDWIC
PEATHOLE

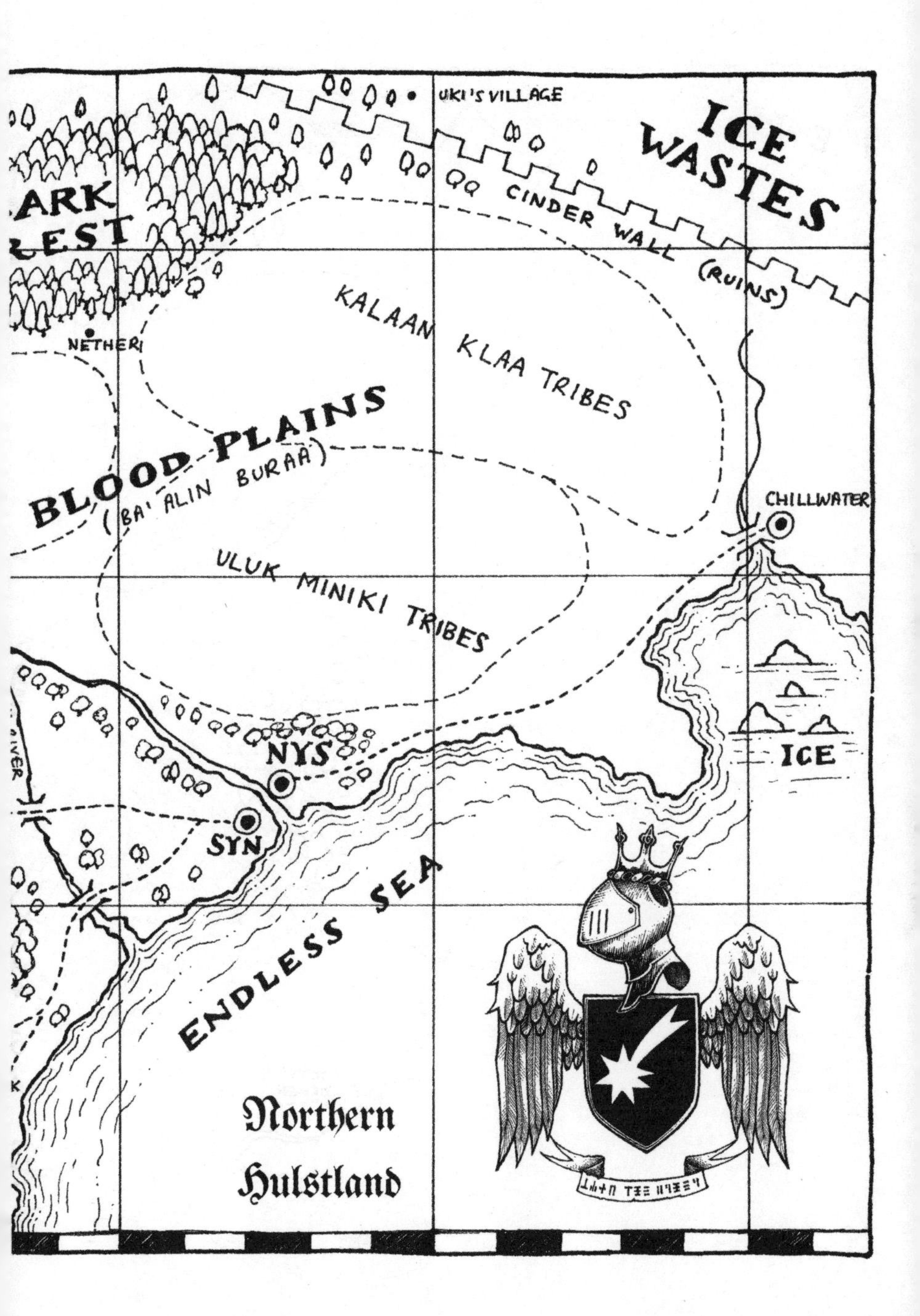
UKI'S VILLAGE
ICE WASTES
ARK
REST
CINDER WALL (RUINS)
NETHERI
KALAAN KLAA TRIBES
BLOOD PLAINS
(BA'ALIN BURAA)
CHILLWATER
ULUK MINIKI TRIBES
NYS
SYN
ICE
ENDLESS SEA
Northern
Hulstland

Prologue

In the Five Realms, even the loneliest places have their secrets.

There is a good one, a dark one, hidden at the edge of the Icebark Forest, in the realm known as Hulstland.

Once a long strip of nothing – a mish-mashed mess of plains, swamps, forests and woodland – Hulstland was stitched together, long ago, by a rabbit called Cinder.

He started off as a chieftain, then became a king, then an emperor.

He gathered all the rabbit tribes and breeds and told them they belonged to him. Everyone from the Merel River to the edge of the Ice Wastes. And just to make a point, he built a wall across the top of the kingdom to keep them all in (and those scary Ice-Waste rabbits out).

The Cinder Wall has crumbled now – just a few broken battlements poking out of the snow. And next to it, the forest.

Not a green, thriving, rooty throng of tendrils and leaves like Grimheart. A cold, bare-branched thing, with ground as hard as iron, and thick, hoary frost covering the trees.

That is where the name Icebark comes from, and it is a harsh, unfriendly place.

The odd crow flaps between the branches. Small, skinny, white-furred foxes dart here and there, sniffing out shrews and mice under the crusts of dead leaves, interrupting their sweet sleeps with a horrible *crunch* and *chomp.*

But the secret . . .

At the forest's edge, where the trees are thin and straggly, is a tower.

Squat and stocky, it sits upon a hill, surrounded by toppled heaps of stone that might once have been buildings. Smudges of soot cover everything. The blackened outlines of old roofs jut upwards, the empty holes of windows and doorways gape. Whatever was once here, it was burnt and smashed to rubble a long, long time ago.

All except the tower itself. Whoever built it, built it well. The walls are thick, the mortar strong. There are four windows at the top, one on each side, all with a carved eye above, staring out over the lifeless forest and the plains beyond.

There are few rabbits that live this far north, but they all know of the place. *Evil-eye*, they call it. *Deathwatch. Doomgate.* They say it is the entrance to the Land Beyond, or the place death itself stares over the world, looking for rabbits whose time is up.

It is not somewhere you would like to visit, and definitely not a place anyone would choose to live. No wonder it has been smashed and abandoned, left to crumble and rot.

Except it hasn't. Not quite. Because just now, amongst the chill shadows of the tower itself, there

is a spark. A flash of light gleaming out of the gaping windows. It quickly blooms and flickers.

A fire. Someone has lit a fire. Which means the tower *isn't* empty. Whoever built it, lived in it, watched from it all those years ago . . .

. . . they are back.

Chapter One

A Strange Game of Fox Paw

It is the first time Rue has seen mountains. So far, the tallest things in his small world have been the Razorback Downs and walking along the top of them always made him feel tiny. Like an ant crawling over an enormous rock.

Mountains, though . . . they are something else.

They look big from a distance, but then they just keep getting bigger and *bigger.* By the time he reaches the feet of them, his little neck is aching from craning upwards. His tongue is dried out from gaping.

'Close that mouth before something flies into it,' the bard says.

'But they're so *big*!' Rue replies. Up and up and up they tower: craggy lumps of rock reaching up into the clouds. If he felt like an ant before, now he was even tinier. A speck of a speck: the smallest grain of sand on a beach.

All that stone teetering over him makes him feel dizzy. 'Might they fall down?' he asks.

The bard laughs. 'They haven't moved for millions of years. I don't think they're going to budge now.' He points with the end of his staff. 'That range on the left are the Arukhs. Them on the right are the Eiskalt Mountains. We're going through the pass between.'

They had left Spinestone a few weeks ago. With nowhere in particular to go (and with nobody wanting to kill him) the bard had taken them on a gentle amble, over the downs into Gotland and along the edge of the forest. They'd stopped at a couple of warrens for a meal or two in return for a tale. The skies had been clear, the days long and sun-filled. Everything was peaceful.

And then one morning the bard had suddenly stopped walking. He'd stood and tugged at his beard.

'You know what I fancy?' he'd said. 'Some Hulstland ale.'

And with that, they had set a course for the narrow pass where the two mountain ranges met.

Several other travellers are on the road with them. There are tinkers and pedlars, even a family of brindle rabbits, tramping on past, stooping under the weight of their overflowing rucksacks. Two or three carts trundle by, towed by teams of giant rats. In return for some rude limericks, the bard manages to get them a lift and they ride all the way through the pass, huge cliffs and ridges of striped rocks closing in on either side of them. The cart jolts and bumps through potholes and over scattered lumps of flint, and by the time they come to a stop at a little trading town, both Rue and the bard are covered with bruises.

'Welcome to Hulstland,' says the bard as they hop down from the wagon.

Rue looks around at the cluster of stone and wood buildings, nestled on the side of a foothill. He doesn't appear to be very impressed.

'I thought you said things were grander here?' he says, frowning. 'Where are the cities and the statues? And what are those square things on the hillside?'

The bard sighs. 'Things *are* grander, further in. This is just a tiny trading town on the edge of the Empire. Pebblewic, if I remember rightly. Those "square things" are the rabbits' houses. I think one of them might even be a tavern . . .'

'Houses?' Rue says. 'You mean they don't live in warrens, like normal rabbits?'

'Look at the ground,' says the bard, poking it with his staff. 'It's granite and flint, peppered with a tiny sprinkle of soil and grass. You can't tunnel into that. Not without muscles like boulders and the patience of a glacier. In this part of Hulstland, the rabbits build houses to live in. Just like the Ancients did.'

Evening is beginning to close in, the sky blushing orange on the horizon. With thoughts of ale tankards and roasted beetroots, they make their way into the town.

One of the buildings is indeed a tavern, although it's really more of a barn that happens to sell ale and food. The tables are rough planks of wood, balanced between lumps of rock. Wooden crates serve as chairs and the floor is a sticky mix of mud, sawdust and spilt beer.

'What's that *smell*?' Rue asks, clamping a paw over his nose as they make their way to an empty table.

'That's how taverns are supposed to smell,' says the bard. 'At least ones in tiny little two-rat towns like this.' They choose a spot by the fire, where the wood smoke overpowers the stink a bit. 'You'll get used to it. Although maybe you shouldn't tell your parents that I brought you here. Or remember any of the language you hear being used. In fact, probably best you close your eyes and pretend you're somewhere else. Drinking dens aren't really a place for young rabbits.'

A hunched old bartender stomps over to take their order. Soon the bard has a clay mug of ale on the table before him and Rue a bowl of vegetable soup (or rather, a bowl of water that has had a turnip briefly waved over it). It's not exactly gourmet cooking, but after their long cart ride, anything is welcome.

'Do the rabbits here speak a different language?' Rue asks, in between spoonfuls of soup.

'No, they speak Lanic,' says the bard. 'That was one of the Emperor's rules when he brought all the different kingdoms of Hulstland together.'

'Will you be telling a tale, then? To pay for the meal?'

The bard shakes his head, then fishes his purse from his belt. While he is rummaging around amongst the different currencies and assorted trinkets inside, Rue clears his throat.

'Then perhaps . . . I mean, seeing as you aren't . . . maybe *I* could perform something?'

The bard pauses in his coin search to give Rue a stare from beneath his brows. 'Trust me,' he says, 'you don't want *this* place to be your first gig.' He pulls out a few copper coins and lays them on the table, each one marked with the face of a very serious-looking rabbit.

'When you're ready, Rue, we'll find you somewhere perfect,' he says, noting the disappointed look on his apprentice's face. 'There's no need to rush, though. Right place, right time. As *I* learnt at Golden Brook.'

He takes a long swallow of his ale, then wrinkles

his nose. It isn't quite the delight he'd been hoping for all the way from Gotland.

'So,' says Rue, pushing his bowl of turnip-scented water aside with a sigh. 'If neither of us is telling a tale for *them*' – he points to the three or four drunken rabbits slouched over the other tables – 'perhaps you could tell one for me? Maybe one about you and your famous brother Podkin?'

'Hush!' says the bard. 'You know that's supposed to be a secret!'

'Sorry,' says Rue, with a wince. 'But you said that the story wasn't over. You said that you all had more adventures. I just want to hear them! Please?'

'And *you* said – in fact, you swore it on your ears – that you would only bother me about Podkin stories once every three days. Have you any idea how long it's been since you last asked me?'

'Three days?' Rue says, hopefully.

'Fifteen minutes, Rue,' says the bard. 'You asked just as the cart was pulling in. And you've been asking ever since we got on the thing this morning. I *knew* it was going to be like this as soon as Sythica let the rabbit out of the burrow.'

'But I love hearing about it! And you were actually *there*! Do you have any idea how amazing that is?'

'A little,' says the bard, rolling his eyes. 'Quiet, now. Somebody's coming over.'

Rue turns to see a cloaked, hooded rabbit, making its way between the tables towards them. He catches a glimpse of brown fur, a braid of long hair, shot with grey. Quick brown eyes, darting left and right, even though their owner is trying to move as casually as possible. Could it be danger? An attack from another assassin? Rue holds his breath and grips the edge of the table.

'Well met,' says the stranger as she pulls up a crate.

'Indeed,' says the bard, with a cautious nod.

'Fancy a game of fox paw?' the stranger asks.

The bard's eyes widen for a fraction of a second, then he nods again. 'I have my own dice.'

'As do I,' says the stranger. Both rabbits then reach into pockets to pull out little cloth bags. The bard tips his up first, spilling three bone dice on to the table. The stranger does the same. Her dice are wooden but Rue's clever eyes spot something strange. The numbers on the faces are different styles, but the fox-paw symbols match. And they aren't the usual type of paws: the centre pad on all of them is a little spiral, unlike any other set of dice he has seen.

The matching dice are some kind of sign between the two rabbits. Rue notices them relax a little, but now the bard's ears are twitching with curiosity.

'Nikku?' he says, reaching a paw out to the strange rabbit. 'Of the Foxguard?'

'Yes,' the rabbit replies, clasping his wrist. 'Good to see you, Wulf.'

'How did you know I was coming?'

'I have eyes on the pass. You were spotted riding in on a cart.'

'I'm guessing you aren't here for a chat,' says the bard, leaning closer and lowering his voice.

'I'm afraid not,' Nikku whispers. 'I was going to send a sparrow to you anyway, but here you are. Kether works in mysterious ways.' She pauses to touch three fingers to her forehead, and the bard copies the gesture.

'Is it the Endwatch?' The bard asks. 'Has there been news?'

'There has,' Nikku says. 'I don't have the details, only that the alarm's been raised. Something's happening in the north.'

'North? In the cities? At the Wall?' The bard reaches out to grab Nikku's arm. 'Not the tower?'

'I don't know. I got a sparrow from our agent in the town of Melt. It's a little river shanty two days from here. I've sent word out to everyone we have in Hulstland but you should still head there in the morning and see what's going on. I was about to go myself but now you're here . . . I can arrange a ride on a trade wagon for you. You'll need to speak to Gant. He runs a store there. He's the one who raised the alarm.'

The bard lets out a puff of air and sits back on his crate. His brow is furrowed and his green eyes flash. *Whatever this business is,* Rue thinks, *it's serious.* He can feel the questions starting to bubble up inside him, but something tells him to wait until this Nikku rabbit has gone.

'Very well,' says the bard. 'We leave in the morning.'

'I'll make arrangements,' says Nikku. 'There's an inn three doors down the road where you can stay. And don't eat anything else from this place. Not unless you want to spend the next three days pooing water.'

With that she scoops up her dice and leaves, giving Rue a quick wink as she passes. Rue waits until she has left the tavern before grabbing hold of the bard's cloak and unloading questions into his face.

'Who was she? What were those funny paws on the dice? Why is there an agent? What's the Endwatch? Who is Kether? What's going on? Is it dangerous? Are we in danger? Are we? Are we?'

'Enough!' the bard shouts. Some of the drunken rabbits raise bleary eyes to glare over at them, which makes the bard feel very uncomfortable. 'Come on,' he says. 'Let's go and find somewhere to sleep for the night. I'll tell you all about it then.'

*

The inn is a lot better than the tavern had been. Not as cosy as a burrow, but it has stone walls, a thatched roof and fireplaces in every room. The one Rue and the bard rent has two straw-stuffed mattresses and a little window that looks out on to the mountains.

As soon as they are inside, Rue jumps on to his bed and sits cross-legged, waiting for the bard to start talking. 'Well?' he says. 'We've found somewhere to sleep. You said you'd tell me all about it.'

The bard sighs and slumps on to his mattress. 'I did, didn't I? That was silly of me.'

'So, what's this Foxguard, then? Is it secret? Why does it have agents? Are you an agent?'

'The Foxguard . . .' says the bard, and sighs. 'It's a group of rabbits and yes, I am a member. And it is a secret. It was set up a long time ago to keep an eye out for something. We have agents all over the Five Realms. We carry the dice so we can identify one another – to make sure we can be trusted.'

'Is this Kether a part of it? Is he who you're watching?'

The bard laughs. 'No. Kether is the god of order and numbers. He's who everyone in Hulstland worships. In fact, they believe he is the *only* god. They think the Goddess and the rest are just fairy tales for savages.'

'They don't believe in the Goddess?' Rue's eyes boggle and his mouth hangs open. How can such a thing be true?

'Relax,' says the bard. 'Different folk believe in different things. It's fine. It's natural. It's only when they start telling others they're wrong and decide to have a war about it that there's a problem.'

Rue blinks for a moment as he digests this. Then the questions start again. 'The Endwatch, then. What's that? Is it something bad? Like the Gorm?'

'Mmm.' The bard tugs at his beard. 'The Endwatch *is* bad. Different from the Gorm, but just as evil. It's complicated, though. It would involve telling quite a long tale . . .'

'A tale?' Rue folds his arms and smiles like a rabbit who has just rolled three fives in a game of fox paw. 'Well, we're going on a two-day journey tomorrow. The perfect chance for you to tell it.'

'I suppose.' The bard lies back on his mattress. 'Although, if I tell that story, it will have to be instead of you hearing about Podkin.'

'Really?' Rue's voice is suddenly not quite so smug. 'Can't I have both?'

'I'm afraid not,' says the bard. 'It's a long story. An important one. Although it is part of Podkin's tale as well, in a way. It takes place a year or so after the Battle of Sparrowfast, while Podkin is busy training and taking care of his Gifts.'

'Is it exciting?' Rue asks. 'Is there danger and villains and fighting?'

'Yes, yes, yes and yes,' says the bard.

'And are there heroes? Will I like them as much as Podkin, Paz and Pook?'

'Maybe not Pook,' says the bard. 'He's extra special. But I'm sure you will like them. We live in a world full of stories, you know. It would be boring only to hear about the same characters over and over, wouldn't it?'

'Is it a real-life story?' Rue asks. 'Will there be actual characters who pop up at the end of our journey to surprise me, like Sythica? And you?'

'Well,' the bard tugs at his beard again. 'I admit there seems to be a pattern of that happening. But I can't promise anything.'

'Very well, then,' says Rue. 'I would like to know everything about the Endwatch. *Everything*.' He emphasises the last word with a glare at the bard.

'Excellent,' says the bard. 'It's probably a good idea for you to know about him. It can be the second story for your memory warren.'

'Wait . . . him? Who's *him*?'

'Uki,' says the bard. 'Uki Patchwork. The Magpie Demon. Uki of the Two Furs.'

'Uki? Magpie Demon? Who's he? Why's he called that? Is he the hero? How can someone have two furs?'

But the bard has rolled over and pulled his cloak across his face. All Rue's questions fall on deaf ears and there is nothing else for the little rabbit to do except wait for morning and the start of a new story.

Chapter Two

The Outcast

Rue sleeps badly that night. Wind whistles around the inn – a sound he has never heard before, being used to burrow life – and he keeps jolting awake as it howls and hoots, as it shakes the thatch roof and rattles the shutters.

When he does sleep, his dreams are full of sinister foxes with wide, yellow eyes, chasing him through mountain passes, always staring, staring. It is almost a relief to see the dawn light peeping in through the window crack, and to nudge the bard awake with a foot.

They each snatch a roll of fresh-baked bread from the kitchen and step out of the inn into a bright, clear morning. The air is sharp and cold and Rue's breath steams, joining with wisps from his hot, buttered roll as he crams it into his mouth, filling his fur with sticky crumbs.

The townsfolk of Pebblewic are just beginning to rise, but one has been up for a while, waiting for them. Rue spots the hooded figure of Nikku stomping over, those quick brown eyes darting to and fro.

'Morning,' says the bard when she draws close. Rue remembers what he learnt about Kether last night and touches three fingers to his forehead. To his delight, it draws a broad smile from Nikku.

'Ninefold blessings to you, little one,' she says.

'Did you find us a wagon?' asks the bard. Rue half hopes she hasn't. His bottom is still bruised from the bumpy cart ride through the pass.

'Better than that,' says Nikku. 'Come.'

She leads them back up the beaten-mud path that winds between the squat Pebblewic houses, back to the gravel road from Enderby. One of the houses by the roadside seems to be some kind of trading station. Rabbits are already leading rats out from the stables and saddling them, or hitching them to carts and wagons. Cargo is being loaded ready to head back to Gotland, or further on into Hulstland itself.

The carts look extremely uncomfortable with thick wooden wheels that will feel every pothole and jolt.

'Not those, little one,' says Nikku, spotting Rue wincing. 'Around the corner here.'

They head around the side of the little trading station and there, all hitched up and waiting to go, is the strangest wagon Rue has ever seen.

It has spindly, spoked wheels fixed to curved bits of metal, and a skinny wooden frame with hide stretched over it. It doesn't look strong enough to hold its cargo of baled-up Enderby tartan, let alone passengers.

It has long shafts, between which two creatures have been harnessed. When Rue sees them, he blinks in surprise. He points and looks up at the bard with a mixture of fascination and horror.

'Jerboas,' the bard explains. 'They live on the plains to the north. A bit like giant rats, but much, *much* faster.'

Rue stares at them again. They have long ears like a rabbit, black eyes and twitchy rat noses, oversized, springy back legs with enormous splayed-toed feet, and graceful, sweeping tails, tufted at the end with sprays of fur. It's like several different types of animal have been clumsily spliced into a very strange-looking mix. Suddenly, the good-old rats and their clumsy wagons don't look too bad.

'These will get you to Melt in no time,' says Nikku. 'Jaxom here is one of us, too.'

She points towards a rabbit who has just emerged from the far side of the wagon. Dressed in leather armour, he has a mane of long, sandy fur, pulled into a topknot on his head. As he turns to greet them, Rue notices the criss-cross lines of scars all over his nose and face, and his fierce grey eyes, like chips of mountain rock. He also spots two long daggers in his belt, and a sword strapped to his back. He looks more like a warrior than a trader.

The bard clasps wrists with him, then nods towards the wagon. 'Fast is she?'

'The fastest,' says Jaxom, his voice gruff but friendly. 'We'll be in Melt by evening tomorrow.'

'Are you expecting trouble?' The bard looks pointedly at the weapons all over Jaxom's belt.

'There's sometimes Arukh raiders about,' says Jaxom. He shrugs as if it's just a minor problem. 'I can outrun them, no trouble.'

Rue gulps. He has heard stories of the fierce Arukh rabbits, with their long, spiked manes and painted faces. None of them were very nice. Most of them involved someone being skinned alive.

'Jaxom here is half Arukh himself,' says Nikku with a grin. 'There's nobody better for getting you there with your fur still in one piece.'

'You have our thanks,' the bard says to her, swinging his pack up on the wagon. 'I'll let you know what we discover.'

'Safe travels,' says Nikku. She lifts Rue up on to the wagon and helps the bard clamber up next to him, and then she is gone. Rue just has time to snuggle himself up between two packages of tartan before

Jaxom leaps on to the driver's board and cracks his whip.

'Off we go!' he shouts, and the jerboas are away.

It is the fastest Rue has ever moved in his life.

The jerboas bound and leap with their long hind legs, sending the cart zipping along the track out of Pebblewic like an arrow from a bow.

The sprung wheels of the wagon bounce and squeal but absorb most of the bumps and dips. What with the bales of material for extra cushioning, the ride is almost comfortable.

Rue looks up at the bard, the wind whipping his tattooed ears back and whooshing through his fur. He beams at Rue and the pair laugh together, whooping as Jaxom cracks the whip and shouts out, 'Hai! Hai!'

Before the sun is properly up, the little town of Pebblewic is completely out of sight.

*

The *hop-hop* rhythm of the jerboas soon becomes natural, soothing even. They whizz along a track of dried mud and gravel, on their left the barren foothills leading up to the snow-capped peaks of the

Arukh Mountains, on their right a wide expanse of empty grasslands. Nothing but the odd little tree – hawthorns and blackthorns, Rue thinks – tortured by the wind into bent, twisting shapes.

It doesn't take long for the little rabbit to get bored.

'So,' he says, after tugging at the bard's cloak for a bit, 'are you going to tell me about him then?'

'Him?' says the bard, a twinkle in his eye. 'Him who?'

'You *know*. Uki Thingy. The one you said about last night.'

'Oh, *him*,' says the bard. 'I didn't think you really wanted to hear about that. I was sure you only wanted more tales about Podkin.'

'I do,' says Rue. 'I *really* do. But first I want to hear about Uki. And the Endwatch, and why you have to guard against them. Come on, you said you'd tell. We're on this wagon for two days. I'll die of boredom if you don't.'

The bard pretends to consider this for a moment, knowing it will at least be nice and peaceful. In the end he grunts and arranges himself on the tartan bales a bit more snugly.

'Very well,' he says. 'I have to warn you, though, it doesn't start off like Podkin's story.'

'You mean with Gorm and chasing and fighting and things?'

'No, none of that. It's a very sad start, I'm afraid. And Uki doesn't seem like much of a hero to begin with.'

'Neither did Podkin,' Rue reminds him.

'That's true,' the bard nods.

'But there will be action, won't there? And daring deeds and fights and things?'

'Oh yes, lots of those,' says the bard. 'Once the story gets going. You have to let it build up first, though. A good story comes to the boil slowly, just like a good vegetable stew.'

'I know,' says Rue. 'I can be patient. I can be as patient as anything.'

The bard gives him a long look which says he knows otherwise, and then shakes his head and smiles to himself. 'Very well, then. Show me your best patient listening and I'll begin . . .'

*

The story starts, as not many nice ones do, in a graveyard.

Not a nice little well-tended Enderby graveyard, with wildflowers and butterflies and benches to sit on. No, this one is north, far north. Up just beyond the crumbled remains of the Cinder Wall, in the frosty tundra and spiky bare trees of the Ice Wastes.

The tribe that lived there had walled off a bit of dead woodland, built a little shrine to Zeryth, their god of storms and snow, and scraped out some shallow holes for their dead.

Grave mounds of broken stone are dotted here and there, marked with carved wooden poles, hung with beads and charms laced on to braided string. The wind that howls through that wasteland blows them, filling the bare woodland with a constant rattling. A sound like the bones of the restless dead, lying in their cold, shallow scrapes in the earth.

On the night our story starts, a poor, starving mother rabbit has braved the darkness of the woods and the clattering of the unquiet dead. She has crept into the sacred space of the graveyard, knowing she would never be allowed in if the tribe knew, knowing they would chase her out with sticks and hurled stones, with screams of ‘outcast!’ and ‘witch!’

But tonight, she has to be there, even though it will mean using up the end of her strength. Even though the bitter northern cold is already eating into her fingers, toes and ears. Even though she knows it is her final night on this painful, miserable earth.

For in her arms, bound in a piece of tattered blanket, is the body of her only child. Nothing more than bones, wrapped in skin – the poor thing wheezed out his last breath that very morning.

‘Uki,’ she whispers to the body, cradling it like she did when he was born eight years ago. ‘Uki.’

She had been so happy then, in that moment. Happier than at any time in her life. That little bundle of fur had completed her in a way she had never thought possible, and she knew, the first moment she saw him, that she would do anything for him, *anything*, for the rest of her days.

Anything, including creeping into a frozen, haunted graveyard to bury him in a hidden corner under a dead oak tree.

Laying Uki's body gently on the ground, she began to paw and scrape at the iron-hard earth. With her fingers first, then with a lump of rock.

'No good,' she whispered. 'No good.' She was too weak to even make a dent on the frozen soil.

Instead, she began to gather rocks, some from the tumbledown stone wall of the graveyard, some borrowed from the burial mounds around her, hoping the spirits of their owners wouldn't be angered.

Slowly, painfully, she started to cover the body of her son.

As she worked, she thought back over his short life, remembering how hard it had been. What suffering they had both been through. Her tears fell amongst the stones.

She wasn't from the Ice Wastes, originally. She had been born in Gotland, in a little warren called Flintle. Her parents had been potters and, when she was about the same age as her son, they had decided to travel to Hulstland where, her father had heard, there was good work for rabbits with his talents.

'Meera,' he had said. 'It will be a new life for us. Things are better in the Empire. They have cities and roads and guards with suits of shining armour. Rabbits will buy our pots and we will have our own shop with a burrow behind it. It will be perfect. You'll see.'

Except they had never got that far. No sooner had they made it through the mountains, the group they were travelling with was attacked by a party of Arukh raiders.

There were spears and flint axes and screaming. Somehow she was separated from her parents, dashing into the shelter of some nearby trees. To this day she doesn't know if they survived. She has hoped many times that they did.

For several days she had wandered through the lifeless trees of the Icebark Forest, surviving on scraps of bark and the odd berry. She was found, half dead, by another raiding party, this time from a tribe of Ice Waste rabbits crossing the boundary of the Cinder Wall to steal food and seeds.

They took her back with them and tied her up, quite possibly getting ready to eat her. It was only because one of them spoke Lanic and found out she was a potter that she was spared.

In return for her skills, making the best pots and bowls the tribe had ever seen, she was adopted. She lived among them and learnt their ways, even taking one of their warriors as a husband.

For a few years, things were good, and she was happy.

And then Uki was born.

She noticed it as soon as he was passed to her for his first feed. Such an unusual baby: it was like a line had been drawn down the middle of him. One side had fur as black as the moon's shadow and an eye of icy blue. The other side was snow white, like his father, but with a deep-brown eye. Burnt umber, like a clay pot fresh out of the kiln.

She blinked up at her husband in wonder – about to marvel at how special their new baby was – and that was when she first saw it. That look of horror, mixed with disgust.

To her, this half and half child was a blessing. She remembered one being born in her home warren, how the priestess of her tribe had called it sacred. The joining of two kittens in the womb, making something new.

But to the Ice Waste rabbits, with their pure white fur, he was a monster. Something different, something wrong. A thing to be afraid of.

They are brutal, the Ice tribes. Their food and warmth and shelter are precious. Too precious for any who are weak or unhealthy. Those that don't fit are simply taken out on to the tundra and left in the cold. Left for Zeryth to claim their souls, the foxes to eat their bones.

That was what they wanted to do to Uki: to leave him in a snowdrift to freeze. She refused, and begged and pleaded with her husband who, despite sharing the tribe's beliefs, loved her truly. Uki was allowed to stay, even though it made life difficult for his parents. Meera, especially.

It took quite some time but she learnt to bear all the evil stares and insults. She took them for her child, who – despite his two halves – grew into a strong and healthy toddler.

They might have still been there now if her husband hadn't died.

He went out on a raiding party, four years ago now, and never returned. The warriors had tried to steal food from one of the Blood Plains tribes and been caught. Those rabbits were fierce, almost as fierce as the Arukhs, and only one fighter had returned alive.

Without the protection of her husband, it only took a few days before they were thrown out of their hut. If it hadn't been for her pottery, they would have been cast out of the village completely. As it was, they were allowed to move into a broken-down, draughty old roundhouse on the outskirts of the tribe. She carried on making pots, which were bought for scraps of food. The tribe put up with her just as long as her demon son was kept hidden away. Out of sight and out of mind.

Uki continued to grow, even though food was scarce. She kept him cloaked and hooded, and only left the house when she knew no other rabbits were about. They haunted the nearby woods at dusk and dawn, foraging for extra food, digging for clay. Like a pair of ghosts with only each other for company.

She'd often thought of leaving. They could head back over the Wall, somehow survive the cold, dodge the plains rabbits and the Arukhs. Maybe even make it back through the mountains to her old warren.

But the risks were too great, she'd always told herself. And they were surviving. Not comfortably, true, but they were alive.

'Stupid,' she whispered to herself as she laid the rocks over her son. 'Stupid, stupid, stupid.'

But back then she had no way of knowing what was to happen.

*

As Uki grew older, he began to notice that he was different. Meera never mentioned it or said anything when he wondered aloud why one of his paws was black, the other white. But he could see his fur was patterned differently to her dusty brown colouring and that his eyes, when he glimpsed his reflection in a pool or puddle, were not the same.

The image of his halves stayed with him, and he grew to think of himself in that way: two parts of one thing.

Happy Uki / sad Uki.

Kind Uki / selfish Uki.

Brave Uki / scared Uki.

He even divided the voice in his head – that little voice we all have chattering to us in the background – into two: the normal part for everyday thoughts and another, darker side for all his worries and fears. It would chirp up whenever a decision had to be made, or when something was about to change, making him doubt himself or panic. Most of the time he tried to ignore it or prove it wrong. Most of the time.

And then there was the bullying.

The village adults all kept well away from their lonely roundhouse with its leaky roof and draughty walls. Children, though, are more curious, especially if there's something they're told to stay clear of.

Every now and then a group of them dared each other to go and find 'the demon'. They would stand outside the hut, at a safe distance, waiting for a glimpse. When they saw Uki peep at them through the doorway, or caught him out fetching water from the nearby stream, they would run away shrieking in mock terror.

But not all of them ran. Some were more spiteful and called out horrible things. 'Mismatch' and 'two furs'. 'Magpie' and 'demon boy'. More than a few times they had thrown stones as well as insults.

It didn't take Uki long to realise that every child in the village hated him and that it was all because of his fur.

'I wish I didn't look like this,' he often said to his mother at night when they were huddled together by their tiny fireplace.

'You mustn't say that, Uki,' she told him. 'The Goddess made you this way. You can't help what you look like. But you can help what your heart is like, what your thoughts are. You have a good heart, Uki, and your thoughts are kind. Don't let those children change that just because they don't understand you.'

She used to pray her words got through to him, or that the tribe rabbits might change their minds and accept him. But in her bones she knew they never would. So she began to make plans to take Uki away to the south, where rabbits weren't so cruel and superstitious. She knew he needed friends to play with to show him the meaning of kindness.

Except life doesn't pay much attention to plans: the weather was never quite right, or she needed just a few more provisions, or there were just a few more pots to make . . . Always a reason to put it off.

Right up until it was too late.

It was just a few weeks ago, during the last days of winter as the weather began to change. They had scraped and starved their way through the harshest, deadliest season, although it had left them both little better than fur-covered skeletons. Now she had an order of pots to finish that would hopefully give them food. Enough, maybe, to put some flesh back on their bones; to build up some strength for a journey. *After that,* she had been telling herself, *we'll be off. Out of the Wastes, over the mountains and back to Gotland.*

Uki, not wanting to get in her way, had gone out to the stream.

He loved it there, quiet and alone, and his favourite pastime was building dams and bridges across the little trickle of water, then balancing his way across them. He had been unable to do it all winter, but now the thaw had begun and the stream was running again.

Using hazel twigs and flat lumps of slate, he

blocked off the flow and watched as the water built up behind it. It grew into a pool, higher and higher, before it began to trickle over the top like a tiny waterfall. That was when his moment came: a few seconds in which to teeter his way across the top before it was too late.

Finally, just as he leapt to safety, the dam would give way with a *whoosh.* A satisfying burst, like a long-held breath being released.

Then he would start again, building it bigger and better.

That day he had been on his third attempt. Quite a big pool had grown behind the dam, the stream in front drying to a trickle. He almost thought his wall would never break, that the pool would grow and grow into a pond, then a lake . . . He made one trip safely across the top, arms stretched out for balance, and was about to head back when, with a *crack*, the twigs snapped and the water burst outwards, *swooshing* down the stream bed in a flood of sticks and dead leaves.

Uki had been about to cheer when a peal of laughter came from the other side of the stream.

Looking up, he saw a girl there. A girl from the village with the snow-white fur and blue eyes of all the other rabbits.

Uki felt a sudden wash of panic, not unlike his dam breaking moments earlier. He tensed himself, ready to face the insults or the hurled rocks, just as he'd done a hundred times over.

Instead, the girl hopped across the stream and came over to him. Uki blinked at her with wide, mismatched eyes. *This* had never happened before.

'That was brilliant!' she said. 'Are you going to do it again? Can I help?'

Another child? To play with? Uki was overjoyed at first – until his dark voice decided to speak.

Don't, it said. **It's just part of some cruel new trick. Another way to hurt you.**

The thought made Uki pause for a moment, but in the end the need for some kind of company won him over. He nodded at the girl, not really knowing how to speak to anyone but his mother, and the pair set to work.

As they gathered twigs and rocks and began

stacking them in the stream bed, the girl chattered away. Her name was Nua and her father was a hunter. She had heard about Uki, and even spotted him once or twice. She knew the other children were scared of him but she wasn't. She didn't believe in silly things like demons and monsters. She knew he would be nice.

Uki could hardly believe his ears. At first he only nodded at her, but as his confidence grew he began to grunt yes or no, and finally started to answer her almost-endless comments and questions.

By the end of the afternoon, they had built a pretty good dam and had taken the first steps of a friendship. It was, he thought at the time, the best afternoon of his life.

He was even going to show her his balancing trick: to teach her how to feel the wood below with her toes and step-step-step as quickly as possible, holding your breath for the sudden snap and splash in case you fell into the water . . .

And then the bullies showed up.

Every warren or village has them: one or more children who, for reasons only they know, aren't happy unless they are making somebody else miserable.

In Uki's village there were two such horrors – a boy and his older sister.

Both were as mean as starved snakes: him with his fists, and her with her tongue. Of the many attacks on Uki over the years, those two had been behind them all, in one way or another.

And today was going to be no different.

They stood on the far edge of the stream, watching Uki and Nua play, with a spiteful glint in their eyes. They watched for a long time, waiting until they couldn't bear the happiness of the growing friendship any more. Just as Uki was about to step out on to the dam, the girl called out.

'Hey, Nua! Don't you know you're supposed to stay away from the outcast? He's a demon!'

'We're going to tell on you,' said the boy. 'Your da is going to beat you with a stick for this.'

Both Uki and Nua jumped clean out of the stream with a splash. Uki's eyes flashed and he moved to pull Nua behind him – out of harm's way – but to his surprise, she stepped in front of *him*, with just as much fierceness, if not more.

'Tell all you want,' Nua shouted back, fists bunched on her hips. 'My da won't mind. Not when I tell him how nice Uki is. He's a much nicer rabbit than either of you.'

'Our ma says he's an evil spirit,' said the girl. 'He should have been left out for Zeryth when he was born.'

'Your ma is nothing but a mean gossip and a liar!' Nua shouted. 'Everyone in the village knows it, too!'

That made the bullies angry. The boy reached down, pulled out a great slab of slate from the bank and, before Uki could yell a warning, threw it towards them with all his might. It hit the surface of the stream and bounced once, twice, before hitting Nua in the stomach.

She fell, screaming, into the water and the two bullies fled. Uki tried everything he could to help his new friend – lifting her to the bank, speaking softly to soothe her – but she was too upset. She staggered off, back to the village and her parents.

Uki had a sick feeling in his gut. And when he went back to the hut and told Meera, she had a sick feeling too.

Bullies are always cowardly as well as mean. There was no way those two would take the blame for what had happened, not when there was a perfectly good scapegoat in the form of Uki. And even if Nua tried to correct them with the truth, it wouldn't help. Not when the villagers *wanted* the bullies' story to be true.

All these years they had been waiting for something like this. A reason to make their fear and hatred of Uki seem reasonable. *That patchwork demon,* they would be saying. *Look what he did to poor little Nua. Threw a rock at her when she was walking by the stream. Nearly drowned her, he did! We knew he was evil all along, and this proves it!*

Sure enough, dusk hadn't even fallen before there was a commotion outside their hut. A babble of angry voices as the village gathered together to *do something* about Uki.

Meera grabbed a blanket and began filling it with what food and clothing they had even as she heard the crash of her kiln being kicked over, the stack of freshly made pots inside it shattering in a shower of sparks.

She thought they might just let them leave, but they had other ideas. Peeking through a hole in the wall, she saw the two children who had terrorised Uki, wrapped in the protective arms of their mother, secretly smiling at the chaos their lies had caused. Rocks were already in their paws and other rabbits were copying them, picking up lumps of granite and slate, ready to hurl.

It filled Meera with rage, but what could she do? Beside her, Uki was sobbing, telling her he was sorry for the trouble he'd caused. Poor, innocent little Uki, whose only crime was being different.

It wasn't long before the stones started flying.

If the roundhouse had been stronger they might have bounced off, but the rocks punched through the battered turf roof like it wasn't there.

They smashed the pots and plates on the hearth, they splintered the tiny chairs and table. One bounced off Meera's shoulder, bringing tears to her eyes. Another hit Uki on the shin, cutting deep into his bone and making him scream.

Meera knew they would die if they stayed in the

hut. Their only hope was that the place was little more than a crumbling shell. Grabbing Uki to her chest, she ran at the back wall, using her weight to crash through the ancient stone.

The rocks, only held together with moss and cobwebs, burst outwards, and they tumbled free. The villagers were too caught up in their stoning to notice, so they managed to half-run, half-stagger, over the stream and into the woods.

Meera's decision to leave had been made for her but without any of the preparation they needed. Even though the thaw had started, it was still winter. The nights were deadly this far north, the days almost as bad without proper food and shelter.

They would have been better off staying put and letting the stones do their work.

*

In the end, they didn't make it anywhere near as far as Meera had hoped.

Past the tribal graveyard (where she now knelt) through a gap in the broken Wall and a little way into Icebark Forest. They were making for Nether – a small trading town at the edge of the forest – but were still deep amongst the trees when Uki's fever took hold.

They had limped for two days, her with her injured shoulder and him with that nasty, deep gash to his leg. They had rested as little as possible, fearing the villagers might be on their trail. Perhaps she should have taken more time to wash Uki's wound, or use clean scraps of cloth for bandages, but all she could think of was getting away.

When they finally stopped, Meera noticed Uki was sweating, his brow hot and fevered. The cut on his leg was edged with angry red skin and wept sticky, yellow fluid.

An infection.

She knew the signs but not how to treat them (she was a potter, not a healer). Frantically, she cleaned the cut and bound it with fresh coverings torn from her cloak, but she didn't know which plants would help. She barely even knew which berries and leaves were safe to eat.

The sorry pair staggered into a clearing and made camp as best they could, but Zeryth must have had his heart set on their souls. That night, winter decided to leave a parting gift. Frost and hail, mist and wind. It didn't let up for days. There was no food to be found, no help or healers within reach.

Already half-starved, they both faded quickly, her from hunger and Uki from the infection in his blood. At the back of her mind, Meera always thought someone would appear – a kindly stranger, a wandering woodsman – offering help and food, as in the stories. But they didn't. And then, that very morning, Uki had shuddered in his sleep, given one last gasp . . . and died.

*

The rock cairn was finished. Uki's skinny little body was completely covered, just a pile of stones like all the others in the graveyard.

Meera should really cry or wail now, she supposed. Tear her clothes, pull her ears, scream at the sky, perhaps. But instead she just felt empty and cold, like a hollowed-out shell of a thing. And she was so very, very tired.

She looked at the roots of the dead oak tree, spreading out and around Uki's grave. They seemed, she thought, like a good place to sleep. Her final sleep: one that would last forever.

With the end of her strength, she planted a kiss on the topmost stone of Uki's grave, and then curled up amongst the root and rock, the dead grass and cold earth, and closed her eyes.

She would open them again when she was in the Land Beyond.

Chapter Three

The Fire Spirit

But how can the hero of our tale *be* a hero if he is dead? (I can tell that's what you're about to ask, so just close your mouth and let me get on with the story.)

Well, Uki *wasn't* dead. Not yet, anyway.

The winter frost began to creep through the stones of the cairn, painting white crystals over the blanket shroud he was wrapped in. It froze his mother's last tears into tiny jewels of ice. It began to freeze Uki's starved, fever-racked body, making him as cold and stiff as the skeletons sleeping all around him.

But, somewhere deep inside the little rabbit's shell, there was a tiny spark of life left. The dimmest of heartbeats, the quiet crackling of neurons in his brain. The fever hadn't killed him. Not yet, anyway. Just stilled his breath and his pulse so deeply, his poor starving mother had thought him gone.

No, Uki wasn't dead, but he would have been before morning had not something quite *amazing* happened.

*

Before I get to that part, though, there's a bit of explaining to do.

Now. You remember how brave Podkin and Paz (and even braver Pook) fought a great battle against Scramashank and the Gorm? And how they destroyed the corrupted Gifts with magic arrows?

And you will also remember how the Gorm warriors fell apart after that blow was struck. You might even recall how Podkin thought he heard a roar from beneath the earth, from the evil iron being that was Gormalech.

Well, Podkin was right.

That creature of living metal, seething beneath the Earth's crust where he had been trapped for millennia, did indeed roar.

The wound Podkin gave him was worse than any he had felt before. His hold on the surface world was broken, and he shrank back into himself to lick his wounds. Down through the caverns and dark tunnels of bedrock, down to where the rocks are soft and safe and warm. There to gather his strength and plan, I expect, his next attempt to break the Balance that was his pact with the goddesses.

Gormalech, Podkin had discovered, was a creature made by the Ancients. One that had warped out of control and driven them up into the stars.

But the Ancients had made many other things besides that ruinous monster. Most of them had been devoured by him, sucked up into his living, boiling mass of iron as if they'd never existed. Some, however, remained. Little nuggets of cunning craft and skill, buried under the ground and either too hard or too poisonous for Gormalech to get into.

The creature had worried and chewed at these, like a badger with a sore tooth. He had squashed and squeezed them over the centuries, ground them this way and that until most had been forgotten, especially in his recent obsession with the rabbits walking about *up there*.

One such treasure had been left behind in Gormalech's sudden departure. Left, as it happened, a few centimetres from the surface in the Ice Wastes of north Hulstland, not far from a certain graveyard we have just been hearing about.

Quite a tiny thing: an amethyst-pink crystal about the size of a small pumpkin.

All the centuries of pressure had worn it down, rubbed it thin as paper like a piece of sea glass, and the things trapped inside it had weakened it even more.

On the very night that Uki was buried, the crystal *popped*.

A tiny, tinkling sound, had there been anyone around to hear it, and a cluster of little glowing things emerged. Five fireflies – minuscule specks of light – floated free and drifted off into the dark woodland, lighting the pale trunks of the trees around them.

One spark, bright orange in colour, drifted towards the graveyard.

It jinked and twitched to and fro, as if sniffing something out. A scent hidden nearby: a spark of life in the cold, dead woodland.

Uki.

Yes, it had sensed the flickering pulse of the young rabbit. It could also tell that, like a guttering candle, it was about to be snuffed out.

Zipping and sparkling, rushing between the graves, it headed for Uki's pile of rocks and slipped in through a gap. It found his cold little body there, and wormed its way between the blankets, over his face, up to the corner of his ice-blue eye. And then wriggled inside.

*

Uki woke up.

There had been fever, he remembered. Such pain in his leg. Cramps in his empty belly.

All that had gone now.

There was something pressing down on him. Lots of somethings. Hard, poky somethings. He sat up, hearing the clatter of tumbling rocks. Somebody had covered him in them, like he was dead. Was he dead?

He blinked his eyes but couldn't see anything. It took him a moment to realise there was fabric over his face. A cloth or blanket. A moment's squirming and it fell away, revealing two things: it was night, and he was in a graveyard.

Waking up buried in a graveyard is not a nice experience for anyone. In fact, Uki was just gathering his breath to scream his head off, when he noticed a shape floating in the air by his face.

It was a little ball of fire, flickering like flames in the hearth: round and round, lighting up Uki's top half as he poked out of his fresh, new grave.

As Uki watched, the flames grew, spreading outwards and twisting into a new form. A figure with arms, legs and a round, earless head. It was small – no bigger than a newborn baby – but perfectly shaped. Eyes appeared, and a gap in the fire that looked like a mouth, opening and closing like a gasping fish. The thing waved its fiery arms frantically, as if it were trying to tell Uki something urgent.

'What . . . What *are* you?' Uki managed to stutter.

The floating fire creature opened its mouth again and Uki heard sounds. Some kind of language, never heard before – not Waste tribe or Lanic. At Uki's blank look, the thing tried again. More gobbledygook.

Uki felt something in his head then, a funny tingle behind his left eye. When the fire creature spoke next, Uki understood it perfectly.

'This?' it said. 'Can you understand this?' When Uki nodded, the thing gave a flicker of relief and then moved closer. 'I am Iffrit,' it said. 'A . . . A spirit . . . and I have something important to tell you.'

'Iffrit . . . ?' Uki said. With another wiggle, he freed a paw and pinched himself. This *had* to be some kind of a dream.

'Yes,' the thing said. 'And you are . . . wait . . . Are you a rabbit?'

'Of course,' said Uki. Why was that so surprising? 'Everyone is.'

'And are there any other . . . beings . . . around? Creatures that look like me? Tall, thin, little ears on the sides of their head?'

Uki thought for a moment. The description

sounded like stories his mother had told him. Tales about the ones who had left strange stone structures all over the Five Realms. 'Do you mean the Ancients?' he said. 'They don't exist any more. Most rabbits think they're just made up.'

'I see,' said Iffrit. His fiery eyes blinked for a moment, as if he was thinking. He looked Uki up and down, seeming to peer deep beneath the skin and fur. 'There seems to be a lot of the "Ancients" in you. Are you sure they are no longer here? Are there stories – legends – in your world about how you rabbits were made?'

'Well,' said Uki. 'The Waste tribes say that Zeryth made us out of snow, so he could feast on our souls . . .'

'No, that's just nonsense,' said Iffrit. His form flickered for an instant, popping out of sight then appearing again. It seemed as though he was having trouble staying in place.

'But my mother – she's from Gotland – she says that the goddesses made us. Right after they tricked Gormalech into going underneath the ground.'

'*Gormalech!*' The name seemed to mean

something to Iffrit. 'So they finally lost control of him. That would explain the damage to the crystal . . .'

Uki watched Iffrit for a moment as he pulsed and flickered some more, digesting this new information. He was speaking to himself, babbling. Whatever he was, he was in some kind of distress. Uki got the impression his mention of the Ancients had upset him somehow. 'Must have been gone for centuries now. More even,' Iffrit was muttering. 'This rabbit thing . . . not ideal . . . but enough of the same make-up, maybe . . .'

'Excuse me?' Uki said, when it seemed like Iffrit had forgotten him. 'Excuse me? Iffrit? Am I . . . Am I dead?'

Iffrit paused in his babbling to look at Uki again. 'Dead? No. You would have been before morning, but I have . . . helped you. I have fixed your body and am keeping it alive. I need you, young rabbit. I have been trapped for so long . . . my own life force has faded and I have been badly hurt by those I was guarding. I'm afraid I don't have much time left. I have joined myself to you so that I can pass on all my powers. So you can finish my task.'

'You've *joined* with me? Is that what I can feel in my head?'

'Yes,' said Iffrit. 'I'm in there. I could have taken you over, but this way is better, I think. I . . . I have a job— What are you doing?'

Uki had reached out a paw towards the floating, fiery figure and was trying to poke him with a finger. There was no warmth there, no burning. His paw passed right through one of Iffrit's legs.

'You can't feel me because I'm not really here,' Iffrit explained. 'I'm inside your head. Literally. This is just an image, so that you have something to talk to.'

'Why?' was all Uki could say. All this – the grave, the spirit, things inside his brain – it was making him giddy and squeamish.

'Because – as I'm trying to tell you – I have a job to do. The Ancients, as you call them, made me for a reason. I was a guard. A prison guard. There were four others, like me, who had done terrible things, and I was supposed to keep them locked away for all time. But they joined together and defeated me this very night, and now they have escaped.'

‘Prison?’ Uki had never heard of the word.

‘A place where bad people – criminals – are kept. As a punishment.’

‘Ah,’ Uki said. The tribe didn’t have such things. If anyone broke their laws, they were taken out on to the glacier and tied down for Zeryth to claim. In fact, that seemed to be their answer to pretty much everything.

‘Listen,’ said Iffrit, flickering with urgency. ‘These other spirits. They *must* be captured again, and *you* must do it.’

‘Me? Why me?’

‘Because you were *here*. I had no other choice.’ Iffrit was floating close to Uki’s face now. His not-there flames licking across his nose. ‘I am going to fade soon. I can feel it. I had enough strength left to fix you, to give you my . . . abilities. They should keep you alive long enough to find the four spirits and capture them. I will show you how. If you can do it, and keep them close to you at all times, you will live and be strong. Very strong.

‘But if you don’t, you will fade and die, along with everything that is left of me. And those things will be free to cause terrible harm to every living thing on this planet. Do you see how important this is? Do you understand?'

'I . . . I . . .' Uki had no idea what to say. Then it occurred to him that, even if he wanted to help this bizarre talking fireball, he couldn't. He had problems of his own to deal with, him and his mother. 'Look,' he said. 'This all sounds very . . . um . . . *serious*. But I can't really help you. I'm sorry, I really am, but I have to stay with my mother. We're on a journey, you see. We're leaving this place and going across the mountains to where rabbits are kind and friendly.'

'Oh.' Iffrit flickered, silent for a moment, then, 'Oh,' again. His mouth opened and closed, as if he was trying to find words for something. And he kept looking over Uki's shoulder.

'What is it?' Uki said. He had an urge to look behind him, but also a sickening feeling that, if he did, there would be something awful there.

'Your mother . . .' Iffrit said. 'I am sorry to tell you this but . . . she is dead.'

*

No, Uki thought. *If I don't turn round, if I don't see it, then it won't be true.*

But there was something about Iffrit's pointed stare, that and the irresistible need to see his mother again, that made it impossible *not* to turn.

Slowly, with every heartbeat full of dread, he shifted round to look behind him.

There, cradled in the roots of a dead oak tree, was the body of his mother, curled in a ball like a sleeping baby, the tips of her fur dusted with frost.

A sound came from Uki's throat that was part wail, part scream. A twisted, animal-like sound that he didn't even know he was capable of making.

He scrabbled free from the rocks around him and half ran, half crawled over to her body. It was as cold as the dead roots around it: hard, stiff, brittle with frost where it should have been soft and warm and . . . *alive.*

'Wake up!' Uki shouted at her. 'Mother, wake up!'

He shook and nudged her, pulled at her ears, and, when nothing worked, turned back to Iffrit.

'Save her! Make her wake up! You said you

brought me back to life – do the same for my mother! Please!'

Iffrit only shook his little round head. 'I cannot. She was dead when I got here. I could only help you because you were still living. There is no trace of life in your mother.'

'Can't you try? Can't you go into her head, like you're in mine? Maybe there's something there you haven't noticed . . . Maybe there's a chance . . .'

'I can't leave you now,' Iffrit said. 'It would mean your death. All the knitting and fixing I have done for you would come apart.'

'I don't care!' Uki yelled. 'I don't care if I die! Just bring my mother back!'

'It can't be done.' Iffrit bowed his head. 'She has been dead too long. There is too much damage. If I tried, you would die as well. I am sorry. I cannot.'

The fiery form of Iffrit flickered once more, then blinked out, leaving Uki to his grief. He screamed again, then cried. He curled up around his mother and sobbed. He told her how much he loved her and begged her to come back. All those things, over and over, until he lost himself in grief completely, not even knowing where or who he was any more.

When he finally came back to himself, the sky was beginning to lighten. Dawn had come, hours had passed. At some point in the night he had buried his mother's body, using the rocks she had once carefully placed around him. Now he sat, paws scratched and bleeding, body numb. Every last tear had been cried out, leaving nothing but a horrid, empty feeling. A great black hole inside him, and he was teetering on the edge of it.

I've lost everything, was all he could think. *Mother, home ... I didn't have much but it's all gone forever.*

There was a flicker of light beside him as Iffrit reappeared.

'Go away,' said Uki. 'You're just a dream.'

'I am sorry for your loss,' the dream said. 'And I have given you time to grieve, but you really *must* come with me. I have things to show you and not much time left. I grow weaker every second.'

'I don't care,' said Uki. 'Leave me alone.'

'*Please.*' Iffrit juddered, his body becoming paler.

Uki could see the rest of the graveyard through it, like looking through a window. But he couldn't move, even if he wanted to. All he could do was sit and stare at the pile of stones that used to be his mother. He could sense Iffrit in the air next to him, gesturing, pleading, begging. He could even *feel* something strange buzzing and fizzing inside his head, but it was as if it was all happening to some other rabbit. As if he were outside himself, looking down on a sad, sad scene in a cold, lonely graveyard.

In the end, it was the voices that made him move. Rabbits entering the wood from the north, crackling through the undergrowth and talking to each other as they marched.

It was his old tribe come looking for him, or perhaps just bringing offerings for their dead. Either way, Uki's numb, empty shell was suddenly pumped with fear. He felt himself struggling to his feet, much to the delight of Iffrit, whose voice swam back into focus.

'Yes!' he said, flying in circles around Uki's head. 'This way! I have to show you the crystal, and there are only minutes left. Quickly! Quickly!'

Uki's only thought was to escape the voices, but he had no idea where to go other than follow the spirit's lead. Leaving his mother and his old life behind, he stumbled out of the graveyard.

Chapter Four

Gaunch

Iffrit led them out of the graveyard and through the woods, back to the heaped mounds of flint which were all that remained of the Cinder Wall.

Once it had stood three metres high, with armoured Imperial troops marching back and forth behind its crenulations, but that was many years ago. The Wall had crumbled, just as the Ice Waste tribes had dwindled almost to nothing. And Iffrit had slept through all this, buried beneath the earth just a few paces away.

Uki clambered over the Wall, his mind still frozen

from shock. He was simply following the floating spirit made of fire now. Just putting one foot in front of the other, unable to think of anything else.

If he had looked closely at the ground, he might have noticed the tracks his mother made the day before, carrying him towards the graveyard wrapped in his shroud. A few faded scuff marks were all that were left to show she had existed in the world. He stumbled past them, on into the forest.

Iffrit took them only a little further, almost as far as the clearing Uki and his mother had been camping in. He swooped down to the tangle of roots and bare earth where an old pine tree had toppled over some winters ago and pointed with both hands.

'Here it is! This is the prison!'

When Iffrit had first described it and mentioned the terrible spirits locked inside, Uki had imagined some kind of castle or tower, like the ones in the tales his mother used to tell. All he could see now was a cluster of pinkish shards where something the size of a melon had burst open.

'Is that it?' he managed to say. 'There were five of you in *there*?'

'It looks small from the outside, but it was made to hold huge amounts of information.' Uki just looked at him blankly. 'I mean, there was a whole world in there. Seas, oceans, mountain ranges. Just like this world, but on a scale so small, your eyes wouldn't be able to see it. The prisoners were each trapped on their own island and I had the job of guarding them. In there, I could change shape to be whatever I wanted. A towering, flaming giant or a colossal winged beast made of fire. I used to soar through the sky above them making sure they couldn't escape.'

Uki could only shake his head. This was too much to even *begin* understanding. Part of him was still sure this was just an awful dream and he was looking forward to waking up, even if it was into a body that was starving and filled with infection.

'Quick,' Iffrit urged him on. 'You must gather up some pieces. At least four of the big bits, to trap the spirits in. And some of the little fragments too. They will probably be valuable to your people. Like diamonds or rubies.'

So this is *a dream,* thought Uki. *And I'm the prince finding the treasure.* He stooped down and picked up five of the bigger shards, stuffing them into the pocket in his trousers. They were smooth, about the length of his paw and with lots of facets and edges. Once they were safely stowed away, he scooped up a pawful of little crystals and poured them into his other pocket.

'Good,' said Iffrit. 'When you get to the nearest town – you do have towns, don't you? – you should find a smith of some kind. Get them to fit the big crystals on to knife handles or spear hafts. They will be easier for you to use like that. And then you will need some kind of chain or belt to wear them on once they are filled—'

'Spears?' Uki blinked at the spirit. None of this was making sense. 'What am I going to do with *them*?'

'They are for catching the spirits! Haven't you been listening?' Iffrit flickered in irritation. The creature *had* been saying things all the way here, Uki realised, but he had been somewhere else, inside his own head. He'd heard nothing.

'I have so little time left. You *must* pay attention.' Iffrit was popping in and out of sight every few seconds now. Each time he reappeared he grew fainter. 'When you find the spirits, you will know them. You will sense them, just like I can. They will probably have merged with bodies like we have. Except they will have taken control of them I expect. Once you are close enough, jab the host with a crystal. The spirits will be drawn inside and my power – I mean, your power – will hold them there.'

'And then what do I do?'

'You must guard the crystals. Keep them near you at all times. They will give you strength at first, but it won't last. Not until you have all four. You *must* not stop until you get all four. Do you understand?'

'All four. Yes.'

'And you must go carefully. I can sense another one of our kind nearby. Another spirit. It may have noticed me, too. And there could be more around.'

'More spirits?'

'Yes. Creatures made by the Ancients. Some may be kind, but others . . . you will have to see. It would be best to be as inconspicuous as possible.'

'Incon-what?'

'Inconspicuous. Hard to notice. Secret.'

'Ah, right. Secret. I see.'

'Good. I— Wait . . . Do you feel that?' Iffrit suddenly turned in the air, his head twitching like a wolf following a scent. To Uki's surprise he *did* feel something too. A kind of sixth sense that something dangerous was nearby. A prickling on the back of his neck, like when the tribe children used to spy on him.

'What is it?' he asked.

Iffrit sniffed some more. 'One of the spirits! Gaunch, I think. He is close. And very weak. If we are lucky, he won't have had time to steal a body. Come, quickly! I only have a few seconds left!'

Rising back up to head height, Iffrit zoomed off through the trees. Uki had to run to keep up. They were following a path he noticed, as he ducked under low-hanging branches and jumped over trailing roots. One dotted with slabs of mossy stone here and there, all broken and jagged, poking up through the layers of mud and leaves. *Some kind of old road,* he thought. *Maybe one the soldiers used when the Wall was new.*

Deeper into the forest they ran and all the time that twitchy, tingling feeling grew stronger and stronger. Like an itch in his head he couldn't scratch.

Iffrit was moving faster, being able to pass through anything in his way. Uki noticed how transparent he had become. Like a ghost, a half memory of the thing that had first appeared to him in the graveyard.

Suddenly Iffrit stopped, darting behind an old silver birch tree, its bark hanging off in papery tatters. Something behind the trunk was glowing. A sickly yellow light that flickered just like Iffrit's flames. Could that be the missing spirit? Uki dimly wondered if it was safe, running up to an escaped creature as evil as the ones Iffrit had described. But then his life had exploded so completely in the last few hours. *What more can go wrong?* he thought as he reached the birch and peered around the trunk. *How can anything be worse than it already is?*

Uki was expecting to see some kind of demon. A winged snake, or something with fangs at least. Instead, there was just a tiny speck of light floating a few centimetres off the ground.

'There!' Iffrit shouted in triumph. 'It is Gaunch, the first of the spirits! Quickly, ready a crystal!'

Uki fumbled in his pocket for one of the shards. He didn't see what all the rush was about. 'Is that it?' he asked. 'That tiny yellow bit of light? It just looks like a baby firefly. Or a flying seed.'

As Uki watched, the thing flickered. For an instant he had a glimpse – an impression – of a creature lying on the forest floor. A thing made up of that yellow light, long, spindly limbs curled around itself. Starved skin stretched over bones and a bald, earless head with huge, terrified eyes. It looked more like a skeleton than an evil monster, and it certainly didn't seem dangerous.

A blink and it was gone again.

'That is it! Gaunch, the Lord of Famine! He poisoned the Ancients' crops, made them grow into warped, twisted things that they couldn't eat. He planned to starve them so he and his followers could take over their world. Quickly now! Press the crystal to the core of light! He will be pulled inside!'

Uki moved towards the yellow speck, holding the crystal in his paw. But that glimpse of the starving thing on the floor made him pause. How was he to know that Iffrit was right? What if it was a perfectly innocent being he was about to imprison? If only his mother was here to tell him what to do. She always knew what was best.

'Why are you waiting?' Iffrit floated down before him, so faint now he was hardly there. 'Do it now, before he escapes!'

'I don't know . . .' Uki couldn't find the right words. 'What if this isn't right? What if *you're* the evil one? I saw him just now and he looked helpless . . . *terrified*.'

'That's what he wants you to see,' Iffrit said. 'Think hard. My memories are yours now. What do you know of Gaunch?'

Uki was about to ask what under earth the spirit was talking about, when there was a flash behind his eyes. That sensation of waking up from a dream with cloudy memories that seem both real and unreal at the same time.

He saw a picture of a tall creature dressed in yellow armour standing amongst a desolation of burnt and twisted plants. Fields and fields of crops, all blackened and dead, stretching to the horizon as far as he could see. When he opened his eyes, the figure of Gaunch was back again, this time his bony face was split by a fierce, evil grin. The sunken, hollowed eyes gleamed with hatred and spite.

Iffrit is right, Uki realised. *This thing must never go free.*

He stabbed downwards with the crystal, aiming for the spot the glowing speck had occupied. His paw passed right through the body of Gaunch and into the soft layers of dead leaves under the birch tree. The image of the grinning spirit blinked out, as did the yellow light all around him. In his paw, Uki felt the crystal burn hot for a moment, buzzing as it was filled with a flow of energy.

And then *he* sensed it too.

A fizzing warmth, unlike anything he had known before, flowed through him, bubbling through his body, arms, legs, even to the tips of his ears. He felt like he could mow down the entire forest around him, just by thinking about it. Like he could leap up to the stars …

'Well done,' came a voice from beside him, and

he remembered Iffrit was still there. Just. 'You can feel the power, can't you?'

'Yes,' Uki nodded. 'It's . . . it's *amazing*.'

'It won't last long,' said Iffrit. 'And the other spirits won't be so easy to capture. Mortix, the Queen of Death; Charice, Bringer of Disease; Valkus, Spirit of War. You must follow them, while you can still sense the trail. This is as far as I can go . . . I can feel myself fading . . .'

'Are you dying?' Uki suddenly felt scared. He didn't want to be alone. Not truly alone, without his mother, without this strange spirit-thing he had thought was really a dream. 'Please don't. I can't . . . I don't want to be on my own.'

'You won't be,' said Iffrit. 'Not really. I am a part of you now. All my memories, all my powers are kept alive in you. I'll always be there, in a way.'

Uki didn't find that very comforting. He would still be alone and with an impossible task to complete. One which would mean his own death if he failed. He reached out a paw to the dwindling spirit. 'I can't do this . . . it's too hard . . .'

'You can.' Iffrit's voice was no more than a

whisper now. 'I believe in you. You . . . You never told me your name . . .'

'Uki.'

'Uki,' Iffrit repeated, as he vanished. 'Be strong, Uki.' And he was gone, leaving the young black-and-white rabbit standing in the middle of a cold, dead forest, feeling more alone than he could have imagined possible.

Interlude

Dusk is beginning to draw in when Jaxom hauls on the jerboas' reins, coaxing them to a halt. He leaps down from the driver's seat and leads them over to a little cluster of hawthorn trees, where he ties them up and puts a nosebag of seeds on each of them.

The bard jumps down as well, performing an exaggerated stretching routine that looks like some kind of slow-motion dance.

'Please don't say you're stopping there,' says Rue. There have been several breaks in the story already – when they had lunch, when the jerboas were rested or watered. Each time Rue had been hopping from foot to foot, waiting for the bard to continue.

'We're camping for the night,' says the bard. 'I'll carry on after dinner. Maybe.'

Rue throws their packs from the wagon and then climbs down after them. 'All right, then. How about some questions in between?'

'Do we have to?' says the bard. He walks over to where Jaxom has already spread his blanket on the ground and is setting some food out on it. Small, brown loaves of bread, dried turnip slices and a clay pot of something that looks and smells like pickled cabbage.

'Just while we eat,' says Rue. 'Just before you start the story again.'

The bard sighs and settles himself next to Jaxom. He adds some pieces of cornbread and a flask of elderberry juice to the feast.

'Aren't we having a fire?' Rue asks. He was looking forward to a big, crackling blaze. It was by far the best place for listening to the bard's stories.

'No fire,' said Jaxom. 'Not unless you want to spend the night having your skin sliced off.'

'The flames and smoke would be seen for miles,' explains the bard. 'Any Arukh raiders around would spot us and come investigating.'

Rue shuddered at the thought and pulled his cloak around him. Even though it was summer, the air was chilly this close to the mountains. 'Are they really that dangerous?'

'Depends,' said Jaxom, spreading some of the disgusting pickled cabbage on to a slice of bread. 'Some of the tribes are friendly – they even come down to towns like Melt to trade – but others are fierce as trapped weasels. They have warlords instead of chiefs, you see. They go through them pretty quick and every now and then you get one who wants to cause trouble. Hasn't happened for a while, though.'

'The last *real* problem was before I was born,' says the bard. 'That was when the tribes all joined up and decided to attack Gotland.'

'Was that when Crom and your father fought their first battle?' Rue asks.

'Well remembered,' says the bard. 'It was indeed.'

'That would make a good tale,' says Jaxom, but

before the bard can agree, Rue jumps up and stomps his foot.

'Hang on,' he says. 'You've got to finish the tale of Uki first! And then you said Podkin's would follow after, don't forget!'

Jaxom laughs and waves Rue back with a paw. 'Relax, little one. I wasn't suggesting he tell it. I was enjoying the Uki story myself, you know. He's a famous hero, here in Hulstland. Ninefold blessings on his name.'

'Oh,' Rue says, remembering to touch three fingers to his forehead. 'Like Podkin is where we come from?'

'Very similar,' says the bard. He has fished three leather cups from his pack and now fills them with juice.

'But there's some things I don't understand,' says Rue.

'Here we go,' mutters the bard, rolling his eyes at Jaxom.

'So, the Ancients made Gormalech and they also made these spirits. Why did they keep making horrible things?'

'Well,' says the bard. 'Those were only some of the things they made and I think it's pretty obvious they were mistakes. They locked the spirits away in a prison that was supposed to last forever. Gormalech, on the other hand, went a bit out of control. That's why the Ancients aren't around any more. But they probably made all sorts of other things as well. Things we can't even begin to understand.'

'Why did the spirit say there was some of them in us? Didn't the Goddess make us?'

'Yes,' says the bard, and is about to say more when he is interrupted by Jaxom clearing his throat. 'At least, that's what *we* believe. Others think Kether is the maker of all things. Ninefold blessings and all that.

'Anyway. There has been some discussion about whether the goddesses (and gods) *are* the Ancients. Or may even have been made by them as well. Just discussion,' he adds quickly, bowing his head to Jaxom, 'but it would explain some of the things Iffrit said.'

'Toasted turnips,' says Rue. He is actually quiet for a moment as this thought sinks in. Jaxom and the bard take the chance to drink their juice and start in on the cornbread. The pause doesn't last long.

'Also,' Rue continues. 'Why are the spirits so dangerous? Iffrit and Gaunch just faded away. Won't the others do that too? And how did they all fit into a tiny prison? What *are* they?'

'That's a lot of questions at once,' says the bard, pouring more juice. 'As I understand it, they had been trapped in that crystal for thousands of years. Hundreds of thousands, maybe. That made them weak. Too weak to carry on without a body to live in. A bit like a flea or a tapeworm, maybe. Perhaps they used to live inside the Ancients' bodies too? Who knows. It's certain that they weren't creatures of flesh and blood like you and me, though. They have a tiny speck that is real – the glowing lights that Uki saw – and the rest is something else. On their own, they probably *would* have faded away. Or gone into a deep sleep like Iffrit did. But if they find bodies to take over . . . well, that's when the trouble will start.'

'*Do* they find bodies? Does Uki capture them all? Does Iffrit come back?'

'Hold your horseradishes!' says the bard. 'That's

the rest of the entire story! A good few days' worth at least!'

'Well, what are we waiting for?' Rue says, settling down and snatching up the last piece of cornbread. 'You've had something to eat and drink, and there's not going to be a fire. We should at least have a story before we go to sleep.'

'He's right there,' says Jaxom, lying back and wrapping himself in his cloak. 'It's been many a year since I had a bedtime story.'

'Oh, very well,' says the bard, glugging down the rest of his juice. 'Just a bit more before bed, I suppose. Now, where was I?'

Chapter Five

Revenge

Uki stood still for a very long time. So long, in fact, that a tiny firecrest flew over to see what was going on. It fluttered backward and forward between the branches of the birch tree, the splash of gold on its forehead glinting in the sunlight, its bright eyes staring at the strange new statue in its forest.

On and on he stood, his only movement the slow blink of his mismatched eyes, until the firecrest lost interest and flew off.

Inside Uki's head, however, it was very different.

All the crazy things that had just happened to him were tumbling over and over, mixed with bits and pieces of memories that Iffrit had left behind. It was too much for Uki's young brain to cope with.

Slowly he lifted the crystal in his paw and stared at it. It was hot and buzzed with energy. Inside the pink shard there were swirls of yellow light, bumping and battering at the walls of this new prison as the trapped spirit tried to escape.

If it wasn't for this one solid piece of evidence, Uki would be sure he had gone mad.

And now I have to track down the other spirits, he thought, *because if I don't they will destroy the whole world.*

That didn't seem real either. In fact, harsh though it may sound, Uki didn't care much about the rest of the world right then. The only thing he could really think of was his mother, lying cold and alone in that graveyard. That, and the cruel rabbits who had put her there. He remembered them throwing stones, the gleeful smirks on the faces of the bullies who had caused it all.

And they would be back there now, safe and

warm by their firesides, probably laughing to each other about what had happened. Maybe they didn't know his mother had died or that he had nearly died too. Maybe they did and they didn't care.

He ground his teeth. Rabbits shouldn't be allowed to do such things to one another! All the years of teasing and misery just because he looked different, and now *this* . . .

As Uki's anger flared, he felt a sudden rush of power. Capturing Gaunch had given him strength, Iffrit had said. He wondered how much.

Reaching out a paw, he grasped one of the birch tree's low branches. He could feel the smooth bark, the sap running through it. Ordinarily, it would take a good few minutes of chopping with an axe to get through wood this thick.

Uki twisted his grip a tiny fraction and the branch snapped off with a thunderclap *crack*. It had been as easy as pulling up a blade of grass.

Uki stared at his paw as he wiggled his fingers. *It won't last long,* Iffrit had said.

Not long, perhaps, Uki's dark voice whispered to him, **but long enough for what you need to do.**

He turned towards the Cinder Wall and started the walk back north.

*

The yellow spirit's power had made him fast as well. He stormed through the woods on legs that didn't seem to ache or tire. His mind was still reeling and he didn't notice the passing of time properly. One minute he was clambering over the Wall, the next he was crossing the graveyard where he had woken just that morning. Everything was foggy, like a dream.

Revenge was the only thing he could think about. The things he would do to the members of his old tribe when he found them. The lessons he would teach them. Call him a demon, would they? He would show them what a demon was really like . . .

And then, somehow, there he was, standing outside the cluster of stone-and-thatch huts, hidden behind a dead, fungus-covered oak tree.

Night had fallen and a northern wind blew flurries of snow crystals round and round in the air. He blinked up at the darkness, wondering where the day had gone.

How did I get here? he thought. *What am I even doing?*

Grief can do funny things to your mind, and this was Uki's first real experience of it. If only there had been someone kind to explain it to him, perhaps he might have been able to cope, or at least understand what was happening to him.

He could see firelight glinting around the edges of the hut doors, hear the mumble of voices within. As he watched, one of the doors opened, and two rabbits stepped out, cloaks huddled tight against the cold.

Uki's breath caught in his throat. It was the two bullies, scuttling across the frosty ground back to their house.

Them, Uki thought, his fists bunching tight. He could see the piggy eyes of the boy peering around the village. His sister was whispering in his ear as they walked. Probably a mean and spiteful nugget of gossip.

They had no idea he was standing just a few metres away. The outcast, back to haunt them. This was his chance to rush out and surprise them. Catch them just as they were heading into the warmth of their hut.

And do what? he asked himself. All the way here, he hadn't been thinking properly he realised. All he could feel was anger at what had happened to his mother. That, and the feeling of power from the crystal still gripped in his fist.

Was he really going to attack those rabbits? He hated them, yes. He wanted to see them punished, but was he actually able to hurt them?

They deserve it, his dark voice told him. **It's because of them that your mother's dead. It's because of them that you have nothing.**

He remembered the branch snapping off in his paw. With that kind of strength he could really injure someone. Kill them, even.

His mother would never have wanted that. She had always told him to be kind and good. Even when the village children had teased and laughed at him, she would tell him to forgive them.

'I'm sorry, Mother,' he whispered into the bark of the dead oak. 'I can't forgive them. Not ever.' But, he realised, he couldn't hurt them either. No matter how easy it would be with this new strength he had. That would make him as bad as them. Worse even.

Instead he would leave them. Leave them alone to their sad little lives. It wouldn't be long before they found another victim to bully. And then another, and another. Eventually, everyone in the village would hate them just as much as Uki did. And then what would they have? They were all alone out here in the Ice Wastes: no other tribes for miles and miles around.

Perhaps they would learn their lesson and change. Perhaps they would lead miserable, lonely lives. Uki took a deep breath and let it out slowly, imagining his anger swirling out with the steam, carried away by the snowflakes. He found he didn't care any more. These were all other rabbits' problems now. He was done with this place for good. There was a whole other world out there for him and, if Iffrit was right, it needed his help.

He turned his nose south, towards the Five Realms.

Chapter Six

Jori

Uki's sleep that night was filled with strange dreams.

He flew through a pink-tinted sky, with blazing wings of fire stretching out on either side of him.

He soared and circled over an endless sea, riding lazy thermals and staring down at the waves below. Every now and then he passed over an island, each with high, jagged cliffs jutting upwards, topped with towering walls of glass.

There were creatures living there, one on each lump of rock. They had built themselves little homes:

a blocky, fortified castle; a smoking workshop surrounded by pools of noxious slime; an empty banqueting hall amongst fields of blackened crops; and a tiny thatched cottage with a skull hanging on the front door.

When they saw him flying overhead, the creatures ran into their homes as fast as they could and locked the doors. They were terrified of him, and it made him feel powerful and yet lonely, both at the same time.

And then there was another dream. Of a stone tower, the four walls carved with open, staring eyes. It sat amongst a group of huts and outbuildings, all built on top of a hill at the edge of a forest.

While the first dreams had been strange and alien, this place seemed almost familiar.

There was someone, a presence, inside the tower. Uki couldn't see it, not yet, but he could *feel* it there. It was searching, peering out across the treetops, looking for . . . *something* . . . with an overpowering feeling of hunger and need.

And then, in the few seconds before he awoke, he sensed the thing get a sniff of what it was after.

A spark like lightning shot through the tower and a bell began to sound . . .

Uki sat up and rubbed his eyes.

The shadows of sleep hung in his head like sticky cobwebs. Those wings, those creatures on the islands . . . they weren't a dream at all, he realised, but memories. Things Iffrit had seen during all those years inside the prison that had now been passed on to him.

But what about the last one? The vision of the tower he had seen just before waking? It had seemed so real, the trees of the forest so much like those surrounding him right now. He even thought he could hear a faint echo of the bell itself, still ringing somewhere in the distance . . .

Uki shook his head to clear it and had a good look around.

He had left the village last night and walked on through the darkness for several hours, no longer afraid of all the hoots and scratchings in the trees around him. Passing the Wall, he had made his way far into Icebark before finally curling up in the hollow of an old, fallen tree and slipping quickly into a deep sleep.

A frost had formed in the night; a light dusting covered the ground and was crusted over his cloak. He brushed it off, realising he didn't really feel the cold at all. *Just as well,* he thought. Without Iffrit's power and the crystal, he would probably have frozen to death.

He didn't know the forest well but he could feel a pull coming from somewhere to the south. A feeling like an invisible thread was stretching from somewhere behind his eyes, off into the distance: tugging, tugging. *The spirits,* he thought. *They are calling out to whatever's left of Iffrit.*

He knew if he followed that faint line, it would lead him out of Icebark and on to wherever the three remaining creatures had gone.

What would it be like out there, away from the Ice Wastes? His mother had told him stories about the rest of the rabbit world. There were five realms, he knew, and the closest one was called Hulstland. She'd said it was made up of lots of different kinds of places: wide open plains where rabbits rode on leaping rat-like creatures called jerboas; swampy fens full of snakes and frogs; hills, mountains, rivers, fields and farms. And not forgetting villages, towns and cities: great underground places where hundreds of rabbits lived together.

Uki couldn't deny he was a little excited at the chance of seeing it all, but to think that his mother wouldn't be there with him . . . A sudden wave of sadness overtook him and he had to sit on a tree stump and sob into his cloak.

After a few minutes he managed to calm himself, and sniffed away the last of his tears. **Pull yourself together,** his dark voice scolded him. **You have to get out of this forest before you go anywhere.**

Uki knew there were some ruins near the centre. His mother had often talked about going to see them someday. After that, there was a day's walk to the forest edge and the start of the plains. There was a little town there, she'd said. A place called Nowhere or Nether or something. Uki thought that would be somewhere the spirits might head for. Somewhere they could find bodies to live in, like Iffrit had done with him.

'To the ruins, then,' he said aloud, making a

blackbird fly off into the treetops, shrieking as it went.

*

It took him longer than he thought to reach the ruins. The forest was thick at its heart. The bare trees with their white bark were crowded together, branches mixed in and meshed with tangled snags of brambles and vine.

There was probably a path somewhere leading just where he wanted to go, but he couldn't see it. He could only follow the invisible call of the spirits, a straight line that seemed to go through every single thorn bush it could find.

Dusk was falling by the time Uki finally saw an uneven block of stacked stones rising up above the treetops. In the failing light it appeared to be just a slab of darkness but its shape was unlike any of the natural ones around it. Two sides joined to form a corner of what must once have been a building, the rest of the structure having tumbled away long ago and been swallowed by the hungry forest.

The ruins, Uki thought. His mother had said they were left behind by the Ancients. Just like Iffrit and his prison, Uki now knew. It made him wonder what other things might be scattered over the world. Bits and pieces of buildings and hidden secrets buried under the ground. How he wished he could have told his mother all about it.

Just thinking of her made the sobbing feeling start to rise up again, and he was about to sit down for another cry when his senses began to tingle.

Even though the forest all around was now just a dim shade of grey, Uki could *feel* that there was something – or someone – else in the ruins. Not quite hearing, not quite seeing – he just had a feeling that there was life pulsing away somewhere inside the stone structure.

A spirit? he thought at first, but this was different from the distant pulling at the back of his head. No, the spirits were far off now. Out of the forest completely, he was sure.

Stepping as quietly as he could, Uki tiptoed around the outskirts of the stones. The sense that someone was there grew stronger and stronger with each step. Sure enough, as he moved around the stone structure, he could make out a figure in the twilight.

It was a rabbit, a young one. Bigger than him, but not an adult. Huddled against the wall, it had its head buried in its paws, and appeared to be crying, just like he was earlier. Pricking up his ears, Uki could hear quiet muffled sobs. A girl's sobs, lost and alone in the dark forest.

What do I do now? Uki wondered. Should he go and see if the rabbit was all right?

Mind your own business, said the dark voice. **This has nothing to do with your quest. Best just carry on through the forest.**

He was standing in the darkness wondering what to do, when he caught sight of a movement in the distance. Just a shifting shadow at first, but as Uki stared through the gloom he picked out an ear, then two. It was another rabbit. A way off yet but heading steadily closer.

Something about the way it moved gave him the feeling it was stalking, hunting. Was it a friend of the rabbit in the ruins, out looking for food? Or was it after *her*?

His answer came soon enough.

He watched as the stalker crept nearer. It was

definitely trying not to let the girl in the ruins know it was there, which was a bad sign. Uki held his breath, curling himself as low as possible amongst the undergrowth so the stalker wouldn't spot *him*.

Closer, closer he came, right to the far edge of the ruins. *He's going to hurt her,* Uki realised, and with that thought came a sudden surge of anger. Another bully attacking someone weak and defenceless. A growl built up in his throat and, in the space of a heartbeat, he decided he was not going to stand by and let this happen. Uki was going to *do* something about it. He carefully reached out a paw, feeling around on the cold forest floor for something he could use as a weapon. His fingers closed over a hunk of old stone half buried in the forest soil.

The girl was still crying to herself, completely unaware of the other rabbits nearby. As Uki watched, the stalker began to draw a long, slim blade from a sheath at his belt as he stepped inside the shelter of the ruins. He was only a few metres from his victim now – ten from where Uki crouched. Any second he would pounce, his blade would flash and the girl would be badly wounded, or worse.

Not if I can help it. Uki saw the stalker tense, ready to strike. There was no time to move closer, no way to block him. The only thing was to throw the stone he was clutching and hope it scared him off somehow.

Uki stood up, ripping the stone from the ground and hurling it in one motion. Except the small piece he was holding was just the tip of an enormous chunk of masonry, more like a boulder. It burst from the ground with a loud, tearing *schlop*! and sailed through the air, trailing clods of earth in a tail behind it.

The sound made the stalker leap up and the rock hit him in the chest, knocking him clean off his feet and back into one of the ruin's walls, where he was sandwiched between the two hard pieces of stone. There was a horrible crunching sound, and then he fell to the floor in a limp heap.

Uki saw the girl had also jumped to her feet and, out of nowhere, a gigantic knife had appeared in her paws.

'Who's there?' she shouted. 'Who did that?' She spoke in Lanic, a language different to that of Uki's tribe, but luckily one his mother had taught him.

Uki paused before responding. The girl wasn't crying any more. In fact she looked quite frightening with that blade and, worse, the terrifying scowl on her face. It made Uki think he might have been wrong about her being poor and vulnerable.

But he *had* saved her after all. And she deserved to know who was out there, hiding in the bushes. He raised his paws and stepped out of the undergrowth. The girl peered at him through the gloom.

'Why is there only half of you?' she said.

Uki wondered what she meant for a second, and then realised his white fur was the only part showing in the gathering darkness. 'It's my fur,' he called back. 'I have different colours.' He turned his head so she could see his blue eye, an icy chip amongst the black velvet of his left side.

The girl cocked her head, her ears twitching. 'Are you a . . . child?'

'I'm eight.' Uki had no idea what else to say. It was unusual enough for him to meet a new person, let alone one whose life he had just saved. What were you supposed to say in this situation? He thought it might be a good idea to introduce himself.

'I'm Uki, by the way.'

The girl ignored him and turned towards the fallen stalker. In a few steps she was by his side, her blade still drawn.

'Is he . . . dead?' Uki asked.

The girl poked him with her foot a few times, then knelt down and listened by his head. 'No. Still breathing. You hit him with a *boulder*. How under earth did you do that?'

Uki didn't know where to start explaining, so he just shrugged. He took a chance and moved closer, into the clearing around the ruins. The girl had turned back to the unconscious rabbit and was rummaging for something in the pouches at her belt.

'I think he was going to hurt you,' Uki said. 'Do you know who he is?'

'He's one of my family's men,' the girl replied. 'And he was probably going to kill me, not just hurt me.' She had taken a vial from her belt and was tipping something into the rabbit's mouth.

'Are you making him better?' Uki asked. It seemed a strange way to treat someone who might have been about to murder you.

'No. Just making sure he doesn't wake up. Not for a couple of days, at least.'

The girl finished dosing her attacker, then stood to face Uki.

She was a good head-and-a-half taller than him, Uki now saw, which would make her quite a bit older. Twelve or thirteen, maybe, and she held herself high with the confidence of someone strong and important.

She wore leather armour, dyed black. It was snugly fitted to her body with buckles and belts all over, hand-stitched with twining patterns that made it look beautiful and very, very expensive. There was a row of pouches at her waist and a flask of carved white wood, stoppered with a silver lid. A cloak of soft, dark wool hung from her shoulders, clasped at the neck with a brooch in the shape of a coiled snake.

Her fur was light grey with a white patch over her nose and mouth, and black tips on the points of her ears. She had fierce, stony eyes, and a deep frown that she was currently using on Uki, as if questioning how he dared to be in the same forest as her, let alone having the cheek to save her from certain death.

He looked down at his own clothes: poorly stitched rat-leather trousers, a patched and darned shirt of hemp cloth he had outgrown last summer, and half an old blanket for a cloak. He felt like some kind of beggar in comparison to her. The thought almost made him want to kneel and apologise for being so scruffy.

'It would appear that you have saved my life,' she said, after the pause was starting to become awkward. 'The blood honour of my clan means that I am now in your service.'

She wrinkled her nose as she spoke, as if the words themselves smelt terrible.

'Oh,' was all Uki could say. 'Thank you. I think.' And then, 'What does that mean, exactly?'

The girl rabbit sighed. 'It means, *exactly*, that I owe you a debt of honour. I have to help you out in some way to repay it before I can get on with my life and forget you even exist.'

Uki blinked up at her for a moment. It was clear he had annoyed her quite a lot, although he had only been trying to help. 'That's very nice of you,' he said. 'But I don't really need any help. I just heard you crying and then that rabbit was about to hurt you . . .'

'I was *not* crying!' The girl slid her big knife into the sheath at her belt with a snap, and then stormed back to the corner of the ruins with a *swish* of her cloak. She knelt down and began striking sparks from a flint so hard they zipped and flew everywhere.

This was Uki's first experience of a teenager and he didn't know whether to try and calm her down or run for cover as fast as his paws could carry him. Instead he stood fixed to the spot, frantically trying to think of the right thing to say.

In the meantime, the girl got her campfire going and then pulled a metal tripod and a pot from her pack. The firelight made her grey eyes gleam even more when she finally looked up at Uki again.

'Well?' she said. 'Are you going to come and have some supper or not?'

'Oh. Um . . . yes. Thank you.' Wondering (and hoping) this might count for repaying the honour debt, Uki crept over and took a seat on the other side of the fire. The girl was putting chopped vegetables and spices into the pot, and the smell was already delicious. It made Uki's tummy rumble and he realised that he hadn't eaten anything for days now. The power of the spirits had kept him going somehow, without the need for food.

As the pot began to bubble and clouds of spice-scented steam started to rise, Uki racked his brains for something to say. This was nothing like being with Nua, whose flurry of questions had almost overwhelmed him. Now it seemed up to him to break the silence. But what with?

She clearly didn't want to talk about being upset, and it seemed nosy to ask why someone had wanted to kill her. She didn't seem at all interested in Uki's unusual fur (which was a huge relief), but then she didn't care about any other part of him either.

Should he talk about the weather? The forest? Compliment her lovely armour? In the end, he was trying so hard to think of something to say that he ended up being silent.

'Here.' The girl spooned some stew into a bowl and handed it to him. Uki blew on it, then began to tip it down his throat with relish, enjoying the warming heat that spread through his chest and marvelling at all the new flavours and spices he'd never tasted before.

'Hungry little thing, aren't you?' The girl was dipping a spoon into her bowl and sipping from it with great grace and control.

'Sorry,' said Uki, wiping his mouth on his sleeve. He couldn't help feeling that everything he did or said around this girl made him seem more and more stupid.

The girl just raised an eyebrow and carried on sipping until her bowl was empty. She placed it beside the fire to which she added a few more twigs, then sat back to stare at Uki. It was a look sharp enough to chop turnips with.

'Well,' she said, leaning forward, curious. 'Are you going to tell me how you managed to crush a grown rabbit with a rock that weighed twice as much as yourself?'

Uki felt a sudden swell of panic. The very first encounter with another rabbit and he had revealed his powers. He really should have been more careful. Cross with himself more than anything, he answered her question with a rude one of his own. 'Only if you tell me why that rabbit was trying to kill you, and what you're even doing out in the forest on your own at night.'

He cringed as soon as the words left his mouth but, to his surprise, the girl gave a flicker of a smile. 'My name is Jori,' she said. 'I am the granddaughter of Toxa, Lord of Clan Septys.'

She paused, waiting for a reaction from Uki. When he didn't show the slightest bit of awe, she frowned and carried on. 'As you *clearly* don't know, Septys is one of the Shadow Clans of Hulstland. Of all the many clans, there are three who are well known for their skills in silent killing. They are used as assassins throughout the Five Realms. All deal death in different ways: Clan Septys are famed for their use of poison.'

'You kill people?' Uki asked.

'Not I,' said Jori. 'And that's the problem.' She looked away, out towards the dark forest, and Uki thought she might be crying again, although this time, silently.

'I was supposed to join the family business,' she said. 'They'd been training me since I could hop. But

I never wanted to *kill* anybody. All the knowledge and skills of the Clan – they could be used to help people instead of hurt them, you see. That's what I discovered years ago, although I didn't dare tell anyone.

'And then the time came for my trials. The tests to become a true assassin. The first parts were easy: our clan style of fighting, identifying deadly plants, mixing potions. Until it came to the final task. They wanted me to actually, really kill someone.

'I couldn't do it.' She looked back at Uki, her eyes gleaming with tears. 'I just couldn't. So I ran away instead.'

'I don't think that's bad,' said Uki. 'Not wanting to kill someone, I mean. I think you did the right thing.'

'My family clearly don't.' Jori flicked an ear at the crumpled form of her attacker. 'Nobody runs away from Clan Septys. It's an insult to their honour. They would rather have me dead than out here, giving away their precious secrets.'

Uki watched as Jori wiped her eyes on a corner of her cloak. He couldn't understand how somebody's own family would want to hurt them. Was that really how things worked out here in the big, wide world?

'What about your parents?' he said. 'Don't they love you? Won't they miss you?'

Jori laughed – a hard, bitter sound – and shook her head. 'You haven't met my parents. They have three other children, older and more important than me. All they care about is the blood honour of the stupid Clan. The whole lot of them. They're as cold as dead fish.'

She spat into the fire then wrapped her cloak tight around her. When she looked up at Uki again, she had returned to her previous self. Calm, elegant and superior. 'Your turn,' she said. 'Tell me how *you* ended up alone in the forest, throwing boulders around like they were pebbles.'

For a moment Uki considered making up a tale – there was no way anyone would believe what had really happened – but he couldn't think of anything convincing enough on the spot. A bear had passed by and thrown the rock instead of him? It was a magic stone that had just leapt out of the ground by itself?

It had fallen from the sky, like a particularly heavy spot of hail?

In the end he just told Jori the truth, starting with his escape from his village and ending up with him rescuing her earlier that very evening.

As he spoke, he watched her expression change. From wide-eyed pity at the beginning, to a frown, then a sneer when he started talking about spirits and crystals. When it looked as though she was about to call him a liar, he reached into his pocket and handed her Gaunch's crystal. For the rest of the tale she sat and stared into its swirling depths, feeling the heat and tiny buzzes of energy with her fingertips.

When Uki finished, Jori sat silent for a good few minutes longer. Finally, she handed him back the crystal then stoked up the fire, adding the rest of the firewood. She pulled some blankets out of her pack and tossed one over to him.

'Sleep as close to the fire as you can,' she said. 'It's going to be cold tonight.'

And with that, she rolled herself up in her cloak and blanket and went to sleep.

Uki sat and stared at her for a moment, trying to

puzzle out her reaction. No questions? No teasing? No asking for more proof?

He thought she might sit up suddenly and start asking him things, but she didn't. Instead, when her breathing slowed to gentle snores, he wrapped himself up too and snuggled near the crackling fire.

Other rabbits, he thought, were very strange creatures indeed.

Chapter Seven

Lak Kriya of the Kalaan Klaa

When Uki awoke the next morning, his first thought was to wonder where the roof of his hut had gone, and why his mother wasn't asleep beside him.

Then he remembered. *That* was his old life. Everything was different now; nothing made sense. With a deep sigh he sat up, ready for another day in this strange, motherless world. At least there had been no more dreams last night. Although the nagging feeling that something was looking for him still remained.

Jori was already awake, wrapped in her cloak and poking at the ashes of the fire. Another frost had come in the night, coating everything in a film of white sparkles. Uki spotted a spider's web hanging from the ruins, transformed into a net of tiny, perfect diamonds.

'Breakfast,' said Jori. She handed him something she had dug out of the fire. Some kind of round vegetable with leathery brown skin.

'Haven't you ever seen a potato before?' she said.

Uki shook his head and bit into it. The centre was soft and fluffy. Hot steam billowed out, covering his face as he chomped away.

Jori watched him, delicately cutting slices from her baked potato with her belt knife. When Uki had finished and licked most of the crumbs from his fingers, she cleared her throat to speak.

'I've been thinking,' she said. 'About what you said last night.'

'Yes?' Uki held his breath, waiting to be called a liar, or worse. He'd known it would be coming, after all.

'You said there are three more … spirits … out there?'

Uki nodded.

'And that they will do terrible things if they aren't stopped?'

Uki thought of the islands and their inhabitants. The poisonous gases, the fortress prickling with spikes. 'Yes,' he said. 'I've got a feeling that it will be awful.'

'Then . . . if you don't mind . . . I should like to come with you. To help, I mean.'

Uki nearly coughed his potato back up. She actually wanted to help him? Even though he'd said how dangerous it was? Even though she was some kind of royalty and he was a scruffy bumpkin from beyond the wall?

'You see,' Jori continued, 'it would be a good way for me to repay my debt to you. And it would keep me far away from my clan's warren. And, if we are successful, it would be a great achievement. I might even be able to return home and show them that my beliefs, my way of doing things, works just as well as poisoning and murder. If not better.'

Uki stared at her, wondering if this might all be part of a joke. 'You do remember what I said, don't you? About the danger and everything?'

'Of course,' said Jori. She patted her belt where the big knife and the flask were. 'I can take care of myself you know. If that rabbit had tried to face me last night, rather than sneaking up on me, I would have sliced him like chopped radish.'

Uki had forgotten about the rabbit. He glanced over to where he lay, still motionless, his fur and clothing covered in a crust of frost.

'There's something else you should know,' Uki said. 'I think there's someone following me. Or searching for me at least.'

'Who?' Jori looked around the forest, ready to draw her big knife again.

'I don't know really,' said Uki. 'It's just a sense I have. I sense lots of things now … ever since Iffrit went into my head.'

'Is it one of these "spirits"?'

Uki thought for a moment. 'No, I don't think so. I mean, it *feels* similar, like it is a spirit. But it definitely isn't one of the things from the prison. They are in my memories now, in my mind. Like I've known them forever. I don't really understand how it all works. Iffrit didn't say anything about me being able to sense *other* spirits, although I suppose they must be around. Perhaps this whole forest is full of them.'

Jori relaxed again. 'It doesn't matter. Like I said, I can look after myself. And you can hurl massive lumps of stone about. I think we'll be fine. What do you say?'

Uki thought hard. Iffrit hadn't said anything about *not* asking anyone for help. And he couldn't deny that it would be nice to have some company. Even if it was someone who made him feel awkward most of the time.

'All right,' he said. 'I accept.'

Jori smiled – looking much friendlier (and actually very pretty) without a scowl – and performed an elaborate bow. 'In that case, partner, I suggest we break camp and begin our quest.'

Uki bowed in return, and they set about packing.

*

It turned out there *was* a path through the forest. The remains of the old road, dotted here and there with fragments of stones like the ones Uki had spotted before. It made their progress much faster, even though it didn't quite line up with the direction Uki could feel the spirits calling from.

'It's definitely that way?' Jori asked him as they walked. 'You can tell where they are?'

'Yes,' said Uki. 'It's like I can feel them pulling on a string that's tied to my head. Another thing Iffrit did to me.' Mentioning the guardian spirit made him remember one of the last things Iffrit had said to him. 'Is there a town near here? My mother said there was one at the edge of the forest.'

Jori nodded. 'Nether it's called. A little trading town full of strays and runaways. Just a few huts bunched together really, but it's the only place the plains tribes will trade with, so my clan visits there every now and then. For plants and herbs to make their poisons.'

'I need to go there,' Uki said. 'I need to find a smith.'

Jori raised an eyebrow at him, so he told her about Iffrit's instructions. She looked a little reluctant at first, but finally she agreed to head there. 'There might be people looking for me,' she explained. 'I was staying there for a bit – I thought it would be the last place in Lanica my family would find me – but

I had a feeling I was being spied on. That's why I was hiding in the forest, trying to throw them off the scent. Not very well, it turns out.'

'Oh,' said Uki, ears drooping. Iffrit's brief instructions were all he had to go on.

Jori fiddled with the silver stopper of her belt flask for a moment, and then sighed. 'But we won't find another smith until we cross the plains. That's a three-day journey at least. I guess we'll be fine in Nether. If we're quick.'

Uki was about to thank her, but she had already turned and was heading down the path, making him trot to keep up.

They walked in silence for a while, Uki simply enjoying not being on his own any more. But as the gap in conversation grew wider and wider, he began to feel as though he should fill it. What did rabbits who hardly knew each other talk about? The weather? The scenery? Uki's eye kept being drawn to the blade on Jori's belt. It was made of a silver metal he'd never seen before. The hilt sparkled in the morning sunshine. The thing was beautiful yet deadly, and it fascinated him.

'That big knife,' he said. 'What is it made of?'

'Big knife?' Jori laughed. 'Haven't you ever seen a sword before?' She drew it and swished it through the air a few times before laying it across her forearm so he could look at it.

'*Sword,*' said Uki, trying the word out. 'The warriors in our tribe had stone axes and spears. Some had knives, but they were of orange metal. Copper.'

'This is steel,' said Jori. 'Made from iron. It's Damascus-forged and this groove down the middle is a "fuller'. It reduces the weight. The metal has been folded over a hundred times to make it stronger.'

The long blade had a ripple pattern running through it, like a babbling stream. The edge looked sharp enough to split his whiskers.

'I thought iron was poisonous,' said Uki. 'My mother said it was controlled by an evil god that lived under the ground.'

'Nonsense.' Jori rolled her eyes. 'That's what they believe across the mountains in Gotland and Enderby. But iron from the ground *is* tainted. In Hulstland we use sky metal. Haven't you heard about Eisenfell?'

Uki shook his head, feeling stupid again. Jori didn't seem to mind and began to explain it to him.

'Hundreds of years ago, a rock fell from the skies – from up where the stars are – and landed in Hulstland. It made a colossal crater in the ground, and when rabbits explored it, they found it was full of workable iron.

'Cinder was the king of the biggest tribe at the time. He taught his smiths to forge steel and used it to make tools and weapons. To build walls and towers with stone. He turned the crater into a city – Eisenfell – and then grew an empire from it, joining all the tribes of Hulstland together. They became the clans that exist today, and Cinder became the Emperor. And all because of metal like this.'

'Amazing,' said Uki, staring at the sword with even more respect. 'A weapon like that must be very special.'

'Very,' said Jori, swishing it through the air in circles again. 'Every year there is less and less sky metal. Owning steel swords and armour is a sign of how powerful and wealthy your clan is. This is only a small blade but it would still cost more than a house.

I bet my father would love to have it back.'

At the mention of her father, Jori's scowl returned. She sheathed her sword, and they walked on in silence again.

*

Even with the extra speed from following the path, the sun was nearing the horizon when they reached the edge of the forest.

The trees had begun to thin a while ago, but the sight of the plains suddenly appearing still drew a gasp from Uki. There had been wide open space in the Wastes of course, but it had been broken up by mountains, twisted trees and – in the far distance – the jagged white and blue streaks of the glaciers.

But none of that quite compared to his first sight of the Blood Plains.

Grass. Red grass. Like a sea. No, an ocean.

Acres and acres of it, as wide and empty as the sky above. No trees, no bushes, just silvery ripples as the wind blew across. It made Uki feel tiny and lost, like when he looked up at the endless stars in the night sky. How could a speck like him make a difference in this vast, dizzying world?

As well as giving him a clear view for miles, the lack of trees made his sense of the three spirits stronger. They were out there somewhere, off to the south-east: an itching behind his eyes when he looked that way, as if they might be specks on the horizon, just too small for him to see clearly. It was a very frustrating feeling.

After a few moments, Jori nudged his shoulder. 'If you've finished gaping, the town is over there.'

Uki looked to his left, where the line of the forest stretched off towards the Wall. Twenty metres away there was a cluster of stone buildings, ringed by a patchy fence of wooden stakes. Smoke drifted up into the sky from several chimneys in thin white streams. The place was scarcely bigger than the village he had come from.

'Nether,' he said.

'Impressive, isn't it?' said Jori, half smiling. 'Truly a wonder of the rabbit world. At least you won't look out of place in your barbarian outfit.'

Uki gave her back a glare as they wandered towards the town.

*

There was a gate in the south of the Wall with an ancient guard-rabbit snoozing on a stool outside. He didn't so much as twitch a whisker when Jori and Uki walked past him. Even if he had, his blunt spear was lying in the dust, well out of reach. Uki was amazed. Weren't there ferocious bands of rabbits out on those plains? And what about his own tribes? Ice Waste rabbits raided south of the Wall sometimes, too.

Jori noticed the shocked look on his face and laughed. 'Don't worry. I think this place is safe from attack. But only because there's nothing here worth taking. Look.'

Inside, Uki saw the 'town' was made up of ten or twelve rectangular buildings, much bigger than the roundhouses of his village. They were built from the same grey stone as the Cinder Wall (in fact, some of the carved blocks looked as though they might have been pillaged from the Wall itself) and roofed with wooden slats or turf. One of them had three enormous creatures tied up outside. Big, fluffy things with giant ears, gangly, folded-up legs and long swishing tails. They nibbled hay from a manger, twitching their noses and occasionally giving a little hop.

'Jerboas,' Jori said. 'The plains tribes ride them.'

'My mother told me,' Uki said. But her description hadn't done justice to how *strange* the things looked.

'That must be the smith.' Jori pointed to a building that had a low shelter attached. There was a brick forge in the middle of the shelter with a tall chimney stack that was belching white smoke.

Walking up to it, Uki could see the smith at work. She wore a long, leather apron, and was holding a pot at arm's length with a pair of tongs that glowed bright orange at the ends. As he watched, she poured molten copper from the pot into a clay mould on her workbench, then set the tongs aside when it was full. She mopped her forehead with a sleeve, then looked up at them.

'Good evening,' she said. 'Can I help you?'

'My ... friend ... has something he needs crafting,' said Jori. She had a way of talking that instantly made the smith stand straighter and listen. If Uki had tried to speak, he expected he might have been told to hop off. 'Tell her your requirements, Uki.'

'Um ... yes.' Uki fumbled in his pocket for Gaunch's crystal shard. When he brought it out, the smith gasped aloud.

'That's the biggest gem I've ever seen! And there's moving lights inside it! Where did you find it? Is it rabbit-made?'

Jori spoke quickly, before Uki could even think of an answer. 'It's a family heirloom. Very old. Very important and valuable. Isn't it, Uki?'

'Yes, yes ... Family,' said Uki, wondering why Jori had interrupted. 'I need it put on to a spear shaft. There are three more as well.' He thought for a moment, remembering Iffrit's instructions. 'And I will need to take the crystals off and put four of them into a belt ... or something. So that I can keep them close all the time.'

He wished he'd given it more thought, but the smith's eyes were already gleaming with the thought of a new project. 'I can make a haft they'd fit to, easily,' she said. 'My husband is a leatherworker.

He should be able to make a belt. Maybe a harness to hold the spears in too . . . When did you want the job done by?'

'Tomorrow morning,' said Jori. 'It's urgent.'

The smith's face fell. 'The morning? I'm sorry, but I don't think I'll be able. I'm just finishing for the night as it is . . .'

'You will be paid well,' said Jori, pointing to the serpent badge on her cloak. Uki thought this was a cue for him to give the smith something. He fished in his other pocket and brought out a few of the small crystals, the ones Iffrit had told him to take for payment.

'Here,' he said, putting them on to the workbench. The smith gasped and staggered, grabbing the bench for support. Even Jori's eyes boggled.

'Are they . . . diamonds?' The smith rubbed her eyes and blinked. 'There's enough there for us to buy a forge in Eisenfell itself! Are you sure you want to pay this much?'

'I'm sure,' Uki said. Then, trying to use the same tone as Jori, added. 'But it must be ready for the morning. Your finest work, if you please.'

'Yes, sir. Of course, sir.' The smith scooped up the tiny gems then ran into the house, shouting for her husband. Uki turned to Jori with a proud smile on his face to find her gawping at him.

'I was going to put it on my clan's account,' she said. 'You didn't tell me you were as rich as the Emperor himself!'

Uki shrugged. 'They were just little pieces of the crystal the spirits escaped from,' he said. 'There were lots of them on the ground.'

'Well, best keep that to yourself,' said Jori. 'If word gets out that there's diamonds or magic crystals buried under the forest, the whole thing will be cut down and torn up before you can blink. Do you have any more?'

Uki reached in to his pocket and pulled out the rest. There were five tiny crystals in his paw, twinkling in the pink sunlight.

'Keep them safe,' Jori said. 'We might need them in future. Perhaps we can change them for coins somewhere. You can't go paying for things with priceless gems. It tends to get you noticed.'

'If you say so,' said Uki, tipping the crystals back

into his pocket. He looked around the other scant buildings in the tiny town. 'What shall we do now?' he asked. It seemed a long time until morning, and his senses told him the spirits were still quite far away. Nether didn't look like a place you would want to spend too much time in.

'That building with the jerboas outside is an inn,' said Jori. 'Actually, it's more like a shack with beds, although it's better than sleeping on the ground. Just. Let's get a hot meal and a room for the night. And let me pay. Keep your gems where no one can see them.'

*

As they neared the inn, Uki could see that it had originally been a single turf-roofed building that had been added on to with extra rooms here and there, all leaning against each other for support. The stone walls were hunks of lichen-speckled granite, and he noticed one had the rough remains of a carved face and some marks that might be writing. Could this piece have been taken from the Ancients' ruins?

He was just about to mention it to Jori when he heard a shout coming from behind the inn. The pair looked at each other, questioning. Was someone in trouble? Was it any of their business?

The cry came again, and this time Uki didn't hesitate. He began running around the side of the inn.

Jori soon caught up with him. 'This could be a very stupid thing to do, you know,' she said. Part of Uki agreed but, almost without him realising, his mind had made the decision that he wouldn't stand by if *anyone* was being hurt. There hadn't been anyone there for him when he needed it, and he knew how awful that felt.

They dashed round the building and came to a splintery wooden shelter with stalls for rats and jerboas. A stable for the inn's customers.

There was one jerboa there now, tied up in a stall, and two adult rabbits standing over something on the ground. One of them gave it a hard kick and it yelled. It was another rabbit, Uki realised, and a small one. A little girl. A child.

'Backchat me, will you? Have *that*, you flea-bitten little rat-riding runt!' The other rabbit kicked the child and the pair of them laughed. Uki felt that flash of rage again, that pounding of blood in his head.

'Leave her alone!' he yelled, gritting his teeth and clenching his fists. He could feel the power there, coiled up like an angry serpent.

The two grown rabbits paused in their kicking and looked up. When they saw Uki, they laughed again.

'Look, Nurg,' said one. 'Somebody's cut two rabbits in half and stuck them back together wrong.'

'Come to save your little girlfriend have you? Do you want a kicking as— Oh.'

The rabbit stopped midspeech and stared at something over Uki's shoulder. He looked around and saw that Jori had drawn her sword. She had also taken the flask from her belt, opened its silver stopper and taken a tiny sip.

'Care to dance?' she said, putting the stopper back and carefully clipping the flask to her belt. With her other paw she span the sword through the air. Faster and faster it went, until it was just a blur.

'A dusk wraith!' The rabbit called Nurg turned to run but fell over his own feet in panic. The other one was slightly braver and pulled a copper knife from his belt.

Uki was about to call out a warning to Jori, but she was gone. She crossed the stable yard so quickly, Uki didn't even see her move.

In the space of a blink, she was at the rabbit, her sword just a shimmer in the air. Cuts and slashes seemed to appear out of nowhere, and then Jori was back at Uki's side as if she'd never left.

The rabbit still stood in the yard next to his fallen friend. It was like nothing had happened, until Uki noticed there was now just a dagger hilt in his paw. The blade was lying over by the stable, sliced clean off. There were also gaping holes in his shirt, no whiskers on either side of his face and, as Uki watched, his belt fell away, cut through in three places.

The rabbit blinked, swallowed and then winced as his trousers slowly slid to the floor.

'Aaah!' screamed Nurg, clambering to his feet and sprinting away from the inn. The other rabbit pulled up his trousers and followed, crying as he left.

'That was amazing!' Uki turned to Jori, his eyes boggling. 'How did you move so fast? And what's a dusk wraith?'

'I am,' Jori said. She suddenly slumped, leaning on her sword for support. 'It's the name of warriors from my clan. We drink a potion before we fight. It makes us ten times quicker than a normal fighter, but . . .'

She patted the flask at her side, then sagged to her knees. Uki grabbed her shoulder. 'What's wrong?' he asked.

'This is what happens . . .' Jori was finding it hard to speak now. '. . . when you take dusk potion. Feel weak . . . afterwards. Don't worry . . . doesn't last too long. See to . . . girl.'

Uki didn't like to leave Jori, but the girl who had been hurt was still lying on the yard floor. With several backward glances, Uki hurried over to her.

She was tiny, he now saw. The size of a five- or six-year-old. She had sandy fur, so short it was like velvet, and big, brown eyes that were blinking up at him. She wore loose leather clothes with glass beads and pieces of bone embroidered on, and she had red stripes dyed into the fur of her ears and cheeks. *A plains rabbit,* Uki thought. The first one he'd seen. He had been terrified by them, ever since hearing his mother's stories about his father's raiding party being killed by a plains tribe. This one didn't look very scary, though.

'Are you all right?' Uki asked, and then suddenly wondered if she might speak a different language. He pointed to her and shrugged his shoulders, trying to mime his question.

'*Nam ukku ulla,*' she said, shaking her head. 'I speak Lanic, you know. Us plains tribes aren't savages.'

'Sorry,' said Uki. 'I didn't know. Are you hurt?'

'I'll be fine. In a month or two.' She sat up, wincing and holding her stomach.

'Are you lost?' Uki made his voice as gentle as possible, thinking it might be the best way to speak to a scared five-year-old. 'Are your parents around?'

'I'm not a *baby*,' the girl said. 'I'm ten years old, you know. I'm just small because I got sick when I was little and now I don't grow properly. And my *parents* threw me out of the tribe when I was eight. They gave me my jerboa and told me to hop off and annoy some other family.'

The sole jerboa in the stable turned around at the

girl's voice and made a little *neek* sound.

'I'm fine, Mooka,' the girl called. 'Go back to your oats.'

'I'm *really* sorry,' Uki said. He had managed to offend the girl twice in about a minute. He felt he ought to do something to make up for it. 'Listen. We're about to have a meal in the inn. Would you like to join us?'

The girl's little ears pricked up and she licked her lips. 'A meal? A hot one? At a table?' She looked past Uki to where Jori had managed to stand up again. She seemed to have regained her strength but was still swaying slightly. 'Ooh, I remember her. She's *rich*. Yes, I will definitely join you.'

Uki helped her to her feet, noting that he was a good two-heads taller. They went over to support Jori, and the three of them staggered into the inn for dinner.

*

They had crowberry soup to start, followed by roast parsnips in a spicy sauce that Jori said was a plains recipe. Once she started eating, her strength began to come back, although she clutched at her head every now and then, as if it ached badly. Despite that, she also ordered some blackberry wine that tasted quite disgusting and made Uki cough.

The inn was small, with lots of little rooms leading off from the main hall. It had uneven wooden planks for a floor and several sets of tables and chairs. There was a roaring fire in the hearth, a minstrel playing quiet tunes on a set of pan pipes and there were even tapestries hung on some of the walls. All in all, it was the finest place Uki had ever seen.

The innkeeper served them at their table, obviously remembering Jori from her previous stay (although he did give Uki several funny looks). He seemed shocked to see the plains girl sitting with them, but she just winked at him and beamed.

While they ate, she told them all about herself in great detail.

It turned out that she was a member of the Kalaan Klaa tribe, who lived in the northern part of the plains. There were two other groups: the Sla Neeks and the Uluk Miniki. At the moment, all three were at war with one another, although it sounded like the situation changed on a weekly basis. The tribes liked fighting almost as much as they liked making up and celebrating.

Since she had left her people two years ago, the girl had mostly been living in Nether. Sleeping in the stable and eating scraps in return for running errands and delivering messages on her jerboa.

'You haven't told us your name,' said Uki, as they polished off their parsnip dish.

'I am Lak Kriya of the Kalaan Klaa,' she said, pretending to bow. 'But you can call me Kree for short.'

'That's a pretty name,' said Uki.

'It means "half a mouse",' said Kree.

'Charming,' said Jori, smiling as she sipped her wine. 'Does your jerboa have a name that is actually an insult, too?'

'Yes. He's called Mooka, which means "buzzard meat". You might have noticed that he doesn't have a tail. That's why he was given to me. They were going to use his hide for leather and feed his meat to the birds. He's still fast, though.' Kree's eyes lit up when she talked about her mount. 'The fastest thing on the plains. It's just . . . he just falls over when he goes round corners. Sometimes.'

Jori surprised them all by throwing her head back and laughing so loudly that the rabbits at the other tables turned round to stare. 'A rabbit chased out of his tribe for having the wrong coloured fur, an assassin who can't kill anyone, a pint-sized rider and a jerboa with no tail. What a fine bunch of outcasts we are.'

Instead of being insulted, Kree laughed along, and raised her cup of wine in a toast. 'Outcasts!' she shouted.

Uki raised his cup too, gagged at the bitter taste, then they all laughed some more.

'You two haven't told me *your* story,' Kree said when the chuckling had stopped. Jori gave Uki a look, as if warning him not to say too much, but something about the bubbly cheerfulness of Kree made him trust her. He liked Jori but her moods could be like black thunderstorms, covering everything in shadow. If there was a chance that Kree might come along with them, it would maybe help balance things out.

For the second time in two days, Uki found

himself retelling the strange series of events that led to him sitting there, in an inn south of the Wall, with two new friends and an ancient spirit nestling inside his head.

It was still almost impossible to talk about his mother's death. It ripped open the wounds again, and tears spilled from his eyes on to the table. Once or twice he felt as though the sobs were going to completely overtake him, and he had to stop and breathe deeply. Each time Jori surprised him by laying a paw on his shoulder, and he found the strength to carry on. When he got to the part about Iffrit, the wave of grief became smaller, his mind going back to half thinking it had all been a dream, that his mother was alive and well, firing her latest batch of pots in her kiln. It was as if he couldn't really believe there was a world without her in it somewhere, even though he knew he was only fooling himself.

And then he finished the tale off with the rescue of Jori and the beginnings of their quest to track down the remaining spirits.

Throughout the whole thing, Kree sat motionless,

a spoonful of spiced parsnip frozen halfway on its voyage to her mouth. Uki was waiting for the moment when she started laughing, or refused to believe him, his paw ready with Gaunch's crystal for proof.

But the moment never came. Instead, the very second he finished speaking, she jumped up on to her chair. 'A quest! You are on an actual quest, like heroes from the stories! Oh, please let me come with you! I'll be your guide across the plains! I'll carry your luggage on Mooka! I'll sharpen your swords and polish your armour and cook your meals and . . . and . . . Oh, please just let me come!'

Uki laughed and was about to agree, but thought it best to look to Jori first. He was relieved to see the older girl smiling too. She caught his eye and gave a tiny nod of her head.

'Yes, Kree,' Uki said. 'You can come with us.'

'*Ukku neekneek bulbu bu!* Three times three thank yous!' Kree leapt from her seat to wrap her arms around Uki in a hug, then did the same to Jori. It was the first time anyone but his mother had hugged Uki. It was surprisingly nice.

'If that's settled, then perhaps we should retire for the evening,' said Jori. 'The innkeeper only has one room, but it has two beds if I remember. Perhaps you two could sleep top-to-tail?'

'Oh, thank you for the offer,' said Kree. 'But I always sleep in the stable when I'm here. Mooka would miss me if I wasn't with him.'

Kree skipped off as soon as the wine was finished, leaving Uki and Jori to share the room. The innkeeper led them there and Jori paid him with a silver coin. She slung her pack on one of the beds then flopped down on it.

'That was the last of my money,' she said. 'So it's a good job you've got those gems. We should change one for coin, the next proper town we're in.'

'Good idea,' said Uki. He climbed on to the other bed and lay back on the straw mattress. It was much softer than the pile of blankets and heather he used to sleep on in his village, and heaven compared to the forest floor that had been his bed recently.

Jori must have felt the same, as she began snoring almost immediately. Uki got up to blow out the candles and make sure the shutters of the small room were fastened tight, then he curled up in his blanket.

Now I have two companions, he thought to himself as his eyes began to drift shut. He knew he should be feeling thrilled at the thought, but he couldn't shake that foreboding feeling of something ominous and evil searching the land for him with its sweeping gaze.

And when it found him, it would find Jori and Kree as well.

Chapter Eight

Blood Plains

'It has to be here somewhere! Search harder, you dolts, or they'll hear your screams in Eisenfell!'

Uki jolted awake, the echoes of that terrible, screeching voice seeming to bounce about the room. He looked around, panicked, but saw only the simple wooden walls of the inn. Jori was already awake, washing and brushing her fur. The shutters were open, letting in bright sunlight, and someone had brought a pitcher of fresh water and a washbowl.

'Ah,' said Jori. 'You're awake. So is everyone else in the inn, what with all the noise you were making.'

Uki rubbed his eyes and blinked. 'It was a bad dream.' Except it wasn't, he knew. Someone, somewhere, had been screaming those very words, and he had been there, listening to them. It was as real as Jori, standing in her vest and *very* short cotton trousers.

Suddenly Uki realised that Jori's leather armour was on her bed and she was only wearing her underwear. A blush started underneath his fur, strong enough to turn his white side pink.

'I . . . um . . . what . . . er . . .' He looked at the ceiling, the floor, the window – anything to avoid Jori. 'Have you been here long? I mean, up? Awake?' *Stop talking now,* his mind told his mouth, but it kept on making stuttering noises anyway.

Jori laughed. There was a rustling, clinking noise. 'Don't worry, I'm putting my armour back on now. I don't know what you're making such a fuss about: I had my underclothes on. It wasn't as if I was *naked*.'

Uki made a strangled, squeaking noise.

'There,' said Jori. Peeping over, Uki saw her buckling the last straps of her armour and fastening her sword belt around her waist. 'Haven't you ever seen another rabbit getting dressed before? In my clan warren, I used to share a burrow with ten other rabbits. Girls *and* boys. It's really nothing to be embarrassed about.'

Uki wanted to explain that he'd only ever lived with his mother. Every day without her was new and strange and being around other rabbits was strangest of all. Instead he went over to the washstand and splashed his face with water. Lots of water.

*

It was not long after dawn, Uki discovered. The innkeeper was the only other rabbit up and he gave them each a freshly baked bread roll for breakfast. They steamed in the sharp morning air as they broke them into pieces in the inn's stable yard.

'Good morning!' Kree called, her painted ears popping up from a stable stall. She was jumping up and down, trying to throw a woven blanket over the back of Mooka, her jerboa. Uki could see his sandy fur and the stump where his tail should have been. Two huge ears twitched as Kree went about her work.

'Oo yoo ont a 'and?' Uki called, his mouth full of hot, fresh bread.

Kree had tied the blanket on and was now trying to put something over Mooka's head. He kept turning the opposite way, being as unhelpful as possible. 'No thanks,' she called back, through gritted teeth. 'I'm fine! Although Mooka is going to be made into a nice pair of leather trousers if he keeps being naughty.'

Uki heard the jerboa give a shrill '*neek!*' of protest, before standing remarkably still while Kree bustled about him.

A few minutes later she came out into the yard, leading Mooka by the reins. She had managed to tie a rope bridle about his head, and he hopped along behind her, nose twitching and shiny, brown eyes blinking. 'Isn't he wonderful?' she said.

'He's lovely,' said Uki, keeping his distance. Jori put out a paw for Mooka to sniff. Uki caught a glimpse of two long front teeth underneath the pink, wiggling nose, which made him step back even further.

'Well,' said Kree. 'Are we off on our quest, then?

I've told the innkeeper not to expect me back for about five years. I told him to listen out for songs and legends about me. And maybe to start working on a statue or something.'

Jori rolled her eyes and tutted. Uki twitched his ears. 'I wouldn't get *too* excited,' he said. 'I don't think we'll be making any legends.' **At least, you hope not,** his dark voice added. Becoming legendary usually meant you'd done something extremely dangerous, and probably died horribly in the process. 'Besides, we have to pick something up first.'

They headed to the smith's and saw that she was up and about, tapping away at her workbench with a hammer. She looked up as they entered the forge and jumped to attention.

'Oh, it's you! Good morning and ninefold blessings.' She gathered a bundle of objects from her bench and brought them over. 'We've just finished your piece,' she said. 'My husband and I have been up all night.' In a corner of the forge, the shape of a rabbit could be seen, hunched over a bench and gently snoring.

‘Here,’ said the smith, laying out her work. There were four spear hafts, each one half the height of Uki. They were made from polished hazel wood, wrapped with leather around the middle for grip.

‘I made short spears,’ said the smith. ‘I thought that would be best for you to throw. And these are for fitting the spearheads.’ She put five little metal cups on to the table, each with a threaded pin on the bottom. ‘If I may?’

Uki took the big crystals from his pocket and handed them to her, watching nervously as she handled the one containing Gaunch. With quick fingers, the smith fitted the cups over the end of each, then tapped and pinched them here and there using a pair of tongs and a little hammer from her tool belt.

When the caps were fitted, she lifted the spear hafts one by one and screwed the crystals into the ends. Now they looked like proper spears, but with pink diamonds for heads, rather than sharpened flint.

Finally she lifted her last piece, and Uki saw it was a set of leather straps, joined together with a round, silver buckle. The smith held it up and gestured for Uki to lift his arms. The smith slid the harness over his head and tightened the straps so that it fitted snugly across his chest, like a crossed bandolier.

'It's beautiful,' Uki said. The silver buckle had a pair of magpies on the front, beak to tail in a circle.

'I hope you don't mind,' said the smith. 'But I was inspired by your beautiful fur.'

Beautiful? Uki had no words. He touched the buckle gently with his fingertips and blinked back tears from his eyes.

'The spearheads fit in here,' said the smith. She took Gaunch's crystal and screwed it into the top of the buckle. Uki could feel three more holes, east, south and west, ready for the others. 'And on the back is a quiver. So you don't have to carry the spears around.' She took the four short spears and slotted them into a pouch on Uki's back. Reaching behind his head, he found he could grab one quite easily, although drawing and throwing it at someone would be another matter.

'It's … it's incredible.' He managed to say. 'Thank you so much.'

'Thank *you*, sir,' said the smith. 'We've already decided what to do with your payment. We're heading south to buy a forge in one of them big cities. A new life for us both.' She beamed and looked Uki up and down, proud of her work.

Uki turned round to show his new friends. Kree gave a whistle that made Mooka's ears twitch. Jori nodded and smiled. 'We need to get you some fine clothes to match now,' she said.

They were about to say their farewells when a crowd of rabbits went past, all heading for the town gate and the plains beyond. They had spears and pitchforks and marched with their heads low, as if about to do an important but unpleasant task.

'What's all that about?' Jori asked, watching them stomp by.

'Search party,' said the smith. 'Three rabbits went missing the day before yesterday. They'd been out hunting in the forest and never came back.'

'Three?' said Uki. He gave Jori a worried look.

'They were Nurg's brothers,' said Kree. 'You know, that rabbit who was booting me around the yard. He said my tribe had come and carried them off for dinner. I told him my people wouldn't eat maggot-ridden rat dung like his brothers if they were starving. Then he pushed me over.'

'Yes,' said the smith. 'They weren't the nicest of rabbits. But we all stick together out here, in the middle of nowhere. We'll find them if we can. And for what it's worth, Kree, I don't think it was any of the plains tribes. Most likely Ice Waste rabbits from beyond the Wall.'

Uki began to cringe, but then realised she hadn't meant him. He didn't look like an Ice rabbit, not with his half-black fur, but the comment still made him feel bad. All this rush to blame other groups of rabbits when something went wrong. He had a good idea what might have happened to Nurg's brothers, and it was nothing to do with any tribe or race.

'Well,' said Jori. 'We must be off. Our thanks again.'

With a final round of smiles and waves, they headed out of the town, stopping at the well to fill their water bottles on the way.

'Are you thinking what I am?' Jori whispered, as she crouched over the well bucket with her waterskin.

'The spirits?' Uki answered.

'Three of them,' Jori agreed.

'Why are we whispering?' Kree asked, in a voice loud enough for the whole town to hear. This time, even Uki rolled his eyes.

*

They waited until they were a safe distance away from Nether before explaining to her. Both Jori and Uki thought that the brothers' bodies might have been taken over by the three escaped spirits. If that was the case, it might make them much more dangerous.

'But easier to track,' said Kree. 'If they'd asked me two days ago, I could have picked up their trail. But nobody in that town asks me to do anything except deliver messages and shovel *neekneek* poop.'

'Can you follow trails that well?' Uki asked.

'Of course,' said Kree, puffing out her chest. 'Us plains rabbits learn tracking as soon as we can hop. We learn to ride jerboas even before that.'

'That's good to know,' said Jori. 'But Uki here has another talent. He can sense where the spirits are, can't you?'

Uki nodded. Although it felt strange to call it a 'talent'. It was all just because Iffrit was in his head. He'd done nothing to earn his new skills.

'Go on, then,' said Kree. 'Show us where they are. We can catch them all and be back in Nether for supper.'

'It's not that easy . . .' Uki started to say, but both girls were staring at him, expectantly. He sighed and closed his eyes, trying to focus, trying to snatch at the invisible threads that led to the spirits.

His breathing slowed as he reached out, imagining himself as the great, fiery bird that Iffrit had been, searching the skies for his prey. That familiar tugging was there, but it felt different somehow: not so strong as before, as if it had spread.

'I think . . .' he muttered. 'I think the spirits aren't together any more. I think they've gone different ways.'

Yes, that was it. He could still feel the pull, but it now came from three different directions. He pointed his arms to show where. The strongest was to the east, the others further off to the south.

'East,' said Jori. 'What's out there?'

'Just the plains,' said Kree. 'Uluk Miniki lands are that way, and then if you go far enough, the twin cities, Syn and Nys.'

'That's it,' said Uki. 'That's where the spirit is going.' He didn't know how he knew this – it was just something he felt inside his head. He also had a flash of memory, of an island beneath that vivid orange sky, with a huge stone fortress on it. Spears and machines of war stood along its wall, stabbing at the sky with points and spikes. The spirit within was fierce and strong, full of the urge to fight anyone and everything.

Before he knew what was happening, Uki had fallen to the ground and began to thrash in the long grass, strange words pouring from his mouth.

'Valkus, the Spirit of War. It's him. He was made to keep one tribe of Ancients safe, but he decided to do it by killing all the others. By fighting and hurting and destroying them. Blades, metal, blood . . .'

'What's he doing?' Kree's voice seemed to come from a long way away.

'He's having a fit,' said Jori. 'Help me hold him.'

Uki felt firm paws on his arms and shoulders,

he smelt the crushed grass beneath him and heard his feet drumming on the soil, but it was all miles away, dreamlike. His head was full of visions of war, mixed with Iffrit's memories of the prison, looking down on the armoured form of Valkus, trapped on his island, shooting bolts of iron up into the air.

And then the vision switched. The hate and bloodlust of Valkus faded and he was back in Icebark Forest again. Stark, white trees everywhere. There were rabbits all around, cloaked in black, hacking through the brambles with axes and cleavers. Searching. He was searching for something.

Uki recognised the feeling from the dreams about the tower. This was that thing again: the being that was looking for him. The being that was like one of his three spirits, yet *different.* By opening his mind to Valkus he had let it in, and now he was in the forest looking through its eyes, spying on it as it hunted along with these black-robed rabbits.

Suddenly one of them shouted and he was dashing over, looking down at the very spot where he'd been standing two days ago. There was the broken earth where the crystal prison had been, one or two tiny crystals still left, glittering in the sunlight.

'That's it!' A voice screeched. The same voice that had woken him that morning. 'It was here! But where is the rest of it? Where are the four? They must be near! Search harder! Harder!'

The cloaked figures began to smash the undergrowth all around, spreading out in their desperate hunt. Uki felt a hunger, a need that seemed to pound through his veins like blood, and that sense of endless searching he had felt with his first vision. It would never stop looking, he realised. Seeking the escaped spirits, seeking *him* . . .

. . . and then it was gone.

Uki found himself lying in the grass, his friends kneeling beside him. He felt exhausted, as though he had just run the length of the Cinder Wall.

'What . . . happened?' he managed to say.

Jori fetched a waterskin from Mooka's back and poured some into his mouth. 'You had a kind of seizure,' she said. 'You were saying stuff about a spirit of war, and then about someone searching for you.'

Uki sat up, rubbing his head, which had started to pound. 'Valkus,' he said. 'That's the name of the spirit that's heading east. He loves war and fighting.'

'Oh dear,' said Kree. 'That's bad news. The plains tribes love fighting too. And if he gets to the twin cities there'll be trouble. They're at peace now, but legends are still told about the war that they once had.'

'Then I guess we should go there first,' said Jori. 'If Uki can capture this Valkus quickly, we might be able to stop any trouble.'

'And I saw others too,' added Uki. 'The thing I told you about. The one that's searching for the spirits as well. I think it's found the remains of the prison. I could see them in Icebark, finding the hole in the ground.'

Jori looked back towards the forest. 'That puts it at least a day behind us,' she said. 'If we make good time across the plains, we can stretch out our lead further. Can you guide us to the cities, Kree?'

Kree nodded. 'It's a straight line,' she said. 'We can go quick. Although it's right through

Uluk Miniki lands. We had best be careful not to be spotted.'

'Are they a bad tribe?' Uki asked, remembering the stories his mother had told him.

Kree shrugged. 'Fierce. Good riders. Not as good as the Kalaan Klaa, of course. They are at war with us, though. Ever since our chief's son refused to marry their chief's daughter because she has the face of a badger's bottom.'

'They aren't at war with *us*, though,' Jori pointed out.

'No, but you travel with me. If they catch us, they will probably stake us out on the plain for the buzzards to peck to death.' Kree shrugged. 'I'm sure it will be fine though. Let's go.'

With several nervous glances at each other, Uki and Jori picked themselves up and started the long walk across the Blood Plains.

*

They walked all day, on into the sunset, until Uki's legs felt like they were about to fall off and even Mooka was making little *neek* sounds of protest. The rattling of his new spears on his back had been a pleasant novelty, but now he was sick of them banging against his ears, and the straps had rubbed his shoulders raw. He had no idea how Jori managed to carry her heavy pack so easily, or how the poor jerboa lugged the bundle of Kree's possessions.

The plains stretched on forever, like a red version of the sky above. Uki began to think the whole world was now made up of those two colours: endless, unbroken. He would have given anything to see a simple tree stump or a lump of rock – just something to break up the scenery a little.

'We should camp now,' said Kree, finally. 'Night falls quickly this time of year and we won't be able to see what we are doing.'

'Did we bring firewood?' asked Uki, looking forward to the heat and hypnotising flames of a good campfire.

'No fires,' said Kree. 'You can see them for miles around on the plains. I can't put up my tent, either. It has Kalaan Klaa markings. If the Miniki see it, they'll be on us before you can say "buzzards' breakfast".'

Uki sighed. That lovely straw mattress in the inn

seemed like a distant paradise.

'A night under the stars,' said Kree, sounding pleased. 'With a warm jerboa to snuggle up to, and some lovely cornbread and elderberry jam to eat. What could be better?'

Uki could think of several things, but both Jori and Kree were unslinging their packs and setting out blankets and food. It made him feel stupid again: he had nothing with him except his spears and his raggedy old cloak. He had set off on an expedition to who-knows-where with no provisions or anything that he might need. How far would he have got if he hadn't met his new companions?

'I haven't got any food,' he said in a small voice. 'I didn't really think . . .'

'Don't worry,' said Jori. 'Between Kree and myself, we've got enough to last us a few days. You can cash in a gem and buy more when we get to the cities.'

'Gems?' Kree said, leaning back against Mooka, who had happily lain down in the grass and was nibbling as much of it as quickly as he could, just in case this resting thing was a trick and he was made to get up and walk for hours again. 'He's got gems?'

'Oh yes,' said Jori. 'We're travelling with a rich rabbit. He'll soon be wearing velvet underpants and treating us to the finest blackberry wine.'

'I don't know about that,' said Uki. The thought of dressing himself in finery made him feel very awkward. He sat next to Kree and helped himself to some cornbread, trying to think of something to change the subject.

'Jori,' he said, between mouthfuls, 'why don't you tell us about that thing you did yesterday? That magic potion you drank that made you so quick . . .'

'Dusk wraith,' said Kree, sitting forward with a gleam in her eye. 'I've heard tales about you. Do you really have the souls of murdered rabbits in your flask? Is that what makes you so fast?'

Jori gave a bitter laugh. 'Murdered souls? Do plains rabbits eat each other for breakfast and marry their jerboas?'

'Of course not!' Kree looked as if she were about to jump to her feet, and Uki had a horrid feeling there was going to be a fight, but then Jori laughed again.

'Not nice when lies are told about you, is it?' She

took a swig from her waterskin, then passed it to Kree, who took it with a nod. 'But I can tell you the truth, if you want. Why should I keep their secrets after they hunted me like a weasel?'

She fell silent then, and Uki thought she might have decided not to tell them after all. He was just about to ask Kree a question about the plains – anything to fill the awkward pause – when Jori cleared her throat and began speaking.

'Dusk angel. That's the name of a mushroom. Small and grey, with black gills underneath. It doesn't grow anywhere except the Coldwood, which is where my clan warren is. It's deadly poisonous. Just one crumb would be enough to kill all three of us in less than an hour.

'They start giving it to you when you're just four. Tiny, tiny amounts, added to your food. It makes you sick at first. I remember lying in my cot for days, just vomiting. Some rabbits even die – one or two every year.

'Then you begin to get used to it, so they increase the dose. More and more as you get older, until you can resist enough to drink the potion.' Jori paused to unclip the flask from her belt and waggle it. 'This stuff. It's made from the mushrooms: a secret recipe that has to be brewed in an exact way.

'Once you can drink a mouthful without dying, the training begins. It's not as simple as just having a swig and being able to fight really quickly. Moving that fast changes everything: how your muscles work, your sense of balance. We have hours of practice every day. You can only call yourself a dusk wraith once you pass the final tests.'

'Was that when you refused to kill someone?' Uki asked, remembering her story from the forest.

Jori shook her head. 'No, that came after. I'm a true dusk wraith at least, even if I'm not an assassin.'

'Mushrooms, eh?' said Kree. 'That stuff must be pretty bad for you. Look at how you felt after just a small sip. What happens if you use more?'

'The more you drink, the longer it lasts,' said Jori. 'And the worse you feel after. It does things to your body over time, as well. After years of being a dusk wraith, you start losing your fingers and toes. Even your ears. The elder wraiths in my clan wear hoods and masks all the time, they look so horrible. None of them lives much past forty.'

Kree let out a whistle. 'And what would happen if I tried some? Or ate a piece of those mushrooms?'

'You would die,' said Jori. 'But not instantly. There'd be hours of agony beforehand. Pain like you couldn't imagine. It's probably one of the worst deaths you could think of.'

Uki had no idea what to say to that. He looked at the ornate flask on Jori's belt, tempted to grab it and hurl it out into the darkening plain with all his strength. But even with all the horrible tales she had just told, Jori obviously thought it was precious. Being a dusk wraith was something she was proud of, maybe *because* it had been so hard for her to achieve.

'Well, on that cheerful note, I think it's time for bed,' said Kree. She pulled her blanket over herself and snuggled up next to Mooka's warm fur.

'Are you *sure* we'll be safe?' Jori asked.

'Trust me! *Bulu naska*, everyone.'

'Good night,' Uki said. He wrapped his tattered cloak about him and thought about snuggling up next to the jerboa for a moment, before he remembered those front teeth as long as his arm. Perhaps it would be best to keep a little distance . . .

He lay back amongst the sweet-smelling plains grass and looked up at the drifts of stars above. *A beautiful night, under the open sky with my new friends nearby,* he thought, feeling safe and warm as he drifted off to sleep.

*

Something hard and sharp jabbed Uki in the leg, making him jolt awake. It was a flint spear, poking him through his blanket. At the other end was a tall plains rabbit dressed in beaded leathers, purple zigzags painted all over his fur.

'Look here,' the rabbit laughed. 'This one has been cut in half!'

Uki raised his head to see ten or more rabbits, all pointing spears and axes at them. Kree and Jori were looking out of their blankets with eyes as wide and frightened as his.

'And this one is Kalaan Klaa,' another rabbit said, prodding Kree. 'An enemy on our lands.'

'They will make good buzzard food,' said the tallest rabbit, one who wore a headdress of feathers and carved bones. 'Many Uluk Miniki will enjoy watching you die. Nobody travels on our lands without permission.'

Jori looked over at Kree and gave her a scowl strong enough to curdle milk. '*Trust* you? You're "sure it will be fine"?'

'*Nam ukku ulla,*' Kree said, and spat on the ground. The Miniki warriors laughed and hauled their new prisoners to their feet.

Interlude

The bard's story continues into the night, until Rue's (and Jaxom's) eyes are closed and their breathing has slowed to gentle snores. The bard lies awake for an hour or so more – listening out for the sneaking footfalls of Arukh raiders come to murder him in his sleep – before he drifts off as well.

As soon as they are up and riding on the wagon again, Rue begs for the tale to continue, and it is not until they are approaching the town of Melt the next evening that the bard draws to a close with Uki and his friends in the hands of the Uluk Miniki.

'Don't stop there!' Rue cries. 'At least let us know if they survive!'

'Always leave your audience wanting more,' says the bard. 'Lesson number … three hundred and something. I've lost count.'

Jaxom begins to slow the bounding jerboas, and they spot Melt itself. More impressive by far than Pebblewic, it has a high wooden wall with watchtowers all around. It stands out as the biggest thing on the broad, flinty slopes that lead up to the mountains, although it doesn't have much competition. There are freshly ploughed fields surrounding it, and the odd shepherd's hut. Here and there stands a cluster of gorse or hawthorn, but little else grows apart from patchy, bristly grass. Flocks of jerboas are being herded back to their pens for the evening and, on the far side of the town, a winding river sparkles, bubbling its way off through the Blood Plains to the sea.

As they near the town, they spot rings of ditches brimming with sharpened wooden stakes. Rue can see archers and sentries up on the walls, ready to fill them full of arrows should they turn out to be anything less harmful than tartan traders. It makes him finally realise how much danger they were in, crossing and camping out in hostile Arukh territory. Even with Jaxom's grisly warnings, the whole thing had seemed like a great adventure. Now he understands that they really *might* have been attacked in the night. The thought makes him shudder.

They are stopped at the gate by two guard-rabbits, both holding spears and dressed in thick, leather armour. They know Jaxom by sight and wave him through, into the town beyond.

Their cart trundles in and Rue peers over the edge. There are lots of houses, all made of wood or stone and roofed with pieces of slate. Tall chimneys trail white streamers of smoke, and at the north side of the town there is a gap in the wall where the river runs through. Boats and barges are tied up there, waiting to take goods downstream. It is the first time Rue has seen proper boats, and he stares for a while, hypnotised by their gentle bobbing.

Jaxom heads straight for the trading post, where he stables his jerboas and heaves the bales of tartan from his wagon, with a little help from the bard. As Jaxom goes to get his payment, Rue watches the rabbits of Melt going about their business. All of them, he notices, are armed with swords or axes, even the old rabbits. They nod and greet each other as normal, but there is a tension in the air, as if they are ready to jump into battle at any moment.

'Why would anyone want to live here?' he asks the bard. 'Wouldn't it be better to build a warren somewhere safe, without neighbours who might want to chop your bits off?'

The bard shrugs. 'This is their home,' he says. 'Most of them have probably lived here for generations. It usually takes a lot to leave all that behind. And this is an important trading post. All the amber in the Five Realms is dug from those mountains and is traded here. All the beads and leather of the plains come here from Nether. And all the tribes in the north of Hulstland get their cloth, wool and everything else from Melt. Even the Arukhs, when they're feeling friendly.'

'But what if we're attacked? Look – they're *all* carrying weapons!'

'Then we'll be safe, won't we? I'm just going to

hide behind that old lady over there. She looks like she can take care of herself.'

The bard laughs at Rue's expression, then gives his shoulder a comforting squeeze as Jaxom returns with his pouch of coins. 'The store is this way,' he says. 'Gant should be expecting us.'

He leads them in and out of the wooden buildings until they get to one with a sign hanging outside. It has a picture on it of a turnip above a pair of crossed pickaxes.

Inside is a little wooden room with a counter along the far wall. The rest of the hut, every spare inch, is filled with shelves and boxes, all overflowing with goods for sale. There are barrels of swedes and potatoes, stacks of firewood, packets of seeds, hammers, axes, spades, boxes of nails, jars of pickle and jam. Rue has never seen such a huge amount of *stuff* crammed into one small space before. It is like walking into a cave of treasures, except with handy, everyday items instead of priceless gems.

'Good evening and ninefold blessings, gentlemen,' says a voice from somewhere amongst the heaps of goods. 'I'm afraid I was just about to c-close for the evening. We'll be open first thing in the morning if you would like to c-come back.'

'I was just wondering,' says the bard, 'if you sold fox-paw dice. I have an unusual set I would like to match.'

There is a rustling and clanking, and two black ears appear from behind a stack of pickled gherkin jars. They are followed by a pair of big, watery brown eyes. 'By K-Kether's sacred nostril hair, I thought you'd never get here!'

With a stumble that almost sends the whole stack of jars tumbling, a short, stooped rabbit hops out before them. He squints and blinks, coming a few steps closer to see them better. 'Thirteen c-curses on my eyes – they get worse each year! Is that you, Jaxom? Have you brought these fellows to see me?'

'Yes, Gant,' says Jaxom. 'This is Wulf the Wanderer, founding member of the Foxguard, and his apprentice, Rue.'

The bard bows his head and ruffles Rue's ears. The little rabbit has puffed up his chest so much, it might burst.

'Founding member, eh? Well you'd better c-come

in. Lock the door behind you, I was c-closing up for the night anyway.'

Gant leads them through the cluttered shop to a little room at the back. It is only a tiny bit less crowded. There is a table, chairs and a sideboard, but everything is covered with wooden boxes crammed with more stock. Rue climbs on top of a crate, while the bard shifts a sack of seeds off a chair. Gant feels his way over to the other side of the table, not even waiting to sit before blurting out his news.

'I'm so glad you c-came. It seemed to take forever! It was weeks ago I heard, you see. As you know, I'm the only Foxguard agent this far north. It's not c-close enough to Icebark Forest to k-keep an eye on things there, but I pay good money for information from some of the woodsmen. There hasn't been any news for . . . well, forever. But two woodcutters c-came to see me nearly a month ago. They said they'd been out in the forest one night and seen a light. Off in the distance they said, through the trees. They followed it, knowing that was the sort of news I was after, and it led them right to the tower!'

'The Endwatch Tower?' The bard says. 'I thought it was destroyed?'

'Burnt down, yes,' says Gant. 'Just a shell now. None of the buildings are left, but the tower still stands. Anyway, they c-crept as close as they dared and that was where the light c-came from! And they said they c-could see rabbits moving about inside.'

'How many?' The bard leans forward, gripping one of Gant's arms. 'Were they just other woodsmen? Ice Waste rabbits? Or something else?'

Gant's watery eyes wobble, big droplets about to spill into his fur. 'I don't know. They didn't say. I think they were terrified of ghosts or spirits and ran off. They're only simple woodsfolk, you know, and that place has always had bad stories told of it. They call it Doomgate and other silly names. I'm sorry I c-can't tell you any more. I would have gone up there to see for myself, but my eyes . . .'

'Don't worry,' says the bard, giving Gant's arm a pat. 'You got the word out, that's the most important thing. Has anyone else from the Foxguard come through here?'

Gant shakes his head. 'No, you're the first. Although I c-can't say who's at the tower now. I told Nikku to send sparrows to all the Foxguard in Hulstland. My woodsfolk returned to Nether and haven't been this way since.'

The bard sits back and pulls at his beard for a minute or two. Everyone watches him closely, not wanting to disturb his thinking. Even Rue manages to keep quiet, although the effort nearly makes him explode.

Finally he speaks. 'I think I need to see this for myself,' he says at last. 'At least from a distance. Could be just someone looking for shelter, but if it's the Endwatch come back . . .'

'It might be dangerous,' says Jaxom. 'No offence, but you're not a fighter. And there's your boy to think of.'

'I'm not scared!' Rue shouts, although his voice wobbles a little, spoiling the effect. The other rabbits laugh.

'I'm sure you're not,' says the bard. 'And don't worry, Jaxom. I'll get no closer than the woodsfolk did and head back if it looks dangerous. There's others in the Foxguard who can take care of the fighting, if it comes to that. We'll just have to run back here and wait for reinforcements.'

Jaxom grunts, sounding less than happy. 'I can take you as far as Icebark tomorrow,' he says. 'But I can't spare the time to go creeping through the forest with you. I've got shipments to take back, rabbits waiting for their goods . . .'

'It's fine,' says the bard. 'I've spent a lot of time in forests. We'll creep in and out quicker than a hare with tummy trouble. I'll send a sparrow to you in Pebblewic, and perhaps you can give us a ride back after?'

'Very well,' says Jaxom, still frowning. 'But I still don't like it.'

After that, Gant insists they stay the night, and sets about cooking them supper on a little brick stove that had been hidden behind a bundle of broomsticks ('buy one get one free'). When they have eaten their fill, they clear a space on the kitchen floor for their bedding. Gant has his own cubbyhole for sleeping, somewhere amongst the clutter of his shop. There is just enough room for the bard and Jaxom to stretch out, top to tail. Rue settles down on top of two pushed-together boxes. With light from several beeswax candles and the embers of the stove, it is very warm and cosy.

'I don't suppose,' says Rue, 'before we fall asleep . . . that we could have more of the story? Just to see if Uki and the others escape the plains tribe?'

The bard lets out a sigh. 'Do we have to? I do have rather a lot on my mind tonight . . .'

'Oh, go on,' says Jaxom. 'This part is my favourite bit of the tale.'

'Hey!' says Rue. 'It's not fair if Jaxom knows what happens and I don't!'

'Well, you've had loads of Podkin's tales that I haven't.'

'But he's *my* master!'

'Woah! Hold your jerboas!' says the bard. 'What's going on? Are you both little children? Well, you are Rue, but . . . can't either of you go to sleep without a bedtime story, just for once?'

'No!' Rue and Jaxom reply together. The bard mutters something rude under his breath, and then sits himself up amongst his blankets.

'Very well,' he says. 'If it will stop you both moaning and fighting. I will tell you what happened when Uki and the outcasts were captured by the Uluk Miniki . . .'

Chapter Nine

The Challenge

They were dragged, stumbling – pulled along by ropes tied to their paws – behind the Miniki's jerboas. Uki tested the knots binding him. Even though the rope was thick, he knew he could snap it like a piece of straw. But what then? There were too many rabbits around them, with too many spears. He didn't think Iffrit's powers would keep him alive if he became a walking pincushion. Besides which, Jori and Uki were still bound. There would be no time to free them, and one of them might get hurt.

In the end he decided it was safest to let the Miniki think he was just a harmless child. There would come a better time to escape, when he could free the others too. At least he hoped so.

They were soon at the Miniki's camp. It was nestled in a dip, almost impossible to see amongst the endless flat grass of the plains, and not that far away from where they had camped. Kree cursed again when she saw it, knowing she hadn't done a very good job of guiding them safely across her own homeland.

Uki was surprised to see so many rabbits. It was like a little town, bigger even than Nether had been. But instead of houses or burrows, the Miniki had tents everywhere. Domed structures made of leather stretched over hazel poles, and painted with purple zigzags and figures of rabbits on jerboas. Each one was bigger than his old hut in the Ice Wastes had been. Whole families lived in them, many of whom were just getting up and going about their daily business. They all stopped to stare at the strangers being pulled along by their warriors.

The Miniki, Uki noticed, had slightly darker fur

than Kree, but it was still short and velvety. Their eyes were deeper brown, and the dye on their fur was purple instead of red. Apart from that, they looked very similar. Similar enough, he thought, to make all this hostility seem a bit ridiculous.

The riders dragged them all the way to the camp's centre, before jumping off their jerboas. Uki and his friends were pushed towards the biggest tent. It was the most ornately painted, and had a wide doorway with two guards standing outside.

'Where are they taking us?' Uki managed to whisper to Kree.

'To the chief,' she replied, through gritted teeth. 'So he can decide how we will be punished.'

The large tent was filled with the chief's finery. Lots of painted skins, shields, spears and, of course, an elaborate seat made of what looked like enormous bones lashed together with strips of hide. The chief sat there, drinking from a carved wooden bowl and watching them closely over the rim. His eyes widened when he saw Jori and narrowed again at the sight of Kree. He put his bowl aside, leaving a ring of jerboa milk around his whiskers.

'A Kalaan Klaa? On my lands?'

'We found her with these other children, Chief Gromak,' said one of the riders. 'They were camped out for the night. Heading south-east.'

Gromak growled. He was a big rabbit, his fur painted with so much purple it was hard to see its real colour. His ears were pierced full of carved bones and wooden discs, and there was a long scar running down the left side of his face. He didn't look like someone you would want to annoy.

'Kalaan Klaa are our enemy!' he roared, making Uki flinch. 'Lying two-faced children of weasels and stoats! They said rude things about my beautiful daughter!'

Gromak pointed to the corner of his tent, where a girl rabbit was sitting on a small stool having her fur painted with purple zigzags by a servant. Saying she had a face like a badger's bottom was a bit rude, but calling her 'beautiful' was stretching it too. Unless, of course, you were attracted to long, yellow teeth and scowls that could wilt flowers.

Uki could sense Kree's hackles begin to rise, but thankfully Jori cleared her throat before she could say anything. She bowed her head to the chief. 'Lord Gromak. Please forgive our trespass on your lands. We did not mean to offend you in any way. I am Jori, granddaughter of Toxa, Lord of Clan Septys. My friends and I have urgent business in the twin cities of Nys and Syn, and are trying to get there as quickly as possible. My guide may wear the colours of the Kalaan Klaa tribe, but she has not lived with them for over two years. She has no part in the quarrels between them and your . . . delightful daughter.'

'Clan . . . Septys?' Gromak rubbed the side of his face where his scar ran. 'Aren't they the poisoners?'

Jori gave him a look that was almost as deadly as the contents of her belt pouches. 'Indeed, we are. And I am sure you would not want to anger my grandfather by harming us.'

Clever, thought Uki. *The name of Septys must fill everyone around here with terror.* **As long as he doesn't find out that the Clan want to kill her as well,** his dark voice added.

'Harm you?' said the chief. 'Who said anything about harming you? I'm just asking you a few questions, that's all.' Uki noticed his eyes had widened slightly, and was that a tremble in his paw?

This might just work, he thought. *As long as Kree doesn't open her mouth and say something st—*

'You'd better not harm us, you fat *neekneek bu*! Children of stoats and weasels? The Kalaan Klaa are better than you stupid Miniki in every way! And as for your daughter, a badger's bottom would be a delight to look upon compared to her squished-up, mouse's armpit of a face!'

If Uki's paws weren't tied, he would have buried his face in them. Jori looked up to the tent roof and growled. As for Gromak, he was so furious his mouth hung open for a minute or more, while his eyes boggled so much they almost popped out of his head.

It was his daughter that finally broke the silence. She burst into tears and ran out of the tent. Gromak watched her go and then bellowed, 'That's it! Septys bedamned! Stake these intruders out on the plain for the buzzards! And get me a chair. I want to sit and watch their eyes being pecked out!'

The guards grabbed Uki and the others and

hauled them to their feet. Uki tensed, ready to break his ropes and fight, but before he could, Kree shouted again. 'A challenge! By the red grass of the Ba'alin Buraa, I challenge your finest rider to a race!'

Gromak stared at the little rabbit, gnashing his teeth. It was obvious that he wanted to do something violent and painful to her, but for some reason he couldn't. *This challenge must be some kind of tradition,* Uki thought. He hoped Kree knew what she was doing. Mooka might be fast, but he had no *tail* . . .

'Very well,' he said. 'What are your terms?'

'If I win,' said Kree, 'you let us go. And take us to Nys as quickly as you can.'

'And if you lose,' said Gromak, 'it'll be the buzzard death for all of you. And I will have your skull for my soup bowl.'

'Agreed,' said Kree, and to Uki's surprise, the guards released them all, even cutting through their bonds to set their paws free.

Gromak stood and pointed one thick arm towards the tent door. 'Then let us race.'

Everyone turned and walked out of the tent. Jori

bent her head down to Kree's ear and whispered. 'What are you doing, you crazy idiot?'

Kree winked back at her and Uki. 'Relax,' she said. 'I can win this race, easy. Nothing to worry about.'

Uki remembered her saying that last night, right before they were captured in enemy territory and sentenced to death. He swallowed hard and followed the others over to the camp edge.

*

Word had spread quicker than a plains fire, and the whole tribe were rushing out of their tents, pointing and shouting as they went. By the time they got to open ground, there was a crowd of spectators ready, waving spears and cheering.

Mooka had been brought over. He gave a little *neek* when he saw Kree and hopped over to nuzzle her neck. 'There's a good boy,' Kree whispered to him, scratching behind his ear. 'You're going to run fast as the wind for me, aren't you? As fast as lightning.'

Uki moved as close to the jerboa as he dared and pretended to stroke him too. He took the chance to whisper in Kree's ear. 'Why are you doing this? Can't we just let Jori talk her way out of it? That chief was scared of her, you know.'

'This is a good plan,' Kree winked at him. 'The Miniki ride short-eared jerboas. Mooka is a long-ear. Everyone knows long-ears are the fastest runners. We will be back on our heroic quest in no time. Trust me.'

'But, Kree, Mooka can't run round corners! You said so yourself!'

Kree tightened the knots on Mooka's bridle and hopped up on to his back. 'It's a challenge race,' she said grinning. 'Straight sprint, no corners!'

There was a cheer from the crowd as the Miniki champion arrived, already on her jerboa. She was a fierce-looking rabbit, her ears tied back and wearing a leather vest covered with animal bones. Her jerboa did have smaller ears than Mooka, but was larger in every other respect. Larger, and much more powerful. A long, tufted tail swished to and fro behind it as it glared over at them, nose twitching.

'I've got a bad feeling about this,' Uki muttered.

'Me too,' said Jori. 'Do you think you could pick

up a jerboa and throw it? If you can knock down the entire tribe in one go, we might have a tiny chance of stealing a ride and escaping.'

Uki gaped at her for a moment, and then spotted the wry smile on her face. A joke. But, jokes aside, it really did look as though they weren't getting out of this one.

'Uluk Miniki!' Chief Gromak had been hoisted up on to a chair that sat on the shoulders of four sturdy warriors. 'We are gathered here to witness a challenge! This brat of the Kalaan Klaa thinks she can outrun Sla-Shan, our champion rider!'

The crowd around them burst out laughing. Lots of plains words that Uki was pretty sure weren't nice were shouted.

'So the two will race,' Gromak continued when the noise had died down. 'The first to go round the flag and back will win the Challenge.' He pointed out on to the plain where, a good three hundred metres away, a rabbit was standing holding up a purple flag tied to a spear.

'Wait, *what*?' Kree shouted. '*Around* the flag? Challenge races are always on the straight!'

'Maybe in your tribe of ferret-licking weasel children,' said Gromak. 'Here, on the true plains, we *always* go around the flag.'

'But . . . But . . .' Kree tried to protest but suddenly a wall of pointed spears appeared behind her. She obviously wasn't going to get a choice about how the race was run.

'That's it,' said Jori under her breath. 'We're buzzard food.'

Kree looked over at them and grimaced. Even if Mooka *was* faster than the other jerboa, he would have to get around that flag without falling over. Uki racked his brain trying to think of a way to help, but came up with nothing. All he could do was stand and watch. And pray.

'Riders!' Gromak shouted. 'Are you ready?'

The Miniki champion gave her chief a nod and hunkered in the saddle, every muscle tensed. Kree made a little squeaking noise.

'Then let the race begin! *Ak, Akka, Akku* . . . Go!'

Uki had seen the way Mooka walked before: that loping hop with his back legs, front paws tucked up in front of him. But he had never seen a jerboa *run*.

As soon as the shout had left Gromak's lips, the two jerboas were gone. Those long, gangly hind legs were now springs, shooting the animals forwards through the air over and over, so fast it was like they were flying. The tail of the champion's animal whirled and span as it leapt, counterbalancing it, while Mooka's bare bottom just wiggled.

At first the jerboas were neck and neck, their riders clinging on to their backs for dear life. Then, as they were halfway to the flag, Kree seemed to pull ahead. Mooka's leaps were just as long as the other jerboa's, but he made them quicker, giving him an edge. His long ears were swept back against his body with Kree crouching in between, shouting at him to go faster.

'She's winning, Jori!' Uki shouted, grabbing his friend's arm. 'She's winning!'

'At the moment,' said Jori. 'She's lighter than the other rider. Must be giving her an edge. But it'll all be lost on the corner.' Jori looked away from the race for a moment to stare at Uki, her grey eyes cold and hard. 'Be ready to fight,' she said. 'We can't win but it'll be better than getting eaten alive by buzzards.'

Uki gulped, turning back to the racers. Kree was a good two lengths ahead now, just coming up to the flag.

'Don't fall, Mooka,' Uki whispered, praying to any god that might hear him. 'Don't fall.' He could see Kree leaning over to shout in Mooka's ear, probably saying the same thing.

He held his breath.

Closer to the flag now. Closer. Closer.

They reached it, Kree still with a good lead. She flung herself over to the left, leaning hard to help tip Mooka round the corner. The jerboa turned sharply, but with no tail to help him balance, his long legs slipped and shot out to the side.

Time slowed, everything in the world vanished except the little plains rabbit, clinging to the back of her mount. Uki could see her mouth open, shrieking. He could see Mooka's eyes bulging, his long legs buckling, the ground coming up to meet him ...

That's it, Uki thought, a lump rising in his throat.

They're falling.

It's over.

We've failed.

Chapter Ten

In the Cities

The slow-motion tumble of Kree and Mooka continued, the jerboa's legs lurching out to the right as his body went the opposite way.

Get your legs back under you, Uki willed, trying to send the thought out across the plain to them. *Kick, hop . . . do something!*

Beside him, he felt Jori tense. Her paws flexed against the ropes binding them.

And then . . .

Clods of earth and grass went flying in the air as Mooka *did* kick. Somehow, he had managed to catch the ground with the tips of his toes. He kicked again, soaring upwards, wobbling in the air and – for a few seconds – was facing his opponent, directly in her path. Then, with Kree swinging across the saddle to alter his balance, he tipped the other way, scrabbled for a second and was off again, heading back towards the camp, even as the Miniki champion was making her turn around the flag.

There was a roar of frustration from Gromak and his guards but Uki didn't care. He was jumping up and down, shouting, 'She did it! She did it!'

He even thought he heard a whoop of joy from Jori, but when he looked round at her, she was standing perfectly still, albeit with a slight smile on her lips.

The race wasn't quite over yet. Mooka still had to cover the ground back to the camp. The champion was forcing her jerboa to give its all, even whipping the poor thing with a wooden switch. It hopped as fast as it was able, black eyes popping as it strained, but it was no good. Kree and Mooka were too far ahead and there was no catching them.

They crossed the line with Kree warbling a

victory shriek. Uki ran up to them and, forgetting Mooka's teeth for once, threw his arms around the jerboa. Even some of the Miniki were good-natured enough to cheer.

As his shame-faced champion hopped across the line, Gromak climbed down from his chair and came over to them.

'You have won the challenge,' he grumbled. 'You have free passage on Miniki lands. And we will take you to the twin cities. That is a fast jerboa you have there.'

'Thank you,' said Kree. 'And I am sorry for what I said about your daughter. She does not look like a mouse's armpit. From the right angle.'

'Hmpf,' said Gromak, and then smiled. 'Come, let us have a feast together. It must be nearly lunchtime.'

Uki remembered what Kree had said about the plains rabbits liking to make up. He had a feeling that lunch might turn into dinner, afternoon tea, and then supper and a midnight snack too.

'That's very kind of you, Chief Gromak,' he said. 'But we really have to get to Nys and Syn. It is very, *very* urgent.'

Gromak put his paws on his hips for a moment, but then shrugged and nodded. 'As you wish,' he said. 'I will get some riders to take you. But it is a pity. We were going to eat that jerboa who lost to you.'

Uki glanced up at Kree, who reached a shaking paw down to pat Mooka's neck. Hopefully he would never realise he had been one stumble away from becoming lunch.

*

Gromak gave two riders the task of carrying Uki and Jori behind them on their jerboas. Kree rode on the victorious Mooka. They headed south-east as soon as they could, hoping to make it across the plains by sundown.

The jerboas loped along, not racing, but at a steady pace that ate up the miles. Uki found the motion very strange at first, and he clung tight to the back of the rider in front of him. But he soon got used to the rocking rhythm and didn't feel the need to hang on for dear life. After an hour or two, he was quite enjoying the ride, watching the rippling grass of the plain slip past, smiling across at Kree as she zigged and zagged Mooka in between the two Miniki riders.

They stopped for lunch and to give the jerboas a meal of seeds. The riders talked to each other in low voices, obviously still not trusting them. Kree managed to keep her mouth closed for once and they were soon off again.

Towards the end of the afternoon, Uki noticed the landscape beginning to change. There was a river to the south and trees grew alongside it. One or two at first, and then clumps and copses, the branches peppered with the bright-green buds of new leaves and the odd patch of blossom.

Then the plain itself began to dip down and finally, on the horizon, a strip of blue sea appeared. The riders kept going until they reached a patch of woodland, then they reined in their jerboas and helped Uki and Jori to the ground.

'This is the end of Uluk Miniki lands,' said one, the first proper words that had been spoken to them all day.

'The chief told us to give you these,' said the other, holding out three strings of purple beads.

'Um . . . thank you,' said Uki, taking them.

'They are tribal tokens,' explained Kree. 'They will let us pass safely over Miniki territory. Very special, as there are other tribes that will not know about the challenge.'

'Please pass our thanks to your chief,' said Jori, bowing to the Minikis. 'And we thank you also, for helping us on our journey.'

This seemed to please the riders – Jori always knew how to say the right thing at the right time, Uki noticed – and they climbed back on their jerboas and rode off.

'Well,' said Kree. 'Here we are. The cities are just beyond these woods. I told you I'd get you here safely.'

'Safely? Ha!' Jori gave a harsh laugh. 'We were almost killed! If you'd just kept quiet I could have talked us out of there easily!'

'Yes, but we wouldn't have had a ride across the plains, would we? We'd still be walking now,' said Kree, glaring.

'Oh, so that was all part of your plan, was it? Almost getting eaten alive by buzzards?'

'Might have been.' Kree poked out her bottom lip. Uki could see that quite a large argument was brewing, so he decided to try a distraction.

'Shall we head towards the cities?' he said. 'It would be good to find somewhere to stay tonight. And we still have to find the spirit.'

'Yes,' agreed Jori with a sigh. 'Let's get on. At least we're here now, I suppose. Uki, do you have any idea where we might start looking?'

Uki shrugged. The little tugging feeling was there still, so constant it had become normal. Most of the time he hardly noticed it. He knew they were roughly on the right path, but . . . *perhaps if I try to focus more.*

He closed his eyes and reached for the connection. He could feel it pulling at him, away to the south. He could sense the surging anger of Valkus, the need to be fighting, the constant rage. It seemed a little different now, more focused. As if it had found some kind of target to war against.

And there was something else. A trace of the same feeling nearby, off to their right, amongst the woodland. Not as strong as Valkus himself, but definitely there . . .

'Aargh!' Uki fell to the ground clutching at his head. A bolt of pain had shot through him suddenly – blinding, scorching. He pressed his paws to his eyes, but he could still see . . . except it wasn't *here* he was seeing. It was somewhere else, somewhere familiar . . . *Another vision,* he realised. *I'm seeing through the eyes of that thing on our trail.* Every time he tried to connect to Valkus, his mind linked with this other spirit, creature – whatever it was – instead.

'Where did these crystals come from?'

That voice again, the one from his dream the other morning. The surroundings swam into focus and Uki recognised the smith's forge back in Nether. Those cloaked rabbits were there, tipping over the benches, tools and bits of metal flying everywhere, and the smith herself was held between two of them, her arms twisted behind her back.

'A customer . . .' she was saying. 'A customer gave them to me . . . Please . . .'

'Tell me more,' said the voice. *'Tell me everything.'*

'I have!' wailed the smith. 'There isn't more to tell! Please . . . my husband . . .'

From the corner of his eye, Uki could see the

smith's husband, his body lying on the forge floor. Dead or just hurt, he couldn't tell.

'Oh, you will tell,' said the voice. *'You will tell Necripha all . . .'*

Uki saw a pair of old, withered paws reach up, remove something from above his eyes. The smith stared, gaping, as some kind of wrapping came away. And then her face became a mask of terror and she screamed . . .

*

'Uki! Uki!' Paws were patting his face. He looked up to see the wide blue sky, then the faces of Jori and Kree looking down on him.

'Urrrgh,' he managed to say. It felt like someone had dropped a rock on his head.

'What happened? Did you find the spirit?'

Jori helped him sit up. His head was still spinning but the feeling was wearing off now. 'I found Valkus,' he said. 'He's in the city, I think. He's got someone to fight against.'

'It's begun then,' said Jori. 'We're too late.'

'There's something else,' said Uki. 'Over in the woods there.'

'What?' Jori asked. 'Another spirit? I thought they went off to the south?'

'I'm not sure,' Uki said. 'I think it's different.'

'What was all the screaming?' Kree asked. 'You sounded terrified!'

'I saw that thing again,' Uki said. 'The one that's following us. I don't know why, but every time I try and connect with the spirits we're after, I form a link with it as well. I can even see through its eyes. It was in Nether, hurting the smith, making her talk ... about us, I expect. Maybe Nurg's brothers too.'

'And you're sure it's not from the prison, like the others?' Jori asked.

'No,' Uki shook his head, trying to find words that explained how he felt. 'It's old and powerful like them, but it's not one of those that Iffrit was guarding. I don't have any memories of it like I do the others. But, for some reason, there's a connection. I can't really explain ... I just feel it seeking us, hunting us ...'

'And it's still on our trail,' said Jori, her face grim.

'Yes, but two days behind at least,' said Kree.

'They still have to cross the plains and they won't make such good time as we did.'

'We should still make haste,' said Jori. 'We need to get to this Valkus before he causes any serious damage.'

'What about the thing in the woods?' Uki said. 'I think we should see what it is first.'

'Whatever you say, fearless leader,' said Kree, helping him to his feet. Despite his throbbing head, Uki laughed, and they set off into the trees.

*

Woodland covered the slopes that led down from the plains. Unlike the tangled mass of brambles and bare, sharp branches that made up Icebark Forest, this place seemed green and gentle. Oaks, hazels and beeches, with mossy trunks and weaving roots. Birds sang, butterflies flitted and primroses gleamed in the patches of sunlight.

'Over here, I think,' Uki said, leading them along a worn path in between the trees. He followed the ghost trace like a hound tracking a scent. It kept blinking in and out, but if he concentrated, he could just about feel it.

When they reached the edge of a clearing filled with daffodils, he stopped. 'It's in there, somewhere,' he said. Jori drew her sword. Kree tied Mooka to a tree, then pulled a little copper knife from her belt. Uki wondered if he should have a weapon, and then he remembered the spears on his back. He pulled one out, not really sure what he would do with it if there was trouble, but at least he didn't feel left out.

'Do we charge in screaming?' Kree asked. 'Because I have a really good battle cry. I've never actually had to use it, but it's really scary.'

'*No* battle cries,' said Jori, pretending to ignore Kree sticking her tongue out. 'Surprise is a better weapon than a sword. Do you think it's dangerous, Uki?'

Uki tried harder to sense ... whatever it was. It was difficult to describe what he was feeling: something similar to the memories he had of Valkus, but much, much weaker. 'I don't think so,' he said, hoping he was right.

'Come on, then,' said Jori. She tiptoed into the clearing and the others followed her.

Daffodils were everywhere and the air was thick

with the sweet smell of pollen. Bees bumbled to and fro, droning noisily. At first, they thought the clearing was empty, but then they spotted a hunched shape in the middle. It looked like a rabbit, draped in a cloak.

'Quietly, now,' Jori whispered, moving closer, brushing through the daffodils. Uki gripped his spear tighter.

When they were a few steps away, they could clearly see it *was* a rabbit. A young male with sandy brown fur and a tufty beard. He was huddled under a blanket, staring blankly out at them. His mouth was half open and his chin-fur wet with dribble. *He's in some kind of trance,* Uki thought. *But why is there a hint of Valkus about him?*

'Hello?' Jori said. 'Are you hurt?'

Kree suddenly shouted, making everyone except the dazed rabbit jump out of their skins. 'I know him! That's Nurg's brother! From Nether. One of the missing rabbits!'

Uki gasped. 'That explains why he *feels* like Valkus! The spirit must have been a part of him. Like Iffrit is with me!'

'But Iffrit never made you walk all the way across the plains,' said Jori. 'And you don't sit around like a stuffed cabbage, dribbling on yourself.'

'Maybe the evil spirits did something different,' Uki said. 'Maybe they took control of those rabbits. Made them do what they wanted.'

'Do you think Iffy-whatsit could have done that to you?' Kree asked. She poked at his head with a finger, as if Iffrit was curled up in there, like a caterpillar in a cocoon.

Uki pushed her paw away. 'Possibly,' he said. 'I guess he was too nice to try it. Look what's happened to this rabbit.'

'So the spirit has left him,' said Jori. 'And gone down to the cities. Why would it do that?'

'It's used him up, poor thing,' said Kree. 'Look at the state of him.' They peeked under the cloak and saw that the rabbit was just skin and bones. His feet were rubbed hairless and raw, with blisters from walking so far without rest.

'It's gone to find someone more powerful,' said Uki. He couldn't say exactly how he knew that, but he did. There were memories of Valkus in his head now that let him know exactly how that creature would think. 'Someone he can use to start a war.'

'Then we had better hurry,' said Jori. 'If the cities start fighting each other, it will be a disaster.'

'What about Nurg's brother?' Uki said. 'Should we bring him with us?'

Jori shrugged. 'Do you think he'll recover? Or will he always be like this?'

Uki didn't know. The trace of Valkus was weak and still fading. Perhaps when it was gone, the rabbit's mind would bounce back. He hadn't been under the spell of Valkus for long. The damage can't have been too bad.

'I think he'll be fine,' he said in the end. 'Whatever happened to him, it's wearing off now. I guess it'll be like waking up and finding yourself somewhere strange.'

'He's a grown rabbit,' Jori said. 'He'll be able to find his way home. Or he could go down to the cities like us – make a new life for himself.'

Even so, they decided to leave some food and a waterskin for him. It was the least they could do. In fact, as they left him in his beautiful clearing amongst the flowers, Uki felt a little jealous. Nurg's brother's troubles were over, while Uki was about to head into the unknown again. A city full of rabbits, an evil creature to capture, and something hideous on his trail.

Necripha, he thought. *Whatever you are, I hope I never meet you.*

*

The outcasts carried on walking, down the slope and on until the trees parted, revealing the twin cities of Nys and Syn below them. Both Uki and Kree stopped dead in their tracks, neither of them having seen anything bigger than Nether before.

The river they had been following all afternoon wound down from the plains, widening and flowing to the sea in the distance. A sparkling line of blue all across the horizon. Before it got there, it cut through the middle of a vast, circular wall of wood and stone many times taller than a rabbit. The wall itself was ringed by a complicated series of mounds, ditches and defences. It looked like a maze built by someone who liked wooden spikes a bit too much.

A wide road led into a giant gate on their side of

the river, and there were more roads spidering out on the other side. The fertile land in between them and the monstrous construction was filled with fields, broken up by burrow mounds, hedges and neat little stone walls. It looked like an enormous, living patchwork quilt of green, brown and yellow.

'There you go,' said Jori. 'The twin cities of Syn and Nys.'

'Which is which?' asked Uki when his voice decided to work again. 'It all looks like one place to me.'

Jori laughed. 'It is really, to be honest. Kether knows why they insist on calling it two different names.'

'I have never seen it,' said Kree, 'but I have heard the tale. It *was* one place when it was first built. Two brothers – twins – named Syn and Nys found the spot. They led their tribe here and built a beautiful town. But then they fell out – over a girl, I think – and there was a fierce quarrel. Each built a fort on either side of the river, and their tribe split, too. For many years there was fighting, until they grew old and realised it had all been a stupid waste of time. Since then, there has been peace, and the two forts grew until eventually they joined into one big city.'

'I have heard a similar tale,' said Jori. 'Except the quarrel was over who was the best at fishing. I suppose there is some truth in it. Certainly both sides still have a strong rivalry against each other. Look at the flags.'

Uki peered closer and spotted many pennants flying from the watchtowers that lined the city walls. On the near side of the river they were black with a white ring in the middle; on the far side they were white with a black ring. There were lots and lots of them, as if it was some kind of competition: who can be the proudest of their city?

Uki rubbed his head, which was still throbbing from his vision. 'I imagine it won't take much for Valkus to start the old quarrels up again. He just has to find the right rabbit and give it a push . . .'

'That's right,' said Jori. 'Each city has its own mayor, each with their own soldiers. Both sides think *they* are the best. I've only been here a few times but I always get sick of all the rivalry and boasting.

Valkus will find it easy to start a fight. We have to capture him quickly.'

Kree groaned. 'But that place is *massive*. There could be a thousand rabbits in there! How will he know where to look?'

'Uki can sense the spirit, remember?' Jori said. 'And I expect it will have chosen someone powerful. Someone close to either of the mayors . . . maybe the mayors themselves.'

As soon as Uki heard it, he knew Jori was right. That was *exactly* what Valkus would do. It was as if he knew the creature like an old enemy.

'What's our plan, then?' he said. 'Go in and start walking around until I can track it down?'

'That might take a long time,' said Jori. 'But I have an idea where we can start. My clan have a house in Nys. We are the furthest clan north in the whole of Hulstland, so the Emperor trusts us to be his eyes and ears here. I am hoping word hasn't got to them about me yet. It's a gamble, but if they don't know, I might be able to use them to help us. What do you think?'

She looked at Uki, who was caught off guard for a moment. He expected Jori to be the one making all the decisions. What did he know about this world of clans and cities? In the end he just shrugged.

'If you think it's safe,' he said. 'Don't put yourself in danger. I . . .' He was about to say, 'I don't want anything to happen to you,' but decided it would sound silly, needy. He blushed instead.

Jori didn't seem to notice. 'Let's hope they haven't sent word by sparrow.'

Watching the skies for fluttering message birds, they made their way down to the road that led into Nys.

*

As they walked along, the city seemed to get bigger and bigger. Uki couldn't imagine how many rabbits it would take to build those walls, how much time they'd have to spend.

They passed rabbits working in the fields: planting and sowing, digging up weeds, ploughing the earth with teams of rats. It made Uki wonder just how much food a city must need. Back in his village, they all just foraged for what they wanted. Winters were hard – sometimes he and his mother nearly starved . . .

Mother . . . He realised he hadn't thought of her properly for the past two days and felt a wave of guilt. What would she make of this place? It had always been her dream to leave the Ice Wastes and come somewhere like this. *I wish you were here,* he silently told her. *I wish it more than anything.*

He felt a paw on his shoulder and looked up to see Jori. 'Don't worry,' she said. 'I know it looks big, but you'll soon get used to it.'

She had mistaken his grief for fear about Nys, he realised. Not that he *wasn't* scared. How were you supposed to act in a place like that? What would all the sophisticated city rabbits make of his patchwork fur or his scruffy clothes?

'I'll *never* get used to this place,' said Kree. 'Fenced in on all sides, walls and buildings blocking the view . . . The sooner we're back in the wide open, the better for me.'

The road led up to a tall gatehouse. Guards in black-leather armour stood on either side. More walked along a parapet above the gate and there were others at the top of watchtowers. So many soldiers. Could one of those be controlled by Valkus right now, just waiting for the right chance to throw his spear?

Uki half expected the guards to stop them at the gates, telling them that demons and savages weren't allowed in. Instead, they barely blinked as they marched through behind Jori, who held her head high with her usual confidence.

Inside the city there were rows and rows of buildings. They lined the road, squashed in against one another. The slope down to the river was a mass of clustered rooftops, smoking chimneys making a haze that hung over it all like a bank of fog. Unlike the simple stone huts of Nether, each house had two or more storeys and were made of thick oak frames, with whitewashed plaster in between. Some even had glass windows. Others had colourful shutters thrown open to let in the spring sunshine.

Signs hung from the front of shops, painted with pictures of the goods within. Uki saw a carved carrot, several boots and hats, crossed swords, scissors and bottles of potion. Rabbits bustled everywhere, in and out of doorways, shouting out their wares, leading carts and wagons up and down the road. More rabbits than he had ever seen in one place before. More rabbits than he'd thought there could be in the whole *world.* His head began to spin with it all.

'This is the main street,' said Jori. She had to shout over the noise of traffic and voices. 'It's where all the shops and inns are.'

'Why are there so many rabbits?' Kree asked. She was clutching Mooka's lead rope very tightly and huddling up against him. 'Why are the buildings so *big*?'

Jori just flicked her ears. 'I guess they just started out as huts and then went upwards. The soil here is soft enough to burrow, but the rabbits that came here were from the plains and places like Nether and Chillwater. They were used to building homes on rocky ground, so that's what they did. Old habits are hard to break.'

Uki saw roads leading off the main street. They looked quieter, with buildings spaced further apart. At the end of one was a huge mound, on top of which perched a walled fortress that flew at least ten of the black Nys banners. He nudged Jori and pointed it out. 'What's that?'

'Ah. That's the mayor's fort. It would be a good place to start looking, but it will be tricky to get inside unless we have some important business with the mayor.'

Dodging carts and rabbits, they made their way down the street. It carried on, more or less straight, all the way to the river where Uki could see the boats tied up at the docks. Big, ungainly, bobbing things with spindly masts and ropes everywhere. His mother had told him about them but he'd never seen one. They didn't look like something that should float, let alone travel out to sea. He thought back to the stream by his hut and the little pieces of wood he used to float there, pretending they were ships. It all seemed so long ago now, so far away . . .

'Here we are.' Jori broke his daydreaming, halting them by a tall, narrow building. The bottom storey was made of stone blocks, the top of timber and plaster. It looked dark inside. The windows were blank, framed by black-painted shutters. A sign in the shape of a coiled snake hung over the doorway, matching the clasp of

Jori's cloak, and the door knocker was the head of a fanged serpent.

'I think I'm going to wait outside with Mooka,' Kree said. 'This place looks a bit creepy.'

Uki was tempted to join her, but he could see the look in Jori's eyes. Her ears were flat against her head: this was a big risk for her, he realised. She had no way of knowing if the rabbits inside would welcome her or imprison her.

'Are you sure you want to do this?' he asked. 'We don't have to. We can probably find Valkus on our own. Your clan don't even have to know you're here.'

Jori swallowed, took a deep breath. 'No,' she said at last. 'This will make things easier for us. And I know the rabbit in charge here. He's my cousin. In fact,' she added, 'he's the only one of my whole family that was ever nice to me.'

Uki didn't know what to say. Jori's clan was obviously completely different to anything he had experienced. They had very strange taste in decoration for a start. He felt bad about her taking such a risk just for him, but she seemed to have made her mind up. And firmly too. In the end, he just put a paw on her arm, then followed her as she opened the door and stepped inside.

*

It was dark in the clan house. Dark and quiet – such a contrast compared to the bustle of the street outside.

They found themselves standing in a hallway. The floor was tiled in grey-and-black squares, and tapestries hung on the walls. One showed a rabbit next to a patch of mushrooms, clutching its stomach and dying. The other had a huge snake, fangs about to sink into a terrified mouse. For the second time Uki wished he'd waited outside with Kree.

Jori grabbed hold of a piece of dangling rope and pulled it. Somewhere in the house a bell jingled, closely followed by shuffling footsteps. A hunched old rabbit with a straggly beard and milky grey eyes appeared at the other end of the hall, dressed in an outfit of black velvet.

'Good day, and welcome to the house of Clan Septys,' he said. 'Secret and professional murders and poisonings at reasonable rates. Agonising deaths are extra . . .' Halfway through his well-rehearsed speech, he squinted at them until he finally recognised his caller. 'Lady Jori! What a surprise! But . . . we weren't expecting a visit from the clan warren until next month. Is there some kind of problem?'

'Hello, Nox,' Jori said. 'Don't worry. This isn't an official visit. I've been travelling with my friend here and we thought we'd stop by.'

Nox gave Uki a look, one eyebrow raised. 'I see. I thought for a moment that a street beggar had followed you in.' He wrinkled his nose, as if Uki smelt of jerboa dung. 'And do you wish to see your cousin? He is in the back chamber doing nothing, as usual.'

'Yes, please,' said Jori, as Uki squirmed beside her in embarrassment. They followed the old rabbit through a door at the end of the hallway. She leant to whisper in Uki's ear as they walked. 'Nox is the head servant here. Been running the house for years and years. He's horribly rude, and very deaf.'

'Not that deaf,' said Nox, holding the next door open for them and scowling.

'Thank you kindly,' said Jori with an exaggerated bow, hiding a smile behind her paw. Uki stepped through behind her, cringing.

‘Cousin!’ A shout came from inside the chamber, and before they had even entered the room, a young rabbit had jumped on them, hugging Jori tightly.

‘Hello, Venic,’ Jori said, trying to untangle herself. ‘This is my friend, Uki.’

‘Come in! Come in!’ said the rabbit. He stepped back, and Uki could see he was almost an exact copy of Jori: the same height, the same leather armour. He even had a flask of dusk potion on his belt. His fur was a darker grey, though, without the white patch over his mouth. And his eyes were icy blue, in contrast to Jori’s grey.

‘It’s good to see you, cuz,’ Venic said. ‘Come, sit! Have wine!’

He motioned to some wooden chairs set out by a quietly crackling fire. The room also had a table with a bowl of dandelion leaves and a bottle of purple-red blackberry wine. A small window looked out on to a courtyard with a neat little garden. It looked like herbs were being grown, but Uki thought there was a good chance they’d all be poisonous.

‘Thank you,’ said Jori, taking a seat. ‘It’s been a long time, hasn’t it?’

'It has!' Venic agreed. He pointed to the flask on Jori's belt. 'I see you've passed your trials. How was it?'

'Oh,' said Jori, shrugging. 'Nothing too difficult.' Uki took a seat beside her and breathed a silent sigh of relief. Venic obviously didn't know that Jori had refused to do the final trial. That meant she was safe, for the time being.

Venic laughed. 'Not difficult! So modest. I remember having nightmares for *months* before mine. And after. So tell me. What brings you to the lovely city of Nys? Are you here on clan business? Or . . . an *assignment*?'

Uki shivered. All the time he had spent with Jori, he had forgotten she was trained as an assassin. And this cousin of hers, maybe even Nox the servant – they all *killed* rabbits. With poison. *Probably not a good idea to drink or eat anything here,* he told himself.

'I decided to have a little break. The trials were quite . . . draining. Uki and I have been travelling around Hulstland. We thought we'd visit the twin cities.'

'Sounds lovely,' said Venic. He looked Uki up and down, his eyebrow raised in much the same way Nox's had been. 'You wish to stay here, at the clan house? We don't have any space at the moment but I can move some of the rabbits around.'

'Oh no,' said Uki. The words just popped out, leaving him feeling awkward again. He had been thinking about the high chance of being poisoned and had ended up being rude. 'I mean, we wouldn't want to be any trouble. We're going to stay at an inn.'

'Yes,' said Jori, coming to his rescue. 'Perhaps that would be best. We're only here for a few days.'

'Very well,' said Venic. 'You must stop by for dinner one night, though. And perhaps I could show you some of the sights.'

'That would be very kind,' Jori smiled. 'We were wondering,' she added, 'if there were any parts of the city we should avoid? I heard there had been some trouble recently?'

Venic nodded. 'There has, I'm afraid. Old rivalries between the city halves. Rabbits in Syn have burnt down one of the bridges and set fire to some of the Nysian banners. There's been fighting in the streets, name-calling, things like that. It's all seemed to happen in the last few days. Hopefully it'll blow over before the match.'

'The match?' Jori's ears pricked up.

'Yes, the neekball match,' said Venic. 'It's in two days' time. Nys against Syn. They have one every month and they're always a sight to see. I can get you some good seats, if you're still in town?'

'That would be wonderful,' Jori said, giving Uki a wink. 'Wouldn't it, Uki?'

'Oh yes,' he said. 'Neekball. Wonderful.'

'It's agreed, then!' Venic jumped from his chair and clasped Jori's arm again. 'And we must have dinner. Now, if you'll excuse me, I have a . . . *job* to prepare for.'

Uki had a horrible feeling he knew what kind of job it was. He was quite relieved when Jori said her goodbyes and they left the house.

Kree was waiting outside, draped across Mooka's back, reaching down to give him seeds to nibble.

'Well?' she said, when they appeared.

'There *has* been fighting,' said Uki. 'It sounds like it's coming from the Syn side.' He looked down the street and across the river. The pull from Valkus *did* seem to be coming from that direction.

'Oh great, so we're in the wrong city,' said Kree. 'We'd better head over there and start looking.'

'Not so fast,' said Jori. 'My cousin can get us seats at the neekball match in a couple of days. That will be the perfect chance. *Both* the mayors and all their men will be there. Uki will be able to find the spirit easily, and then we just have to cause a distraction and he can . . . catch it, or whatever he's supposed to do.'

'Neekball! *Pok ha boc!*' Kree spat into the street. 'I have heard of this sport. It is very cruel to jerboas!'

Mooka gave a sad *neek* sound, and Kree patted him.

'Perhaps,' said Jori. 'But we won't have a better opportunity to get at the leaders of Syn. This will be much easier than trying to sneak around the mayor's burrow. What do you think, Uki?'

Uki blinked. Decisions again. How was he supposed to know what was best? Two days of waiting, but a better chance of catching Valkus . . . What if those two days were long enough for Necripha to catch up to them? Or for Jori's clan to find her? But the alternative was even more dangerous: they would have to get inside the mayor's fortress in Syn, discover Valkus, jab him with a spear and then escape again. All without being caught.

'I think we should go to the match,' he said, finally. 'It's less risky. And if Valkus is going to start a war, he'll probably do it there with everyone watching. If we're quick, we can stop it before it even begins.'

'Excellent,' said Jori, rubbing her paws together. 'I'll pop back here later and get the tickets. Once we've found somewhere to base ourselves.'

'So exciting!' said Kree, hopping up and down. 'We will have that spirit locked up on your lovely belt in no time, Uki.'

Uki smiled and nodded, although he couldn't help giving a little shiver of unease. They might think this was all a great adventure, but they didn't have Iffrit's memories jumbled up in their heads. Valkus was dangerous, he knew. Seriously dangerous. And if they got hurt – or worse, killed – it would all be because of him. He didn't think he could bear losing someone else he cared about.

He thought of his mother, lying cold and stiff in that lonely graveyard. *Never again,* he told himself. *Never again.*

Chapter Eleven

Neekball

Despite the thrill of adventure, Kree was less than happy at the thought of spending two whole days in the city. 'You can't see where the sky ends,' she kept saying. 'You can't see the sun rise or set. All there is are buildings. Buildings, noise and *stink*.'

Uki found it just as peculiar, but to him it was a feeling mixed with wonder. All these different rabbits from far-off, fascinating places. Fur of every colour and length, new sights, sounds and smells. And the shops: each one of them packed with things he had never seen before. There was always something new to stare at.

Jori, of course, strolled through the streets like she owned them. Even though she might not have visited Nys for years, she seemed to know every alley, every turn. Without her they would have been completely lost, or perhaps still standing just inside the gate, too frightened to move.

The first thing they did was to visit a jeweller's. Uki gave him one of the tiny crystals and was stunned when it was swapped for a leather bag filled with silver coins. He'd never even seen money in his village, let alone owned any. 'Are you sure it was worth this much?' he whispered to Jori, feeling as though he'd cheated the jeweller somehow.

'More, probably,' said Jori. 'But we need money if we're to sleep and eat. Besides, I quite fancy a hot bath. And you two actually *need* one. Preferably two or three.'

They found an inn that looked out over the river, giving them a good view of the other city. They had plenty of coins for a room each and the best stall in the stable for Mooka.

They also had enough to buy a new set of clothes and a pack for Uki. Jori chose him a pair of black trousers and matching shirt, a leather jerkin and a cloak of the softest grey wool. His spear harness and magpie buckle no longer looked out of place on him. He tried some boots on, but they didn't feel natural on feet that had never worn shoes, so he stayed bare-pawed, like Kree. It was just city rabbits that wore shoes, after all.

It was only after he was back in his room, looking at the strange, smart new rabbit in the mirror, that he realised his old clothes were the one thing he had left from his mother. Tatty and threadbare as they were, there was nothing else – apart from some broken pots back beyond the Wall – that showed she had ever existed. He folded them carefully and stowed them in the bottom of his new pack, along with his blankets, water bottle, bowl and pocketknife.

On the second day in the city, Uki decided he wanted to surprise his new companions with a gift. He wasn't used to giving things, having never had friends before, but he felt the need to show them how grateful he was somehow. How important it was to him having them there, helping him, worrying about him, even though they didn't have to.

He crept out that morning, with his purse, and wandered about the shops searching for the perfect presents. He had no idea how to bargain or haggle, and probably ended up paying far too much, but eventually returned to the inn with a brightly patterned saddle blanket for Kree and a whetstone in an embroidered leather pouch for Jori. He silently left them outside their rooms, just like the Midwinter Rabbit his mother had told him about.

When they met at their table for breakfast, Kree threw her arms about him and hugged him for at least a minute. Jori gave him a bow and touched three fingers to her head, then her heart. Uki wasn't sure what it meant, other than she was pleased. Making them happy gave him a warm, sweet feeling inside, like when his mother had praised him for firing his first clay bowl or thanked him for cleaning the hut. *Friendship,* he thought. *It's the nicest thing. How did I live without it for so long?*

But there was more to their two days than shopping. From their room windows, or the riverside itself, they kept a constant eye on Syn. They saw more and more flags going up, the black circles on the white backgrounds like a thousand staring eyes. The walled mound that held the mayor's fortress was draped almost totally in banners.

'Waving flags is never a good thing,' Jori had said. 'It comes just before waving swords.'

And it looked like she was right. There were more and more soldiers marching back and forth, stopping many rabbits from crossing into the city, and where the bridge had burnt down, a blockade of sharpened wooden spikes had been built.

Mrs Twittle, the landlady of the inn, was a good source of information about what was happening. She had grown up in Syn before moving across the river to marry her husband. He seemed to spend all his time asleep by the fire while Mrs Twittle bustled her way around the inn like a whirlwind of aprons and dusters.

'It's terrible, it is,' she would say to them every mealtime. 'As long as anyone can remember – longer even – there's never been a whiff of trouble between the cities. The odd joke, of course, and a bit of rivalry on the neekball pitch, but we've always got on like family. And now they're burning the bridges! And yesterday there was rocks fired over the river, would you believe? Nearly knocked down two houses! There's talk about building an army ourselves, just in case, you know. My nephew Minty has gone and got himself a spear and everything. Before you know it, there'll be proper fighting, just like in the old stories. Kether save us!'

Uki had also managed to ask her about neekball itself (much to Kree's disgust). She turned out to be quite an expert.

'It's a sport, my dear,' she said. 'Two teams of riders, all on those hoppity jerboas what the plains rabbits ride. They cover them with armour, so's they don't get hurt. The riders wear armour, too. They need it, what with those big wooden clubs with the pointy bits they carry. Bash each other to pieces, they do.'

'So all they do is try and hurt each other?' Uki asked.

'No. Well ... yes ... but that's not *really* what they're s'posed to be doing. They have this leather ball, see, and they've got to try and throw it into the other team's box. There's different holes to chuck it in. The higher up they are, the more points they get. Most of the time they just knock each other's brains out, to be honest.'

It sounded like a strange way to pass the time to Uki. And an even stranger thing to want to watch. 'I guess the match is important,' he said, 'if the mayors are going to be there.'

'Oh, bless my turnips,' said Mrs Twittle. 'It's quite the event. We has a match every month. Sometimes in the Nys Nighthawks' stadium (that's our team), sometimes in the Syn Smashers'. This time it'll be here, and I shall probably have all my rooms booked out. Although Kether knows what'll happen, now we're having all this trouble with one another . . .'

And there had been more dreams, too. The restless spirit, Valkus, somewhere across the river, was leaking thoughts of war and battle. Uki tossed and turned in his bed, his sleep peppered with the sounds of clashing blades and piercing war cries. He woke each morning in a tangle of blankets, feeling as though he had spent the night fighting for his life. And then there was that other thing. The one that was hunting him. *Necripha.* He could feel it out there, on the plains somewhere, searching, searching. Every hour it got a little closer. It woke feelings in him from his distant ancestors, hiding under bushes and in burrows, watching the sky as hungry kestrels circled above.

It was following the trail of the crystals, he knew. But was it really after him? Or Valkus and the other escaped prisoners?

Perhaps all of you, said his dark voice. **And when it finds you? It will make the flash of feathers and crunch of bones your forefathers dreaded seem like a midsummer picnic.**

*

The evening of the match arrived. Uki dressed in his new clothes, folded his cloak into his pack and slung it over his shoulder, next to his spears. He practised drawing one and throwing it, trying to make the action as smooth as possible. Every attempt he fumbled, or got it tangled in his ears. The twelfth time his spear had clattered to the floor, he gave up. Perhaps whatever rabbit Valkus had taken over would be nice enough to jump on to his spear end for him. Even then he'd probably make a mess of it.

He met the others downstairs and paid Mrs Twittle the money for their stay. She was draped in black-and-white bunting, with flags poking out from the top of her bonnet. She had even painted a Nysian flag on Mr Twittle's face as he snoozed in his armchair. 'I'm not actually going to the game,' she said. 'But I does like to support our team.'

She had kindly allowed them to leave Mooka in the stable with their belongings, harnessed and ready in case they needed a quick escape. Luckily, the stadium was only a few streets away. In fact, they could hear the noise of the crowd building already. A dull rumble, at the back of their hearing, that peaked every now and then into a roar.

'Goodbye, then. It's been lovely having you here,' said Mrs Twittle. 'Such polite and sweet young rabbits. Your parents must be so proud.'

'My parents want me dead,' said Jori. 'Uki's *are* dead, and Kree's threw her out on to the plains when she was eight.'

Mrs Twittle's mouth opened and closed a few

times. In the end she decided to change the subject. 'Have fun at the game, won't you, my lovelies. Cheer on those Nighthawks for me.'

Kree growled. 'It is a cruel spectacle of harmless jerboas being tortured for the pleasure of heartless rabbits. I will be cheering no one.'

'Oh,' said Mrs Twittle. 'Well. Goodbye anyway. Do come again.' And she hurried off to polish something.

*

As soon as they walked around the corner from the inn, they were swept along amongst a crowd of rabbits. Most were wearing scarves of black cloth marked with the white circle of Nys. Some waved matching flags or had dyed their fur in black-and-white patterns.

'It looks like you were born to be a neekball supporter,' said Jori, having to raise her voice over the noise of so many rabbits. She was right. For the first time in his life, Uki blended in perfectly.

The crowd bustled its way down the road to the stadium, singing songs as it went. Uki held on to Jori with one paw, Kree with the other, keeping them together in a chain. There were so many rabbits, bumping and squashing up against one another. He'd never imagined there could be so many bodies in one place. How would he ever spot the rabbit that carried Valkus in this crush?

The stadium looked like some kind of wooden fortress from the outside. Once they were in, Uki could see that it was an enormous ring encircling a rectangle of grass in the middle. The river of rabbits flowed in through the gate, reached the edge of the pitch, and then began to spread out into the seats on the right-hand side. There were rows and rows of benches, rising up in tiers, and it looked like each city was going to take up a separate half of the arena.

'We should try to be as close to the Syn side as possible,' said Jori. 'That will give Uki the best chance of spotting Valkus.'

They made their way to the front, Uki using some of his strength to push other rabbits aside. He felt bad, but as Jori said, they needed to be close. There was no sign of the Syn fans yet. Their half of the stands were empty.

'What if they're not coming?' he said. 'We'll have wasted those two days for nothing!'

'At least the jerboas won't be harmed in some stupid game,' said Kree, although she too looked worried.

Jori took a seat in the front row, resting one paw on her flask, the other on her sword hilt. 'Relax,' she said. 'They'll be here.'

Sure enough, no sooner had Uki and Kree sat down than the gates at the other end of the stadium opened. A tide of white-clad rabbits marched in. They stomped along the rows of seats with a purpose. Even from the other side of the pitch, it was clear to see that nearly all of them were carrying weapons. They looked more like an army than a group of sports fans. And there was something else: a swell of anger and hatred came with them. Uki could feel it, taste it. It made his fur stand on end – it was like sharp salt in his mouth.

'Can you feel that?' he said aloud, getting a funny look from Jori.

'Valkus?' she asked.

'Yes . . .' Uki thought for a second. 'But more than that. It's coming from *all* of them.'

Jori flicked her ears. 'Maybe he's infected them somehow. Some kind of smoke-borne poison, maybe? I know of ones that can make a whole room of rabbits go mad.'

That could be it, Uki thought. *Valkus has them all under his power. He'll make them fight against their neighbours for no real reason. They might not even know they're doing it.*

'*Pok ha boc.* This does not look good,' said Kree. 'We're going to be caught in the middle of a battle!'

Uki gulped. Jori stared steadily across the pitch. 'If fighting starts, stay behind me,' she said. 'Let Uki and I deal with any trouble.'

'Uki?' said Kree. 'He's not a fighter!'

'You haven't seen him in action,' said Jori.

Uki hadn't heard her. He was directing all his attention on the opposite stands, trying to pick out the presence of Valkus from amongst the overflowing anger. He could definitely feel something – that scratchy tug behind his eyeballs . . . somewhere in the centre . . . halfway up the terrace. That box in the middle . . . there!

'He's in that box thing!' Uki shouted, jumping out

of his seat and pointing. 'Right there, in the middle!' Jori dragged him back down again.

'Don't give us away!' she hissed. 'That's the mayor's box. It's full of his councillors and captains. Valkus must be inside one of *them*.'

'We said it would be someone important,' said Kree. 'And we were right. Look what they've done already!'

Uki nodded. Just a few days to turn a peaceful city into *this*. Imagine what damage Valkus could do if they didn't stop him. Imagine what damage the other two spirits were doing *right now*.

As soon as the seats were full, the chanting started. There were roars and whoops from the Nys side, with the occasional song about how amazing the Nighthawks were. The Syn supporters simply stamped a rhythm out on the wooden floor, shouting their city name, over and over.

'Boom, boom! Syn! Boom, boom! Syn! Boom, boom! Syn!'

They were all joining in, drowning out the Nys side completely. Uki peered at the box opposite and saw a large rabbit in the middle leading the chant.

That must be the mayor, he thought. *I'll bet my whiskers Valkus is in* him.

Just as Uki was wondering how under earth he was going to get close enough to the mayor to be sure, there was a roar from the crowd as the jerboa riders came on to the pitch. They hopped out from a tunnel, spreading out to take up their positions: ten in black, ten in white.

Kree hissed in disgust when she saw them, and Uki could understand why. The jerboas were clad from head to foot in thick panels of painted wooden armour. It was even buckled on to their paws and legs, and their tails had been tipped with spiked metal clubs. Their eyes peeped from holes in their heavy helmets, showing whites all around as they were kicked and pulled into place.

'*Nam ukku ulla,*' said Kree. 'Those poor animals. Look how scared they are!'

The riders were also heavily armoured. Grilles covered their faces. They had spiked helmets, shoulder pads and bracers. The only part uncovered were their ears, which were torn and tattered, even missing in some cases. In one paw they held their jerboas' reins, the other clutched a heavy club with jagged copper studs.

The chanting stopped for a moment, and Uki saw some rabbits walking out into the middle of the pitch. One was dressed in a fine black robe, with a gold chain about her neck. She was flanked by two guards and followed by a twitchy, armoured rabbit who held a large leather ball in his paws.

'Good evening, citizens!' shouted the robed rabbit.

'That's Nilla, mayor of Nys,' Jori whispered in Uki's ear.

'Welcome to Nys stadium for this month's Twin-City Challenge!' Mayor Nilla waved her paws. Only the Nysian rabbits cheered. 'We extend the paw of sportsmanship to Mayor Renard and the rabbits of our neighbours in Syn. May the best team win!'

Again, cheers only from the Nys supporters. The white-clad rabbits of Syn stood silent, their paws on the weapons at their sides.

Any minute now, thought Uki. *Be ready.* His paw went to the magpie-etched buckle at his chest. He could still feel the heat of Gaunch's crystal. Was it juddering slightly in the presence of another spirit, or was he just imagining it?

Mayor Nilla and her guards walked off the pitch, leaving the armoured rabbit with his ball. He waited until they were clear, then gave a shrill squeak and threw the ball into the air, before running away as fast as his paws could carry him. He barely made the edge of the pitch before the neekball players kicked their mounts into action.

Despite Kree's growling next to him, Uki had to gasp. The game really was a sight to behold. The jerboas, leaping at full speed, dashed across the pitch, slamming into one another with loud cracks of splintering wood.

The riders on their backs kicked their mounts on, swinging their clubs as they flew through the air. They bounded past one another, smacking bats against heads, knocking sparks from armour. Somewhere in the middle was the leather ball, held in a rider's paws one moment, then thrown across the pitch the next.

Uki tried to track it with his eyes. He saw one of the Nighthawks knock the ball from a Smasher's grip, catch it as it fell, then flip it across to his teammate, all in mid-air during a split-second jump.

The second Nighthawk tucked the ball under one arm, then yanked hard on his reins, spinning his jerboa round. He whacked the poor thing's rump with his club, making it leap for the other end of the pitch. Two Smashers tried to stop it, but the club on the end of the jerboa's long tail swiped them both about the head. One of them tumbled from his mount, hitting the pitch with a *crump* and a shower of muddy turf.

The Nighthawk with the ball reached the end of the pitch, beating another Smasher out of the way with his club. There stood a tall wooden box with five holes cut into it. The player stretched high in his stirrups and threw the ball into the top one with a bang. A roar went up from the Nysian crowd.

'Ten points!' Jori yelled, then looked sheepish when she saw Kree scowling at her.

Uki found himself caught up in the moment too. He felt a buzz of excitement at Nys scoring, found himself hoping and praying that they won. In another life this might have been an exciting event, but he

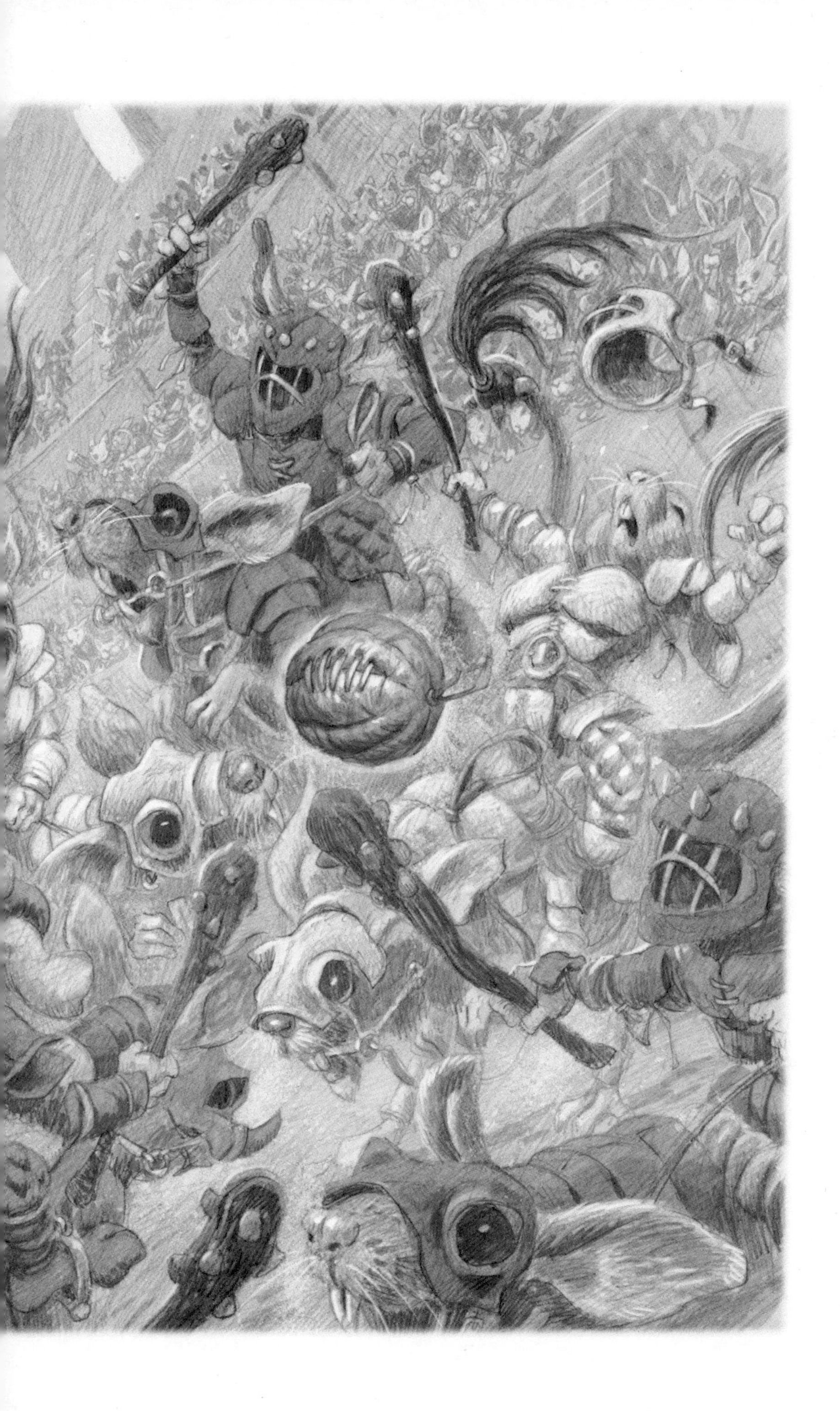

wasn't here tonight for fun . . .

He looked back to the mayor's box and was horrified to see it empty. Where had he gone? *Why* had he gone?

The answer came soon enough. There was a deafening roar from the Syn crowd and they all surged forward as one, leaping over the barrier and on to the pitch, charging towards the Nysian stands with their weapons waving.

'This is it!' Jori yelled, drawing her sword. 'The battle's started. Let's get to the other side!'

'The mayor!' Uki shouted back. 'He's gone!'

'Use your senses!' Jori leapt across the barrier on to the pitch. 'Find him!'

Uki tried to concentrate. He could still *feel* Valkus somewhere inside the grounds. There was still time to get to him.

Uki followed Jori, leaping over the low wooden fence, Kree close behind him. He was suddenly faced with a horde of rabbits charging towards him and screaming. The neekball riders were galloping left and right, trying to get out of the way. It was like facing an oncoming stampede and his first thought was to was run away as quickly as possible. If it hadn't been for Jori's example, he might have done just that.

She stood in a fighting stance, her sword held out in front, her other paw on her flask of dusk potion. Before she could even unclip it, the wave of Syn rabbits was upon her.

'For Septys!' she yelled, and Uki saw several rabbits dodge out of her way, terror at that name overriding their fury. Others were forced into her by the crowd behind them, and Jori began to parry and block their clubs and spears, her deadly steel blade slicing straight through the wood.

But Uki didn't have time to stare. There were suddenly screaming rabbits everywhere. Some surged around him, leaping the barrier and chasing the fleeing Nys fans across the benches. Others weren't as worried about attacking children.

'Syn forever!' yelled a white-armoured guard three times Uki's size, and hurled a spear right at him.

Just as when Uki had seen that clan rabbit stalking Jori, he felt the tingle of his new senses surging. Everything slowed. He could see the spear tip wobbling slightly as it sliced through the air towards him. He could *feel* it fly, knew its path and its target as if it had already struck.

It was going to hit him square in the chest, so he stepped sideways, bringing his arm up to snatch at the shaft. In a blink, he plucked the spear out of the air, then snapped it with both paws. It broke like a stick of raw celery, leaving the spear thrower gaping at him.

Uki took the blunt end and threw it back. His power didn't seem quite as strong as it was in the forest, but it was enough to send the shaft of wood screaming faster than an arrow. The blunt end of the spear hit the Syn rabbit in the centre of his forehead with a *crack*. He toppled to the ground, out cold.

Kree was staring at him, mouth open. 'How did you do *that*?'

Uki only had time to shrug before another rabbit was rushing at him, all gnashing teeth and wild eyes. Uki didn't have time to think about what he was doing. He grabbed hold of the rabbit's head and pushed him to the side, just as surprised as his victim was when the rabbit went flying through the air and into the pitch fence, smashing into a cloud of splinters.

'Come on, fight me!' Kree had picked up the other half of the spear Uki had snapped and was waving it at the charging Syn rabbits. All of them dodged past her, apparently thinking she was too small to bother with.

'There's too many to get past!' Jori sliced another rabbit's club in two and then hit him in the nose with her sword hilt. There was a pile of unconscious bodies at her feet, and she still hadn't had time to drink from her flask.

'Here come the Nys guard,' Uki said. The gates at the end of the pitch were open and black-armoured soldiers were pouring through, forming a wall for the neekball supporters to escape behind. The Syn rabbits had seen them too, and turned to attack. Things were about to get serious.

'Uki,' Jori shouted. 'Lead us to Valkus!'

A wave of Syn soldiers ran through them, rushing to get to the Nysian force. They swiped at Jori as they went, forcing her to block blow after blow.

Uki could still sense Valkus, but the connection

was fading. He must be leaving the stadium, getting to safety. Uki had to be quick, had to stop him before he escaped. But it would be dangerous. Who knew what guards he would have, how well protected he would be? Uki had a sudden vision of his friends facing elite soldiers armed with blades and shields, of them lying bloody on the floor moments later. The risk to them would be huge. Deadly.

That was the moment he realised: there was no way he could ask them to do this. He had to face it alone to keep them safe, to stop them from being hurt.

You have to go now, Uki's voice told him. **While Jori's too busy to follow.**

'I'm sorry!' he yelled. 'It's better this way!' He dashed into the press of bodies, using his strength to shove rabbits aside, flinging them behind him to block his path.

'Uki! Where are you going?' he heard Kree yell as she was blocked off by all the Syn soldiers.

'Stop! Wait for us!' Jori was yelling too.

He hoped they would get clear of the battle, keep themselves out of danger. He hoped he might see them again, and that they would forgive him. But he had to do this. There was no choice.

Uki put his head down and charged further into the squash of bodies, leaving his friends far behind him.

Chapter Twelve

In Enemy Hands

It felt awful to leave his friends behind. The worst kind of betrayal. *What if they never forgive me?* he thought as he powered through a cluster of soldiers in their white-painted armour. *What if I never see them again?*

As he pushed and shoved his way past the oncoming rabbits, Uki nearly stopped and went back to them several times. It was only the constant pull of Valkus, somewhere ahead, that kept him going. *I'm doing this to keep them safe,* he reminded himself.

Even if it means losing my friends . . . at least I know they won't be harmed.

With a final heave, he ducked his head down and burst out of the back row, emerging on to the end of the now empty neekball pitch. He ran past the wooden scoring box towards the gates at the far side.

Risking a glance over his shoulder, he saw a mass of white- and black-clad bodies clashing with each other. Jori and Kree were nowhere to be seen, lost somewhere amongst the huddle.

Please be all right, he thought. *Goddess, Kether . . . Zeryth even. Somebody protect them.*

He ran up to the gates and found them firmly shut. Even though they were three times his height and made of heavy oak, he put his shoulder to them and pushed. He could feel the buzz of the spirits' power running through him as whatever barred the doors on the other side strained, flexed and then gave way. The gates ground open a sliver, large enough for him to poke his head through.

Outside was a street much like the one they had followed to enter the stadium. It was dark now, lit by the odd torch or lantern hanging from the clustered buildings. Uki could see figures out there, on the road. Most were rabbits running away from the stadium, trying to get home and hide from the violence, or shouting for guards to come and help. But there was one small group walking slowly away – Uki could see they were dressed in white cloaks and armour, carrying spears and shields. In the centre of them was a large, ginger-furred rabbit. It *had* to be the mayor and his men.

He squeezed further between the gates, feeling the senses that Iffrit gave him jangling. He stared at the mayor, searching for some hint, some clue, a final piece of evidence that he contained the escaped spirit Uki was searching for.

And sure enough, as he squinted through the torchlight, Uki saw it. Writhing inside the figure of Mayor Renard was a mass of spikes and blades. Just as when he'd seen Gaunch in the forest, it was a ghostly image. There, but not there. Like it was painted on glass laid over the top of reality.

Still, it had a face twisted in a mix of joy and anger, with jagged metal teeth and flaming eyes. And the whole thing glowed with a transparent red light. It flashed into being for an instant and Uki saw it look along the street, right at him. There was a moment of connection, as each of them recognised the other, and then the image blinked out again.

'Hurry!' Uki heard the mayor shout, and the rabbits began to move away at double time. With a final shove, Uki burst out of the doors, reaching over his shoulder for a spear.

This is it, he thought. *If I'm quick enough, I can run up and surprise them. His men won't be expecting an attack from a child.*

He gritted his teeth, clutched his spear tight and took a leap out of the gateway, only to find his path blocked by a rabbit who had appeared from the shadows like a ghost. Uki looked up into a grey-furred face he recognised from somewhere. That wispy beard, those pale, watery eyes.

'Nox?' he said, remembering the old servant from Jori's clan house.

'Now,' said the old rabbit to someone behind Uki.

There was a *clump* as something hit him hard on the back of his skull. His spear clattered to the ground, light blazed in his head and he passed out.

*

Dragged.

I'm being dragged, Uki thought.

His arms were being held, tight enough to hurt, out on either side. His legs were stretched behind him, toes scraping along the packed earth of the road.

He opened his eyes a crack and saw the ground sliding away. There were rabbits either side of him and another in front, leading them.

Nox, he thought. That had been the last thing he'd seen. But why would a servant of Jori's clan want to hurt him? Had they found out about Jori running away? Maybe they wanted to stop him from catching Valkus . . .

But how would they know about that? The only rabbits he'd told were Kree and Jori, and *they* wouldn't have said anything. Would they?

He remembered Jori had gone back to the clan house to get the neekball tickets. **She could have told them then,** his dark voice whispered.

Stop it, he told himself. *She's your friend. You trust her.*

He *did* trust her he realised, and felt a sudden rush

of guilt at having left them behind. If they were here, perhaps he wouldn't be in this fix right now.

'Bring him this way,' Nox was saying to whoever held him. Clearly they had no idea he was awake. They had hit him hard enough to knock him out for hours, but they hadn't reckoned on Iffrit's healing power. It must have fixed him quickly, just like it did back in the graveyard when he was almost dead.

If they don't know about that, they can't know about Valkus either, Uki thought, his mind racing. So Nox must be working for someone else. Jori's cousin, maybe? Perhaps Venic wasn't all that he seemed.

Uki tried to flex the muscles in his arms, wondering if he had the strength to escape, but he couldn't move them properly. His head still swam, recovering from the blow. He would have to wait until he got his strength back, and then burst free. If he tried too soon, they would just hit him again. Much harder, probably, to make sure he didn't wake up.

Maybe Kree will find the spear, he thought.

Maybe they will be able to work out what happened to me.

But how would they know where he was? They would think he had followed Mayor Renard, not been rabbit-napped by Nox.

Thinking of Kree reminded him of what she had said back in Nether, about tracking Nurg's brothers across the plain. Would she be able to do the same thing in a city?

Uki looked down at the road again. It was just dried mud. Too well trodden to leave any tracks on it by walking, but maybe . . .

As carefully as he could, Uki dug the claws of his feet down into the ground. He felt them bite into the earth and scrape along. The rabbits hauling him carried on, regardless. They hadn't noticed a thing.

Uki did it again, and again. He couldn't see behind him to check whether he was leaving enough of a trail but it felt like he might be. Would Kree be able to follow it? Would his friends even want to, after he had left them so selfishly?

'We're here,' said Nox, stopping in front of an old building. This was not the smart clan house Uki had first met him in. It was an old tumbledown building in a dirty, dingy part of the city. Uki could hear the river close by and thought they must be at the docks.

'He's awake,' said one of the rabbits holding him, and Uki cursed under his breath. He'd been looking around, forgetting to pretend he was still knocked out.

'Hit him again,' said Nox. 'Harder this time.'

Uki struggled, trying to break free, but his arms were still too weak. The last thing he heard was the *swish* of a club heading towards the back of his head.

And then nothing.

*

This time when he awoke, he was in a room. It had low wooden beams and plank walls. There were lanterns somewhere, casting flickering shadows everywhere except the dark corners. Uki saw crates stacked around the walls, most splintered and broken. Cobwebs thick with clumps of dust hung off everything in swathes, and the whole place smelt of damp and mildew.

Uki's head throbbed where he had been hit, twice. He could feel lumps there when he moved, and there were little flashes of light going off behind his eyes. But it wasn't the only thing that hurt.

His arms were being yanked above his head, his shoulders and wrists burning. He tried to look upwards, his vision still swimming, and saw metal shackles holding him to one of the roof beams. His feet were dangling in the air, the floor almost a metre below.

Would he be able to break the metal cuffs that held him? He summoned what strength he had and pulled, but nothing budged. He was still stunned, and his restraints weren't forged from copper or bronze. It was that hard, silvery metal, the same stuff that Jori's sword was made of. He would have trouble breaking it even if he wasn't so dizzy.

'Nox. He's awake.' A voice came from behind him, deep and dim-sounding. The perfect voice for a henchman.

'Already?' There was some shuffling and the figure of Nox came into view. He walked up to Uki and peered into his face. 'You're a very tough young rabbit, aren't you? Hurk hit you so hard that second time I thought you might never come round.'

Uki tried to speak, but his tongue felt too fat for his mouth. He swallowed a few times, then managed to croak, 'Why?'

'Why did we capture you?' Nox shrugged. 'I have no idea. We simply follow orders. I can't think what the mistress wants with a mismatched scrap of a thing like you, but the sparrow she sent said you were important.'

'Mistress?' Uki said. Who was he talking about? 'Don't you work for Venic?'

Nox laughed, a cracked, bitter sound. 'Venic? Please – that idle, good-for-nothing whelp? I've had many masters come here from the Coldwood to run the clan house over the years, but he is the absolute *worst.* All he cares about is going to parties and drinking blackberry wine. Besides, I only pretend to work for that bunch of poisoners. My *real* loyalty is with the mistress.'

He reached up to his cloak, where the serpent badge of Clan Septys was pinned, and turned back the collar. Hidden underneath was another symbol: a wide-open eye, cold and staring. Uki had seen it before somewhere, but his head was too fuzzy to think. In the city? In Nether? The Uluk Miniki camp?

Then it came back to him. That eye had been above the windows of the tower he saw in his first dream. Which meant it was something to do with that *thing* hunting him. Could Nox be working for that? And what had its name been … Necro … Necra …

'*Necripha,*' he said.

'Yes!' Nox's milky eyes widened in surprise. 'How do you know her name? Have you met her before?'

He came close to Uki's face, hungry for answers. Whoever this Necripha was, Nox was clearly in awe of her, and desperate to meet her. He was almost dribbling at the thought. Uki turned his head away, disgusted.

'No matter,' said Nox, shuffling over to the doorway and peering through a crack. He rubbed his paws together, as excited as a young rabbit on Bramblemas morning. 'You will see her yourself, soon. To think, all these years serving the Endwatch and tonight I will finally get to see the leader herself! We had word this morning that they were nearly at the city. She should be here any minute!'

The thought of that filled Uki with terror. He struggled against his shackles, kicking and wriggling, but they didn't budge. It only made his shoulders burn and grind more, his arms feeling like they might pop out of their sockets at any moment.

Nox laughed again. 'You won't escape that easily,' he said. 'That's Eisenfell steel those shackles are made of. I had to steal every penny in the clan strongbox to pay for them.'

'No!' Uki writhed and struggled for a few minutes more, but even his great strength couldn't help him. His eyes kept flicking to the doors, hoping that Kree might have followed his trail and was about to burst in, ready to rescue him.

No one came.

Finally, he gave up and slumped, dangling. There was nothing he could do except wait for Necripha to arrive.

*

He wasn't waiting for long.

Nox had taken to pacing the floor, and there were snores coming from somewhere behind him.

The other two rabbits who had dragged him here, Uki presumed.

Then, out of nowhere, there was a sudden rap at the door, making every rabbit in the room leap out of their fur. Nox dashed to draw back the bolts, and a crowd of black-cloaked figures pushed their way into the room.

There were six of them altogether. One, in particular, stood out: a broad, hulking rabbit, his cloak barely covering his sloping shoulders and craggy boulder of a head. He looked around the room with narrow eyes almost lost beneath his heavy brow, one paw on the hilt of the dagger at his belt.

The others were all identical copies of each other – the same size, faces hidden by the cowls of their hooded cloaks – apart from one, who was hunched and bent over. A knobbled staff was clutched in one paw, and Uki could see patchy grey fur, knuckles swollen and twisted with arthritis.

That one is even older than Nox, Uki thought. *Surely that can't be Necripha?*

But he was wrong. Nox dashed from the doorway to bow and scrape before the gnarled figure. 'Mistress

Necripha,' he said, simpering. 'I have captured the black-and-white child as you commanded.'

'Is he unharmed?' The voice was the same as that in his visions, Uki realised. The fur on his neck prickled.

'Yes, Mistress,' said Nox. 'Well . . . mostly.'

With small, shuffling steps, the hunched rabbit moved closer to Uki. He held his breath as it reached up, lifting back its hood. Underneath was the face of an old, old she-rabbit, her head covered in a black scarf. Skin hung in folds from her neck and cheeks. Bones showed through the patchy fur. Her front teeth were an ochre brown and jutted from her mouth. Her eyes were deep set and a dark shade of crimson. They flicked over Uki, taking in every detail, lingering on the crystal in his harness buckle.

She doesn't look so scary, Uki thought. *What was the smith screaming at? Those red eyes? Her disgusting teeth? Or something under her scarf?*

'The fire guardian is in him,' Necripha said. 'I can feel it there. It has merged with him somehow . . . given itself to him.'

Nox scurried over to Necripha's shoulder, still

bowing and nodding his head. 'We found some spears on the child, mistress. And there's a crystal in his buckle.'

'I'm not blind, you dolt!' Necripha waved a paw and her big servant grabbed Nox by the ears and yanked him out of the way.

'Gaunch is in the crystal. Do you see, Balto?' The big rabbit grunted. 'The guardian must have told him how to catch them. But without them all, he will fade and die. He has trusted his task to this child rabbit! Why would he do such a thing? Why not just crush the brat's mind and take his body?'

The big rabbit, Balto, grunted. It appeared to be the most intelligent thing he was able to say. *They're talking about me like I'm not even here,* Uki thought. *I'm just a piece of meat to them: a thing that holds Iffrit inside.*

'Mistress,' Nox was back again. 'You should know that this child is friends with a daughter of Clan Septys. He came to the house with her. They may be looking for him even now. I have told you how powerful the Clan is . . .'

'I don't care about the clans of Hulstland!'

Necripha shouted, making Nox cringe into a ball. 'Not even the notorious Shadow Clans! I have seen them rise, I will see them fall. Besides, how will they know where we are? They can't search both cities in a night. We are safe here for the moment.'

'What shall we do, mistress?' Balto asked. He was staring at Uki with something that looked like hunger.

Necripha tugged the wispy whiskers on her ancient chin. 'I'm not sure. When those rabbits in Nether told me about this child, I assumed the fire guardian had simply possessed him. I also assumed it would be stronger than it is. All those years in the quantum prison must have weakened it.'

'Can we get it out?' Balto rubbed his huge paws together.

Necripha stared hard at Uki again. 'It's not as simple as that. The guardian and this . . . boy . . . have become meshed together. You may have to kill him to find it. When he's dead, the guardian should come out. It'll be a small grain of light, no bigger than a seed. Once we have it, I will try to make it bond with you. You will get its power. If it's too twined up with the child, then we shall have to use my other plan.'

'Other plan?' said Balto, sounding disappointed.

'Yes,' said Necripha. 'We shall just release Gaunch from his crystal and then persuade him to join us. Once we have him on our side, it will be easy to convince Valkus as well.'

'You mean I won't get the magic?'

'No, Balto,' said Necripha. 'Not if you don't have the guardian's power of binding. I'm sorry. We shall just have to make the spirits work with us. Once they see I will allow them to do their evil work, I am sure they will agree.'

Balto drew a curved dagger from his belt and glared at Uki. It looked like he had set his heart on having Iffrit's powers and through them, the strength of the spirits. Now Uki had ruined it and was about to pay a harsh price.

'Wait!' Uki shouted. 'You can't!'

Necripha ignored him, as if he wasn't even there. Balto took a step closer.

'Why are you doing this?' Uki shouted. He kicked and wriggled but the shackles didn't budge. Balto was reaching out for him now, the dagger in his other paw, glinting in the lamplight.

'Who are you people?' If Uki was going to die, he at least wanted to know who was killing him, what they planned to do with his power. 'Why were you in that tower in the forest?'

'Wait!' Necripha held up a paw, making Balto freeze. 'How do you know about the tower? That place is secret!'

'I saw it,' Uki said. 'In a dream.'

'You *saw* it?' Necripha moved to stand in front of him again. 'What else did you see?'

'I saw you hunting in the trees,' Uki said. He racked his brain, while he still had it, thinking of other things to say. He had to buy some time … think of an escape … pray that Kree would find him. 'And I saw you in Nether, talking to the smith …'

'The boats. Did you see the boats we sailed here in?'

Boats? Thought Uki. *I didn't see that. That must be how they got to Nys so quickly.* 'No,' he said. 'Just the other things.'

'Interesting,' said Necripha. 'There is more to this than I thought. I need to look at this young rabbit more closely.' She reached a paw behind her head and began fiddling with her scarf. A feeling of sick horror started to rise in Uki's throat. He remembered seeing this through Necripha's eyes when she had made the smith shriek so. Now he was going to see exactly what she had . . .

Necripha's scarf fell away and it was indeed Uki's turn to scream. There, in the centre of her forehead, was an extra eye. Blank and crimson, like her others, it blinked at Uki, twitching as it peered *into* him. He could feel its gaze, boring through his mind like a burrowing mole. It tunnelled through his thoughts and memories, rooting around, plucking at the juicy ones. He could sense the part of him that was Iffrit, buzzing and tingling in anger as if it were being poked and prodded, every last fragment of it peered at.

The feeling went on for minutes, the longest minutes of Uki's life. Finally, Necripha pulled the black scarf over her forehead again, tying it tight behind her wrinkled ears. Uki breathed a sigh of relief. He wasn't really looking forward to what Balto might do, but it would be better than going through *that* again.

'We seem to have a connection, you and I,' Necripha said. 'That guardian spirit in you must be related to me somehow. We must have had a link in the time before. That is how you've been able to see through my eyes.'

'Time before?' asked Uki. If he could keep her talking for a bit longer, maybe help might come.

'The time before the Ancients left,' said Necripha. 'Before Gormalech. How much did the spirit tell you? Do you know its name?'

'Iff something, I think,' said Uki. He didn't want to give too much away. 'It didn't really tell me much. Apart from that I had to catch the four spirits.'

'Iffrit.' Necripha stroked her whiskers again. 'Yes, I do remember. But everything is so muddled. Bits and pieces missing. It was so long ago . . .'

'So there were rabbits around then? In the time of the Ancients?'

Necripha laughed. 'This body is aged, but not *that* old! No, I am a spirit too. Somewhere in this head is a little spark of a soul. I was made by the Ancients, just like your Iffrit. Just like Gormalech. He is related to me too. You might even call him my brother. When he went crazy and ate the whole planet, I hid. For thousands of years. Can you imagine what that was like? Dodging and sneaking, creeping this way and that. And knowing that if he found me, he would guzzle me in an instant, suck me up to be a part of his squirming metal body.'

'What happened then?' Uki asked. 'Why did Gormalech stop eating everything?'

'Those beings known as the goddesses came,' said Necripha. 'Estra and her sister Nixha. They fooled that fat iron lump, somehow. They found a way to bind him under the earth. Some pact or truce, it is said. "The Balance" they call it. A piece of trickery, more like.'

'I bet you were happy about that,' said Uki. *Keep her talking, keep her talking . . .*

'Happy? That one horrid ruler had been replaced by another?' Necripha opened her mouth to laugh. A hideous, croaking sound, like a frog gargling with sand. 'I wanted this world for myself. If my brother could have it, why not me? Instead, I was made to sneak about like a common thief, hiding away like a shadow.'

'So you took over that rabbit's body? Went and lived in your secret tower?'

'*This* body?' Necripha pulled at the saggy skin of her face. 'This is just one of many I have used. They only last for a hundred years or so, then they fall apart. I took the first one not long after the goddesses made your kind. So small and . . . *furry* compared to the bodies of the Ancients. And with these stupid, flapping ears. But there is always another disciple willing to give their body to me. And so I go on.'

'Why didn't you just make friends with the goddesses?' Uki asked. 'I'm sure they would have been glad to see you.'

'Glad? Glad? They sealed my brother under the earth. What would they have done to me? No, I didn't want them to find me. I hid away again and built up my secret church, my Endwatch. We have hidden in that forest, watching, spying, ever since. Gathering every piece of information we can, searching out the old magic of the Ancients.'

'Why?' Uki asked. 'What for?'

'For the moment we can use it, of course! The

Balance between Gormalech and the goddesses can't last. One day there will be a winner and then . . . then my Endwatch will strike and I shall seize the power! I shall be the one that rules over this Earth!'

'And Nox,' said Uki. 'Is he one of your . . . Endwatch?'

'Yes,' said Necripha, nodding a head to her grovelling servant. 'I have spies and agents in every rabbit town throughout the whole Five Realms. It has taken me hundreds of years to build up my network. Every scrap of information about the Ancients gets fed back to me.'

'Is that how you learnt about the crystal and the spirits?'

Necripha shook her head. 'No, that I sensed myself. And now I know why. This Iffrit and I share a link from the past. To think, all those years and he was so close to me, trapped underneath the ground. If that pesky one-eared rabbit and his family hadn't weakened Gormalech so, he might never have been discovered.'

'What one-eared rabbit? How did he weaken Gormalech?' Uki kept on firing questions, trying to buy precious time. But a glint in Necripha's eyes told him his ruse had been discovered.

'So many questions,' she said. 'Trying to keep me talking until morning, is that it? Think I might turn to stone like a troll-rabbit from one of your fairytales?'

'No,' said Uki, desperate. 'I just wanted to know. I just needed—'

'Enough!' Necripha snapped her fingers. Balto raised his dagger again, a spiteful smile spreading over his face.

'Please,' Uki started to cry. 'You don't have to . . .'

'Oh, but we do, I'm afraid.' Necripha stepped back, leaving room for Balto to do his work. 'If that stupid spirit had just taken over your body, like I do with my vessels, he might have been able to pop himself out without too much damage. But he must have been too scared of hurting you. Scared and weak.'

'He was kind,' Uki said, wishing Iffrit was here now, or Jori or Kree. Anyone who could tell him what to do.

'Well, his kindness has cost you dear, my patchwork friend. He can't hear or see us, which means he isn't coming out. Not until you're dead, anyway.'

'I like dead,' said Balto. He grabbed Uki's neck with one paw so he couldn't struggle. All he could do was stare upwards, at Balto's paw and the dagger it held, the hungry blade twinkling as it came closer, closer . . .

Interlude

'You're not going to stop *there*!' Rue shouts.

'Do you want more?' asks the bard.

'Yes!'

'Then that's where I'll stop. Lesson two hundred and eighty-five. I believe I mentioned it earlier.'

'You said it was three hundred, actually,' says Rue, with a huff. 'But it's only really lesson five or six.'

'Every word I speak to you is a lesson,' says the bard. 'I hope you're paying attention.'

From somewhere near the bard's toes comes the sound of Jaxom snoring. He had drifted off around the time Uki bought his new clothes.

‘Master?’ Rue peers down from his perch at the pile of blankets and ears below him. ‘That horrible Necripha . . . she won’t be at the tower we’re going to, will she?’

The bard looks up at his scared eyes and realises he should perhaps have edited his story a little, this close to bedtime. He reaches out a paw to pat Rue’s shoulder. ‘Her? No. I’m sure it’ll all turn out to be a false alarm. Some woodcutters got lost and camped there, or something. I just want to see for myself, to make sure.’

Rue continues peering. ‘But the Endwatch must still be around, or you wouldn’t need a Foxguard to look out for them.’

Sometimes the bard forgets how sharp his new apprentice is. He tugs his beard for a moment before replying. ‘We never really knew all that much about them. What you’ve just heard in the story – that was pretty much all we ever learnt. After . . . well, you’ll find out after what, we were never really sure exactly how many of them there were, where they were hiding . . . The Foxguard was formed to keep an eye out. Just in case they tried to come back. And to keep certain things safe . . .'

'What things?'

'Never you mind.' The bard rolls over, nudging Jaxom's feet out of his face. 'Time for sleep now, little one.'

'Hang on,' says Rue, making the bard groan. 'I don't understand. Why do the Foxguard have to be so secret? If the Endwatch really are gone, why all the dice and codes and things?'

'Because,' says the bard, 'we don't want them to know we are watching. If they knew we were looking for them, then they'd be hiding even more. This way, if they're still around, they will hopefully slip up. Then we can catch them.'

'One more question,' says Rue, pretending not to hear the bard curse. 'If the Foxguard are so secret, how do you get members? How does anyone know that there's an Endwatch to guard against?'

'From the stories, of course,' says the bard. 'Every time the tale of Uki is told, rabbits learn about the Endwatch. That's one of the reasons stories exist: they have very, *very* long memories. And sometimes, after a telling, the bard will spot a rabbit who asks the right questions or shows the right attitude. Then they take them aside for a quiet word, and maybe make them part of the order.'

'Are all bards part of the Foxguard, then?'

'Not all,' says the bard. 'But quite a few. And yes – before you ask – *you* can be a member, too. I'll give you some dice in the morning.'

Rue, who had indeed been about to ask, squeals with delight, and is still smiling when he falls asleep a few moments later.

*

They rise early to find that Jaxom has been up before them and got his jerboas harnessed and ready. Gant gives them a quick breakfast of bilberry jam on thick slices of bread, before they set off north again. He has filled their packs with supplies, and even given them a little sparrow in a wooden cage, so they can send word when they need collecting.

The cart travels much more quickly without its cargo of tartan bales, and they are soon whipping along the dirt track to Nether, bouncing this way and that as they rocket over potholes. There is a cold wind, blowing down from the mountains to the west, and there are no signs of any rabbits on the road. At one point they surprise a herd of wild jerboas, who go bounding off across the plains, as fast as lightning.

Without the bales to sit on, the ride is very bumpy. Trying to speak without stammering or biting your tongue is very difficult, so there is no chance of any more storytelling. Instead, the bard and Rue stare out as the bleak landscape rolls by, Rue tightly clutching his new pouch of Foxguard dice.

Just as afternoon is approaching, they spot a dark smudge on the horizon. It grows steadily, until they can make out a huge swathe of trees that must be Icebark Forest. An hour or so later and they come to a fork in the road. One branch heads towards the forest itself, the other turns east, along its edge.

Jaxom hauls on the reins, stopping his jerboas. 'This is as far as I can go,' he says. 'The road to the left goes into Icebark, the other to Nether. The best way to get to the tower, so I've heard, is to skirt the western edge of the forest. It's in the Arukh foothills. You won't be able to miss it – there's nothing else there.'

They jump down from the cart and the bard and Jaxom clasp wrists. 'Be careful,' Jaxom warns again. 'No fires during the daytime, and if you do light one at night, make sure it's small. And within the shelter of the forest. There can be Arukh scouts around this time of year.' He smacks his paw with a fist. 'I would go with you, but . . .'

'Don't worry,' says the bard. 'You have to make a living, I understand. We'll be fine. And I'll send the sparrow when we're done.'

Jaxom nods, his brow furrowed. Rue can tell he isn't happy.

'You look after this old one, Rue,' he says, ruffling the little rabbit's ears. 'Don't let him do anything stupid. You're Foxguard now.'

'Yes, sir!' says Rue, giving his bag of dice a shake. Jaxom manages a smile before climbing up into his cart again. With a final warning to take care, he shakes the reins and is gone. Rue and the bard watch him until he is just a speck in the distance.

'I'm sure we'll be fine,' says the bard. 'It's just a stroll around the forest and back. Nothing out of the ordinary.'

'Except for the tribes of bloodthirsty, savage rabbits,' says Rue. 'And maybe an evil order of villains led by a three-eyed monster.'

The bard rolls his eyes and looks over to the mountains. Towering, cold, timeless slabs of rock draped in strings of mist. Could there be pairs of rabbit eyes up there, looking down on them now?

'It *is* going to be fine, I promise,' says the bard, more to himself than to Rue. 'Even so, when we get back to Thornwood, best not mention all this to your parents, eh?'

*

They march to the forest edge and begin making their way along it. Whatever road there was soon vanishes, and they have a tough time picking their way between clumps of brambles and tufty tussocks of coarse grass. Before they know it, dusk begins to fall and they are still nowhere near the foothills that hide the tower.

'We haven't got very far,' says Rue. 'And it's getting dark now.' He is carrying the sparrow in its tiny cage. It sits on its perch with its feathers puffed up, giving sad little cheeps every now and then.

'Thank you for pointing out those incredibly obvious facts,' says the bard. He is beginning to wish he had left this task up to another agent. 'I suppose we had better camp for the night.'

They both turn to stare at the forest. It looks very brambly, with lots of dark, unpleasant shadows between the white trunks of the trees. The beds in Pebblewic, even the kitchen floor of Gant's shop, seem very appealing right now.

'Come on, then,' says the bard. He takes Rue's paw and gives it a squeeze. 'Let's just go a little way in and build a fire to warm ourselves.'

'Just a little way in,' says Rue. He gulps.

*

Half an hour later, and the bard is leaning on his staff and breathing heavily. He has been whacking at brambles and prickly gorse bushes for quite a long time, trying to make enough space to sit down, let alone build a camp. Rue and the sparrow are looking on, keeping as quiet as possible.

'Perhaps,' Rue says, wincing, 'Perhaps there's a path somewhere? One that leads in amongst the trees?'

'Path? Path?' The bard waves his staff in the air, scattering broken bramble leaves and bits of twig everywhere. 'If there was a path, why would I be spending five hours hacking through the thickest patch of thorn bushes in the universe? Just for fun? Or perhaps because I've decided to take up bramble beating as a hobby?'

'I was just saying,' mutters Rue. The sparrow gives a sad *cheep* in reply.

'Good evening.' A voice comes from the bushes behind them, making both Rue and the bard shriek in surprise.

'W-who's there?' calls the bard. They both scan the scrub with terrified eyes but can't spot the voice's owner anywhere.

'I was wondering,' says the voice. 'If either of you would fancy a game of fox paw?'

'Oh, thank Clarion's codpiece,' says the bard, leaning on his staff again and panting for breath. 'I nearly had a heart attack.'

'Fox paw?' says Rue, and then realises what the mystery speaker means. 'Ooh! I do! I do! I've got the dice! Look!'

The bushes rustle and a grey-cloaked figure steps out. It picks its way between the brambles, then reaches up to remove its hood. Rue looks up at an elderly she-rabbit with smoke-grey fur, marked by several scars. She has a white patch on her nose and piercing grey eyes, deep set under furrowed brows. Beneath her cloak she wears patched and battered leather armour, and a sword hangs at her belt along with . . . a silver-topped flask.

Rue stares at her face again, taking in the tattered, torn ears. When she holds a paw out in greeting, he notices she is missing one finger, and another is wrapped in a bandage. She is as old as the bard, maybe older, and so scarred and worn. But the sword, the flask – can it be?

'Jori!' cries the bard, rushing over to hug her.

'Pook,' she says, squeezing him back. 'It's good to see you.'

'You too,' says the bard. 'I was beginning to think I'd made a mistake coming out here on my own. How did you know to meet us?'

'I didn't,' Jori says. 'I was in the twin cities when Nikku's sparrow arrived. I came straight here. I'd just made camp in the forest for the night, when I heard the most incredible noise. Smashing and crashing, shouting and yelling. I came to see who or what was being killed and found you two.'

The bard looks a bit sheepish for a moment, trying to hide the broken-down brambles behind his back. 'Um . . .' he says. 'I don't suppose you've had a chance to look at the tower yet? To see if the rumours are true?'

'Not yet,' says Jori. 'I was going to sleep in the forest for the night, then investigate tomorrow. You're welcome to join me.'

'Yes *please*,' say Rue and the bard together.

'This way,' says Jori. 'There's a clear path straight into the forest just over here. I've no idea why you were trying to thrash your way through those bushes.'

Rue opens his mouth to say something, but the look on the bard's face makes him snap it shut again. Relieved beyond measure, they follow Jori into the depths of Icebark.

*

'An apprentice, eh?' says Jori, after being introduced

to Rue. 'And the youngest member of the Foxguard ever. I'm impressed.' Rue puffs out his chest, making the bard give a proud, secret smile.

She has made a neat little camp, with a small fire already burning in a deep pit, lined with stones. A wall of lashed-together branches blocks the whole thing off from sight, making them almost invisible. A pot hangs over the firepit, with spicy vegetable stew bubbling away inside.

'I'm learning tales for my memory warren,' says Rue. 'And going on dangerous adventures. I'm going to be the High Bard's champion one day.'

'Don't get ahead of yourself,' says the bard. 'And less of the "dangerous adventures". I'm taking very good care of you. Just like a responsible master should.'

'Well,' says Rue. 'Not really. You got us captured by bonedancers and nearly killed. Then we camped out overnight in Arukh territory. And here we are, in the middle of a forest, heading for an evil tower of doom.'

The bard gives a nervous laugh at Jori's surprised expression. 'Very good, Rue. Exaggerating danger, just like I taught you. Good use of your imagination.'

'Do his parents know about all this?' Jori asks. 'Or the Council of Bards? Aren't there rules for looking after an apprentice?'

'Look,' says the bard, 'it's fine. He's never been in any real trouble. Except perhaps for a few minutes ago. But you're here now. We couldn't be safer.'

'I suppose,' says Jori, stirring the stew. Rue notices she is missing a finger from her other paw as well.

'So tell me,' says the bard. 'What have you been up to all these years?'

'This and that,' Jori says. 'I worked as a bodyguard for Clan Sheth for a few years. Did some sellsword work in Enderby, fighting and soldiering for money. I had a pirate ship running out of Chillwater. That was fun until the Emperor's navy sank it.'

'What happened to your paws?' Rue asks. 'And your ears?'

'Rue!' snaps the bard. 'That's none of your business!'

Jori holds her scarred paws out in front of her, giving a bitter half-smile. 'It's all right. I suppose I do look quite shocking these days. *This*, little one, is what happens when you use dusk potion for too long. First, your toes fall off, then your fingers and ears. No dusk wraith has ever survived as long as me, so I've no idea what will drop off next.'

The bard nods at the flask on Jori's belt. 'Do you still . . . fight with the potion?' he asks.

'As little as possible,' says Jori. 'And I have found ways to make the mixture weaker over the years. Probably how I've survived so long.'

Rue stares at the silver-topped flask, wondering why anybody would want to drink something that would make their bits drop off. Then again, the power of the potion had probably saved her life a few times. It made him think of the story, of how Uki had been captured.

'I've been hearing about your adventures,' he says. 'Uki and you and Kree.'

'Oh yes?' says Jori. 'Is your master making a good job of it?'

'Very,' says Rue. 'And I knew someone from the tale would pop up in real life. It kept happening when he was telling me about Podkin.'

'Perhaps the words are calling them,' the bard says, his eyes lost in the crackling flames of the fire. 'They have a strange magic, you know.'

'Or perhaps,' says Jori, 'the story isn't finished yet.'

She shares a troubled look with the bard, and Rue knows somehow that they are talking about the tower. The thought makes him shiver.

'Well,' says Jori, breaking the tension, 'seeing as we have some food and a fire, perhaps your master should continue? I'd love to hear about my old friends again.'

'Yes!' says Rue. 'Yes, please!'

'Very well,' says the bard. 'But no interrupting to correct me, Jori.'

'I shall be the perfect audience,' Jori smiles. 'As long as you make me look good.'

'That,' says the bard, 'may be beyond even my powers . . .'

Chapter Thirteen

To the Rescue

Uki held his breath.

He could feel the dagger's blade along the edge of his scalp, a sharp slice of pain that he knew was just the start of something much, much worse.

His face was inches away from Balto's. He could smell his stale breath, see the spark of horrible excitement lighting up his dull eyes. He looked like he was going to really enjoy what came next.

Goddess help me, Uki prayed. *Mother always believed in you and she was never wrong. Please, save me.*

The worst thing, worse even than the fact that it was all about to be over, was the knowledge that he had failed. Failed his friends, failed Iffrit, failed the whole rabbit race. He hadn't even managed to capture one single spirit on his own.

Iffrit was wrong to have trusted you. Uki's dark voice sounded almost smug. **He should have chosen someone else.**

Uki closed his eyes, waiting for the moment that the dagger did its horrible work. His little heart beat once, twice . . .

Kerr-ack!!

A slamming, splintering clap of thunder shook the whole warehouse. Dust and cobwebs poured down from the rafters and Balto jumped away, giving Uki a clear view of the wide-open doors.

Blocking the gap was the rear end of a jerboa, its giant legs bouncing back from the colossal kick which had smashed the doors off their hinges. A jerboa with a bald little pink stub for a tail.

'Mooka!' Uki cried, even as rabbits ran past the jerboa into the warehouse. Five, ten, fifteen of them, all wearing the grey cloaks and black-leather armour of Clan Septys. At their front was Jori, with Kree peeking out from behind.

'Get away from my friend!' Jori shouted, before taking a huge mouthful of potion from the flask in her paw. Two of the other Septys rabbits did the same. The others had spears and clubs at the ready.

'Nox, you sneaky old weasel!' One of Uki's rescuers was Venic, he noticed. He stared at his old servant with a grin that was half amused, half spiteful. Nox began to stutter a reply but was interrupted by Necripha's furious shrieking.

'Don't just stand there! Kill them!'

The four Endwatch rabbits who had accompanied Necripha into the warehouse all drew blades from beneath their cloaks. They were joined by Nox's two henchmen.

'For Septys!' yelled Venic, and the two forces charged at one another.

Jori and the other dusk wraiths clashed with the Endwatch rabbits first. Uki gasped as he watched the three blurred forms zip in and around the black-cloaked rabbits, their swords flashing as they caught the lamplight, leaving streaks of orange glow across his vision.

He saw three of the Endwatchers fall almost instantly, then gaped as he noticed Nox drinking from a flask himself. *Nox is a dusk wraith, too,* he realised. Uki had assumed he was just a servant.

Or perhaps he was? After swallowing from his flask, Nox choked and coughed. He dropped it to the ground and a gloopy grey liquid spilled out, smoking as it mixed with the dust and air. And then Jori was upon him. The old rabbit raised his sword and blocked Jori's blow. He blocked again and again, the potion he had taken allowing him to move almost as fast as his attacker.

Clangclangclangclang!

The clashes of their swords were too fast to see. There were sparks blossoming everywhere and a rattling of metal.

A splintering of wood drew Uki's attention away. On the east side of the room, the hulking figure of Balto had smashed open one of the wooden shutters. He had Necripha clutched in his arms like a baby, and the two were climbing to safety.

‘She’s getting away!’ Uki shouted, but no one could hear him. The warehouse was full of crashing metal, grunts and screams.

‘No!’ Nox’s voice cried out. Jori had slashed him across his arm and his sword clattered to the ground. She span around, faster than the wind, kicking out her leg and knocking the old rabbit off his feet and into a stack of crates.

By the doorway, the Septys rabbits had nearly finished off the Endwatch. The two other dusk wraiths dropped one in a flurry of blades. Venic’s men clubbed another to the ground, and Venic himself blocked a blow and then swept his sword low, taking out the last rabbit’s feet. It crashed to the floor in a cloud of straw and dust, then Kree stepped in with a plank of wood she had found and clonked it on the head.

Everything was still and silent for a few moments, all except for Nox’s groans of pain.

Uki looked around at the splintered pieces of wood everywhere. At the empty hole of the window Necripha had escaped through. She would probably be long gone, now.

Venic was looking around, too. He nodded at the dangling form of Uki and then took command. 'Tie them up,' he ordered his rabbits. 'Someone find the key for those shackles. And bring me that traitor, Nox.'

The Septys rabbits rushed to obey, all except the dusk wraiths, who slumped to the floor, their energy spent. Uki looked down on his friends, tears spilling out of his eyes. *They came for me,* he thought. *They really came.*

The keys were found and then Kree clambered on to a crate to unlock Uki's iron cuffs. He felt himself being passed from rabbit to rabbit, and then he was on the floor, his shoulder joints burning like fire.

'Uki!' Kree hopped down from the crate and grabbed him in a fierce hug. Jori was suddenly there too, flopping against him, fighting for breath.

'I'm sorry,' Uki managed to gasp through sobs as the tears spilled from his eyes. 'I'm so sorry.'

'Why did you run off?' Kree asked. 'Why didn't you wait for us?'

'I . . . I just . . .' Uki looked away, ashamed. His tears fell on the dusty floor, making tiny little puddles of mud. 'I didn't want you to be hurt. Not because of me. I knew it would be dangerous and something . . . something might have happened to you. I've never had friends before and . . . and I couldn't stand the thought of losing you.'

Kree punched him on the shoulder. 'What do you think friends are for? We know about the danger. We're ready to take the risk. *Pok ha boc!* Don't ever run off on your own again!'

Jori grabbed his arm. Her eyes were almost closed, blinking and blinking as she tried to keep Uki in focus. 'Don't . . . don't you think . . .' She was struggling to get each word out. 'Don't you think . . . we're worried about you too?'

'I'm sorry,' said Uki. The tears kept coming. 'I'm so sorry. Please don't be angry with me.'

'Stupid . . . rabbit . . .' Jori said, then wrapped an arm around him. Kree grabbed both of them in a tight squeeze and the three of them sat like that for a long while.

*

'That's the last of them,' said Venic. His rabbits had bound the paws of all the Endwatchers and dragged them out of the warehouse. Venic himself was propping up the groaning figure of Nox.

'What will you do with them?' Uki asked. The blood had started flowing back to his arms, and the worst case of pins and needles he'd ever had was beginning.

'Clan Septys has some very deep, very dark dungeons,' said Venic. 'Or perhaps Mayor Nilla might like to ask them a few questions.'

'And what about Nox?'

Venic passed Nox over to his rabbits and they dragged him out of the warehouse. 'Oh, he'll be taken back to the clan warren, I should think. He's in for a very unpleasant time. That's if he lives long enough. He must have been stealing dusk potion for a while, taking little sips to build up his resistance. Even so, the amount he drank tonight will probably kill him. It takes years and years to handle the stuff properly, doesn't it cuz?'

Jori managed a grunt. She was sitting up by herself but had her head in her paws, still recovering.

'Don't go anywhere,' said Venic. 'It's not safe

outside. I'll just see this lot on their way and then I'll be back.'

He left them sitting on the warehouse floor and stepped out into the night.

'What's going on out there?' Uki asked. Now that the fighting was over, he could hear some strange noises. Shouts and yells and things crashing about.

'It's chaos,' said Kree. 'The fighting in the stadium has spread to the cities. They are both trying to burn each other to the ground.'

'How . . . how did you find me?'

Kree beamed. 'Kalaan Klaa tracking skills!' she said. 'We ran to the gates but you were gone. Then Jori spotted your spear. We knew you wouldn't have left it behind, so we thought something terrible had happened to you. That's when I spotted your claw marks on the ground. Scratches every twenty paces – I thought you must be leaving a trail.'

'I was.'

'That was good thinking! It was easy to follow. We got to the warehouse and peeked in through a gap in the shutters. That was when we saw Nox. Jori was furious – she thought her cousin had taken you, until we heard him talking about this End of the Watch. She realised he had betrayed Septys and that they would want to punish him. So we ran back to the clan house and told Venic all about it. He was kind enough to bring all his soldiers, otherwise . . .'

They both shuddered at the thought of what might have happened.

'That she-rabbit is the one who's been following us,' said Uki. 'She's after the spirits too. And she wants to take Iffrit out of my head.'

'Well, now she has no rabbits to help her,' said Kree. 'Apart from that big, fat one of course.'

'I think she will find more,' Uki said. 'She told me there were lots of them, hidden all over the Five Realms.'

'No time . . .' Jori muttered. Uki and Kree both leaned forward to hear her faint words. 'No time to worry . . . about that. We must . . . must get Valkus . . . before it's too late . . . Finding him comes first.'

'I don't think you'll be doing that, cousin dear,' Venic stepped back into the warehouse, his rabbits having disappeared with Nox and the Endwatchers.

'What . . . what do you mean?' said Jori.

'I mean, you'll be coming with me as well.' Venic gave a smug smile and preened his whiskers. 'Did you really think I hadn't heard about your little ... disagreement ... with the family? Ran off because you didn't like the idea of killing anyone? A granddaughter of Lord Toxa himself? How do you think our clan has become so powerful over all the years? Killing rabbits is in our blood.'

'Not ... mine,' said Jori through gritted teeth.

'Brave words,' said Venic. He sniggered. 'But I've totally outfoxed you all. Did you notice how I let you and the others take dusk while I didn't?' He patted the flask on his belt. 'You're in no state to fight back, and if your friends do, I shall make short work of them. A toddler from the plains and a funny-furred ragamuffin from Kether-knows-where. They have no hope against a trained dusk wraith. You were their only chance and now you couldn't even lift a spoon. If only grandfather could see you now. He'd be so disappointed.'

'*Nam ukku ulla!*' Kree shouted, about to leap up, but Venic's sword was out of its sheath and pointed at her throat before she could blink.

'I don't think so,' he said. 'Not if you desire to live. Besides, the clan will probably want nothing to do with you. It's Jori who'll be spending the rest of her life in the warren dungeons. Or perhaps in the poison kitchen, testing out deadly new concoctions. While I get a lovely reward for capturing her, of course.'

Jori let out a sob. Her paw reached for her sword hilt, but it was shaking too much to hold it.

'Yes, you and the magpie-rabbit will probably be spared. Unless of course, Jori has been stupid enough to tell you any of the clan secrets.'

Uki thought about the dusk potion and how Jori had told them about her training.

'What if she has?' Kree asked, obviously thinking the same thing.

'Then,' said Venic, his blue eyes twinkling, 'I hope for your sake whatever poisons they try will kill you quickly. Although that isn't very likely. Not very likely at all.'

Chapter Fourteen

A Spot of Midnight Swimming

The tip of Venic's sword moved lazily between Uki and Kree.

He doesn't expect either of us to do anything, Uki realised. *He thinks Jori is the dangerous one and that she's been dealt with. He hasn't even wondered what Necripha wanted with me, or why I was chained up.*

Venic was a very arrogant rabbit and, like most arrogant creatures, he assumed anything smaller than him wasn't a threat.

Jori had realised the same thing. She leant as close

to Uki as she could and whispered, 'Uki . . . throw him. Throw him through the wall.'

'What's that?' Venic said. 'Planning an escape? It won't do you any good. Unlike *you*, cuz, I finished my training and am a qualified ass—'

He never got to finish his unfortunate sentence. As Venic leant over to sneer, Uki jumped up and grabbed his waist. Even though his shoulder muscles still burnt, he had enough power to hoist the bigger rabbit over his head and hurl him across the warehouse. He hit the far wall with a *crump* and flopped to the ground. A stack of crates tumbled on top of him for good measure.

'*Pok ha boc!*' said Kree, her eyes boggling.

'Sorry he didn't go *through* the wall,' said Uki. 'I think my strength is fading a little. And my arms are still quite sore.'

Jori managed a little laugh. 'Oh, I think that's good enough,' she said. 'Help me up. We have to get out of here.'

Uki pulled her up from the floor and let her lean across his shoulders. With Kree leading the way, they shuffled out of the warehouse to where Mooka stood waiting in the street.

'Put Jori up on Mooka's back,' said Kree. 'And here is your lost spear.'

Uki heaved Jori up and draped her over the jerboa's back. Mooka gave a little *neek* and licked Kree's fingers. Then Uki took his spear and slotted it into his harness, next to the others.

'What now?' he said. The streets of Nys were filled with smoke and the stink of burning houses. Screams and yells echoed down the alleys, seeming to come from everywhere.

'Valkus,' said Jori, her voice still weak. 'We get him . . . then run.'

Uki nodded. All the fighting would have created confusion in both cities. They might be able to use it to their advantage. They could sneak into Syn, try and get into the mayor's fortress. And they had to do it quickly. Once Venic awoke he would be after Jori again. And he wouldn't underestimate Uki twice.

'Let's go,' he said. 'The river is near here. We might be able to find a way across.'

*

The night was painted orange by fire. They passed several houses that were alight, with teams of rabbits throwing bucket after bucket of water over them.

Balls of flame kept soaring over their heads, fired from catapults on the Syn side of the river. The Nysian rabbits were replying with waves of fire arrows, whooshing across like flocks of burning birds.

Dodging smoke and clouds of sparks, they made their way to the river. Its black surface was lit up with the reflection of burning buildings in Syn. On both sides of the bank, rabbits were scrambling to scoop up water, all the while dodging rocks and arrows from their enemies opposite.

'This is awful,' Kree said. 'I never liked all these buildings, but to burn them down – and all because of a neekball game.'

'The game was just an excuse,' said Uki. 'This is all Valkus's doing.'

'Even so,' said Kree. 'I told you neekball was bad.'

'Can we … get across … a bridge?' Jori struggled to raise her head from where she lay on Mooka's back.

'Not a chance,' said Uki. The remaining bridges

were guarded at both ends by soldiers hiding behind shield walls and popping up every now and then to throw spears. 'We might be able to take a boat . . .'

'Mooka can swim,' said Kree.

Uki looked at the dark water gently lapping at the riverbank below. It hinted at great depth, maybe with slinking, hidden water creatures. Leeches, fish and eels. 'I don't think I can,' he said. 'At least, I've never tried.'

'Just hold on to Mooka,' said Kree. 'He will pull you across. Won't you, boy?'

'*Neek,*' said Mooka.

It didn't seem as though there was any other option. Uki helped Kree tie Jori in place with Mooka's reins, and then they all edged down the bank towards the river. It lapped at Uki's toes as he stepped in, chilling his fur like liquid ice.

'I'm not sure about—' Uki began to say, and then the ground suddenly disappeared from beneath his feet. One second he was breathing smoke and feeling waves of heat against his fur, the next he was under the water, choking, flailing, no idea what was up or down.

He felt the icy river flow up his nose, into his mouth. He coughed and more rushed in. He could feel his clothes and his harness pulling him down to where tendrils of reeds lashed about his feet. There was thick, sucking mud there and things that slithered between his toes.

He tried to yell for help, but nothing came out of his mouth except bubbles. Gulps of river water flowed in to replace the precious air. Uki flung his arms out to where he thought his friends might be – grasping, desperate.

It was only by chance that one of his flailing paws caught hold of something large and furry. *Mooka!* he thought, grabbing tight. He brought his other arm across and began scrabbling up the side of the jerboa, until at last his head broke free of the surface and he sucked in great lungfuls of beautiful, smoky air.

'You're pulling me under!' came Jori's voice. Uki stopped gasping for a moment to see that he had grabbed tight hold of his friend's back and was tipping her off, into the river.

'Sorry,' Uki managed to say, in between coughing.

'Ig eggeryun all ight?' Kree called from

somewhere. Blinking his eyes, Uki could see they were all in the water, powering towards the far side of the river as Mooka kicked with his huge legs. Kree was keeping pace, the jerboa's lead rope gripped in her mouth.

'Yes,' called Uki. 'Apart from I nearly drowned.'

'You were only under . . . for a second,' said Jori. It had seemed a lot longer than that.

'Eerly dare,' said Kree. Uki held tight to Mooka and felt the water whooshing past him. Moments later, Mooka was clambering up the bank on the other side, dragging three soggy rabbits with him. They had made it.

A brief pause to catch their breath and then they were ready for the next part of their ordeal.

A few steps into the territory of Syn and Uki could feel it. The air was thick with smoke and soot but also something else. It was the rage of Valkus, hot and bitter. It crackled everywhere, infecting all the rabbits of the city, driving them on, making them want to fight and hurt their neighbours.

Mooka squeaked and tried to back away. Even Jori and Kree could sense something was wrong.

'This place,' Kree said. 'It feels bad!'

'It's Valkus,' said Uki. 'He's doing this. It's how he made all the Syn rabbits want war.'

They looked around them, seeing a scene almost identical to the one on the other side of the river. Rabbits were scooping water to put out fires, while clashes of soldiers were raging. They had come ashore near the docks where things were a bit quieter, but there was still smoke everywhere. Lumps of soot were drifting down from the sky, clinging to their wet fur.

'What shall we do now?' Kree asked. She was struggling to keep hold of Mooka, who wanted to get away from this strange, new place.

Uki watched the rabbits upstream running back and forth with buckets. He spotted some empty ones lying on the ground near the smoking remains of a hut.

'Let's grab those buckets,' he said. 'If we look like we're fighting the fires, nobody will ask us questions.'

'Good idea,' said Jori. 'Get me down and I'll help.'

With fingers struggling to untie the wet knots,

they managed to free Jori and help her slither down into Uki's arms. She was able to stagger a little by herself now, but she still had to lean on Uki for support. Together, they hobbled over and collected a couple of leather buckets, then scooped some water into them from the river.

'I think you two are going to have to go on without me,' said Kree. Mooka was starting to buck and hop, and she was having trouble controlling him. 'I can't get him to calm down.'

'Thirteen curses,' muttered Jori. 'I can hardly walk, either. This isn't looking good.'

'It'll be fine,' said Uki. The more upset his friends became, the more he felt the need to be calm. They were here together, they had each other. They would *do* this. 'Kree, you stay here with Mooka. If you can calm him, meet us outside the mayor's fort. Jori and I will find a way in, I know it. Then we can escape through Syn and head south. Venic will have no idea where we are.'

'I wish ... I shared your confidence,' said Jori, which he took for an agreement. Kree didn't look happy at being left behind but stayed where she was, singing quiet songs to Mooka, trying to soothe him.

Carrying their buckets as best they could, they headed into the streets of Syn.

*

It was like stepping through to a mirror world of the city they had just left. Same shops, same houses, except these had white-on-black flags and banners hanging from them, instead of black on white.

The screams and chaos were the same, too. Rabbits threw water over burning buildings. Squads of soldiers ran to and fro with spears and shields. Once or twice they nearly charged into Uki and Jori. The pair held their breath, waiting to be arrested, but the soldiers simply ran on past.

'Get out of the way, pesky kittens!' one soldier shouted at them.

'They think we're just annoying children, getting in the way,' Uki whispered.

'And why shouldn't they?' said Jori. 'Who would suspect their mayor was in danger from a pair of little things like us? We can do things that huge warrior rabbits can't. Iffrit must have known what he was doing when he chose you.'

Uki had never thought of that. Adult rabbits would never suspect a child of doing anything except playing silly games. Iffrit must have guessed the spirits might make the same mistake.

'Just because we're young, doesn't mean we're easy to beat.'

Jori gave a chuckle. 'I think Venic would agree with you there. And that rabbit you flattened back in Icebark.'

Uki gritted his teeth. 'And Valkus will too, by the end of the night.'

*

The fortress was easy to find. It was a giant mound of earth inside a compound walled with wooden stakes, most of which were conveniently on fire. Uki and Jori merged with the crowd of rabbits who were trying to put it out, and then slipped inside the gates while nobody was looking.

The grounds inside were full of shouting rabbits and burning buildings. Those wearing white armour were ordering the others about, making them form chains and heave gouts of water everywhere.

'The river's going to be running dry soon,' said Jori, as Uki dodged sideways to avoid a team of rabbits carrying a full water trough.

Uki didn't comment. He was too busy homing in on the presence of Valkus. It was definitely somewhere inside the fort on top of the mound. He could feel the waves of hate and bloodlust pulsing out of it like some kind of poisonous heartbeat.

'We have to get up there,' he said, pointing.

Jori looked at the fort and groaned. There was a narrow path leading up the mound, and it was thronged with soldiers.

'We could try going around the side,' Uki said. 'Maybe I can break through that wall. It's only wood.'

'Only wood,' Jori muttered. 'Well, if you think your magical muscles can handle it . . .'

They slipped around the side of the mound, away from all the noise and shouting. It was darker here, with nobody to see them creep up to the fortress walls, Jori still leaning on Uki for support.

The hill was rabbit-made, and steep. Uki had to dig his feet in hard to avoid slipping and use one paw to grasp at clumps of grass. His other arm was wrapped around Jori, who was struggling and panting beside him.

The climb seemed to take hours but finally they reached the top. Uki let Jori rest against the wooden wall, and she slid down into a heap at the bottom.

Uki caught his breath, and then laid his paws against the fortress wall. To his dismay, he saw it was made of huge oak trunks, each one thicker than his own body. They were lashed tightly together and must have stood here for many, many years. The wood had hardened like iron. There was no way he was going to break through, even with all his spirit-enhanced strength.

Still, he tried.

He dug his fingers in and pulled. He put his shoulder to a trunk and shoved. He summoned every last scrap of energy he had, felt it tingling and buzzing in his muscles, and pounded on the wall with both fists.

Not even a crack.

'That's it,' said Jori. 'We can't get in here. And there's no way we'll get through the front gate. I can hardly stand.'

'What?' Uki leant his head against the wall, panting for breath. 'Are you giving up?'

Jori nodded, ears drooping, and rested her head in her paws. 'I think we should just admit it,' she said. 'We've failed.'

Chapter Fifteen

The Longhouse

Uki turned his back to the wall and let himself slide down until he was sitting next to Jori. So far that night he had been knocked out – twice – hung up by his arms, almost burnt to a crisp and half drowned. And all with the constant pulse of Valkus's war rage rattling in his head. He was tired.

They both looked out at the view across the cities. If it hadn't been for all the screaming and shouting, it might have been quite beautiful.

Blossoms of flame were everywhere, lighting up the clouds of smoke from beneath. More fire arrows and missiles were swooshing up into the air before tumbling back to earth in showers of sparks, and behind it all was the night sky with its clouds of stars and a glowing full moon.

Uki could see the tiny shadows of rabbits, silhouetted against the flames as they ran about, waving their arms in panic. Down below in the compound they were still fighting fires. There was also a strange machine launching fireballs up and across the river. It was a wooden frame with a giant spoon in the middle. Rabbits wound the arm of the spoon down, then heaved a bundle of oil-soaked rags into the bowl. This was set alight and then a catch was released, flinging the burning ball up into the air. Uki found it sad to think that someone had created such a clever machine only for the purpose of destroying things.

'Have you really never had any friends before?' Jori asked, interrupting his thinking.

He shook his head. Hearing Jori say it made him feel like it was his fault. Like he had something wrong with him. Hidden by the night's shadows, he blushed.

'Neither have I,' said Jori, surprising him. 'Except maybe my cousin, Venic. Although I never really liked him that much. He was always so smug and rude.'

'I thought you would have had loads of friends,' said Uki. 'You're always so confident and strong.'

'Me? Confident?' Jori laughed. 'Maybe I seem that way to you, but it's only because I'm older. And because of my clan. Rabbits treat you differently when they know you could make their eyes melt with a pinch of the right poison in their supper. I certainly don't feel confident, not on the inside. I don't think anyone does, really.'

'Not even Venic?'

'No. He doesn't have a clue what he's doing, same as us. Some folk are just better at hiding it, that's all.'

Uki looked down at the compound again. One of the buildings was completely engulfed by flames now. Two teams of rabbits had thrown grappling hooks into the blaze and were now heaving on the ropes, trying to pull it down before it spread to the hut next door.

Rope, thought Uki. As if to signal something,

there was a burst of panicked cawing and two magpies flew up from their roost in the hut's rafters, flapping their way over Uki's head. His fingers went to the magpies etched on his chest buckle. Could it be a sign?

'Jori,' he said. 'Do you think you're strong enough to hang on to the wall if I throw you up?'

Jori flexed her arms and gave Uki a puzzled stare. 'Maybe. Why?'

'And could you keep hold if I climbed up you?'

'What are you planning, Uki?'

'We can't go *through* the wall,' he said. 'But we might be able to go *over* it.'

'We don't have any rope. What are we going to do – stroll down and ask to borrow some?'

Uki just grinned.

*

Uki's plan was simple. They didn't have any real rope for climbing, so Jori would have to do instead.

With many apologies, he helped her up and then grasped her around the waist. Summoning all his strength, he bent his knees and then threw her upwards. She sailed up into the night sky, four metres or more, higher even than the palisade fence. As she came down, she stretched out her arms and caught hold of the top of an oak trunk. For one horrible moment, Uki thought her grip was going to fail and he braced to catch her. But she clung on, dangling down, her feet not far out of Uki's reach.

'Hurry,' she whispered down to him. 'I can't hold on for long.'

Uki stepped back as far as he could without toppling down the steep slope of the mound, and then ran forward. He leapt upwards, imagining himself kicking like a jerboa.

His feet hit the wall and he kicked again, boosting himself up as high as Jori's shoulders. Uki grabbed hold of her cloak, her jerkin, her ears – anything he could get a pawful of – and somehow clambered upwards.

Jori bit back grunts of pain as Uki climbed over her, until his fingers reached the top of the fence. He pulled himself over, finding – much to his relief – a walkway on the other side. As quickly as he could, he leaned back over the wall and dragged Jori over with him. They both lay panting on the walkway for a moment.

'Don't *ever* do that again,' Jori managed to say.

'I hope I don't have to,' said Uki. He rolled over and took a peek at their surroundings.

They were safely on the ramparts of the fort wall. Beneath them was another compound, much smaller than the one below. In fact, the whole thing was taken up by one single structure. A slate-roofed longhouse with side buildings and lean-tos jutting out all around. The main house itself looked ancient, and it had clearly been added to with countless extensions over the years.

'This must be the original fort,' whispered Jori. 'The one the brothers built, when the city was first started.'

Uki nodded. He was looking around for guards. There were some at the gate and others beyond, guarding the path that ran up the mound. The compound itself seemed empty.

'Everyone must be fighting the fires,' Uki whispered.

'What about Valkus? Is he inside?'

Uki closed his eyes and focused. He was instantly hit by a wave of rage. It flared in his skull, giving him the sudden urge to push Jori down from the ramparts and scream up at the stars. He blinked open his eyes, gasping for breath. It had been so *powerful*, so *raw.*

'I'll take that as a yes,' said Jori. She pointed to the longhouse, at the side nearest them. 'There's a window there. That outhouse below it will be easy to jump to. We can walk along the top of the roof and climb in.'

'Do you think you'll be able to make it?' Uki asked. Jori seemed to have recovered a little, but her eyelids were drooping, her ears limp.

'I'm sure I can,' she said. 'If you help me.'

They crept along the rampart until they were above the outhouse. It was roofed in slate, with quite a wide ridge pole along the top. If they were careful, they should be able to cross it.

Uki dropped down first, landing as quietly as he could. He reached up for Jori and caught her as she leapt. She landed a little awkwardly and they wobbled left and right for a moment before finding their balance.

‘That was close,’ whispered Uki when he dared breathe again.

‘Keep going,’ said Jori. ‘Before I get any dizzier.’

Like a pair of drunken tightrope walkers, they wove their way along the top of the roof. Uki was reminded of the way he used to walk along the tops of his dams back in the Ice Wastes. Who could have known how useful that little skill would turn out to be?

With a final teeter and a leap, Uki grabbed hold of the windowsill, holding Jori up beside him. Keeping their heads low, they peered inside.

It was an old, primitive window, with no glass pane. They could see right inside the longhouse, which was furnished as a feasting chamber, complete with a roaring firepit in the centre. Waves of smoke were drifting up to the rafters, but it was nothing compared to the stink of burning cities outside.

On the far side of the chamber was a dais with a throne on top. Benches and tables lined the walls. Uki could imagine the mayor holding court here, or toasting a feast, but tonight the room was mostly empty. There were just three figures standing by the fireplace. Two armed guards and Mayor Renard himself.

'That's him,' Uki breathed the words, quieter than a whisper. 'That's Valkus.'

The mayor was talking to his men, giving orders of some kind. It was difficult to hear over the crackle of the fire. But Uki wasn't interested in that. His connection with the spirits allowed him to see what wasn't really there. Just as in the street outside the neekball stadium, there were two figures, one overlapping the other. The tubby, triple-chinned figure of the mayor with his white cloak and, imposed over the top, the ghostly mass of red-tinted spikes and blades that was Valkus. The image of the spirit was faint, transparent, but Uki was still hypnotised by its writhing coils and the glimpses of its glowing crimson eyes.

'Do you think you can hit him from here with one of your spears?' Jori asked. Without Uki's extra senses, all she could see was the mayor himself. He was a pretty big target to aim for, though.

Uki shook his head. Perhaps if he'd had a few months of practice, but he barely knew how to hold one of the things, let alone throw it across a room and hit someone.

Jori pointed at one of the heavy wooden beams that held up the roof. It ran from just below their window, right across the longhouse. 'If we crawl along that, maybe you can drop down and jab him.'

Uki again thought back to his balancing feats in the stream where he grew up. He should be able to manage the beam. There *were* a few other complications, though.

'What about his guards?' Uki whispered back. 'They'll slice me into pieces before I can do anything!'

'I might be able to do something about that.' Jori, her fingers still trembling from the dusk potion, fumbled open one of the pockets at her belt. She brought out a small roll of leather and unfurled it. Inside were rows of tiny packets and vials.

'Poison?' Uki asked.

'Most of it's still dry,' whispered Jori. She pulled out a thin glass tube filled with blue powder. 'This should do the trick. If you can crawl along the beam and drop this into the fire, it will burn into a cloud of smoke. It's not the best way to deliver a dose. It might knock them all out, or it might just make them dizzy. Depends how much they breathe. Either way, it'll give you a chance to jump down and get at Valkus. Maybe.'

'Aren't you coming?' Uki's eyes were wide and frightened. He could feel his throat clenching in terror. Was he really about to do this? On his own?

'I don't think I can crawl along that beam,' whispered Jori. 'Too risky. I can hardly keep my eyes open. If I fell . . . it would ruin everything. I'm sorry.'

'It's all right,' said Uki, although it really wasn't. *Come on,* he told himself. *You can do this. Climb the beam, drop the powder, trap the spirit. It will be fine.*

Except it won't, said another voice. **You're just a scared little rabbit. This is a job for a hero, not a funny-furred nobody from a scrappy stone hut in the middle of nowhere. You should have stayed in that graveyard, where you belonged. Now you're going to fall off that beam or drop the powder or start crying. Everything will be ruined.**

'Uki.' He felt Jori grip his shoulder, and realised he'd been staring into the air while both sides of himself argued. 'You can do this Uki. Iffrit trusted you. *I* trust you. I know it's frightening, but difficult things always are. Here. Take the potion. Climb the beam. Go now, while you have a chance.'

She pressed the vial into Uki's paw and nudged him to the window. Uki took a deep breath and somehow, even though the terrified half of his brain was screaming at him not to, he found himself climbing through the window and on to the beam.

Chapter Sixteen

The Spirit of War

Just breathe.

And move.

And do them both really *quietly.*

The beam was about thirty centimetres wide, made of heavy oak, stained black with centuries of smoke and soot. It was rough and uneven, with bumps and dips that made Uki feel like he was constantly about to slip and tumble to the longhouse floor.

That's because you are, said his cruel voice.

Be quiet, he told it.

He could hear the mumble of speech from below

growing louder with each shuffle. The fire snapped and hissed as if it was hungry for him to tumble into it.

One paw forward, then another. You're back in the Ice Wastes. You're walking across the top of a dam. You've done this hundreds and hundreds of times.

The vial of poison was clutched – *very* carefully – between his teeth. If he did fall, he would probably bite into it. He wondered what would kill him first: the fall, the fire, a mouthful of poison, or the spears of the guards. Such a wonderful range to choose from.

You can do it, he told himself. *This is your one chance to catch Valkus. Think of all the rabbits whose houses are burning right now. Think of your friends. They all need you.*

How strange life is, Uki marvelled. A few days ago nobody but his mother cared that he even existed. Now, two whole cities were depending on him.

Breathe.

Move.

He chanced a look down, trying to ignore the sudden dizziness he felt at how far away the floor seemed. It felt like he had crept a mile or more, but it was only twenty paces. The good news was that he had reached the fire. It was time to drop the poison.

Trying to lift his paw from the beam was almost impossible. It was as if it had been glued there, his mind telling him that moving it would instantly tip him off, into the flames. With a *push* of willpower, he managed it, taking the vial from his lips with trembling fingers.

Down below, Mayor Renard was still talking to his men. Snatches of words drifted up to Uki, such as 'crush' and 'attack'. It was hard to focus on what they were saying when he kept seeing glimpses of Valkus overlapping the figure of Renard. A ghostly shape, winding round and round upon itself like a nest of thorny snakes. If it happened to look up and spot him . . .

As quickly as he dared, Uki tipped the vial up and shook it, watching as the blue powder trickled down into the flames. There was a tiny hissing noise as it hit the fire and Uki held his breath – against the smoke, and in terror that one of the rabbits would notice it.

He had half expected a billowing cloud to burst out, filling the hall with toxic fumes, making the guard rabbits choke and retch. The flames sparked a few times where the powder landed and then . . . nothing.

Uki chanced a look over his shoulder, back to where Jori waited. He waggled his eyebrows, trying to signal her without speaking.

'Is that what's supposed to happen?' he wanted to ask, but all he could see of Jori was a slumped shadow at the window. It looked as though she had finally passed out. Now he really *was* on his own.

He looked back down at the guard rabbits and Mayor Renard. None of them had fallen over yet. In fact, nothing at all had happened.

What do I do now? he thought. He could feel the panic beginning to swell, his breathing getting faster and faster. *Shall I jump down anyway? Shall I try dropping a spear on Renard's head?*

Everything he thought of sounded stupid. He was on the verge of crawling back to Jori, shaking her awake and asking her what to do, when he noticed one of the guards put his paw to his mouth and yawn.

Uki bit his lip. He stared down, watching the rabbits below so intently he was surprised they couldn't feel his gaze burning into them.

The guard yawned again. And so did the other one.

'Am I keeping you fools awake?'

Renard's raised voice was loud enough for Uki to hear it clearly. The image of Valkus blazed into view: a mass of spikes jutting out in anger, red eyes burning.

One of the guards mumbled something and then stumbled, almost falling into the fire. The other one was leaning heavily on his spear, but the poison didn't seem to have affected the Mayor.

Perhaps the spirit inside him makes him stronger, Uki thought. *Like Iffrit does to me.*

'What is wrong with you idiots?' Renard/Valkus shouted. 'I'll have your heads for this! Guards! Arrest these rabbits!'

Uki's heart almost stopped beating. If more soldiers came, he would never get to Valkus. This was it. Now. This very instant. He *had* to do something.

Mother, help me, he prayed, hoping she was

somewhere, looking down on him, protecting him.

Without even a scrap of a plan, he jumped to his feet and ran along the beam, trusting his balancing skills to keep him from stumbling.

As soon as he was clear of the fire, he leapt, heading for the hard floor below and relying on Iffrit's strength to stop his leg bones from shattering when he landed. His stomach seemed to remain up on the beam as he fell, as graceful as a bellyflopping badger, to land just a few paces away from Mayor Renard.

Thump!

His feet hit the floor and he tumbled, leaping up as quickly as he could.

Thank the Goddess, he thought, realising all his limbs were still intact, and fumbled behind his head for a spear. The mayor – or his body, at least – turned to face him. But Uki couldn't see any trace of the portly, ginger-furred rabbit. His vision was filled by the bristling shape of Valkus, rearing up like a cobra, spikes jutting out all over in a fan of prickly fury.

He's not really there, Uki told himself. *He's just*

a speck of light somewhere inside the mayor's head. The blades and spikes – that's just what he wants you to see.

'You!' Valkus shouted. 'I saw you at the match! You stink of Iffrit, that cursed fire spirit! And what is that on your chest?'

Valkus stared at the crystal in Uki's buckle for a moment before shrinking back in terror. He realised what it was, what it meant.

'Gaunch? You've captured Gaunch?'

'Yes,' said Uki. He grasped a spear and drew it from its sheath, thankfully avoiding getting it tangled in his ears. 'And I'm going to capture *you* too!'

'No!' Valkus writhed. His jaws gnashed, razor-blade teeth striking sparks from one another. 'It's not possible! You can't stop me now! You're just a child! Where is Iffrit? Let him show himself and face me!'

'I am Iffrit!' Uki shouted back, sounding much braver than he felt. 'And he is me! We're going to stop you, and the others. You're going back into a crystal, and this time you're going to stay there.'

'Never!' Valkus's body twisted and vanished in a blink. Uki stared in shock for a moment, before realising that the mayor was still there. Moving swiftly towards him with a drawn sword. Valkus was using Renard's body to fight back.

This definitely *wasn't part of the plan,* Uki thought as he jumped backwards, just in time to avoid the blade that was whistling towards him. Why hadn't they thought Valkus would attack them? Why hadn't Jori taught him some sword moves? At least the two guards weren't joining in. They were still stumbling backwards and forwards, shaking their heads, trying to clear them. Not that it mattered: Valkus was going to be more than enough for Uki to deal with.

The mayor's body swung the sword sideways, making Uki duck. That one had skimmed his ears, shaving a little patch of white and black fur from each. He raised his spear and hopped backwards again. He could hear voices from somewhere within the longhouse now, and footsteps. More guards were on their way. They could be here any second. He had to trap Valkus before they arrived, or it was all over.

'I am War!' screamed Valkus. 'You will never catch me! I will fill this whole planet with battle and

blood and death!' He let loose a surge of rage that almost knocked Uki off his feet. It was backed up with a sword thrust aimed right at Uki's heart.

'No!' Uki cried. Pure instinct made him sweep his spear across, blocking the blade. Valkus roared in frustration. He rotated his sword, flicking it around Uki's spear and slamming it down, pinning the shaft to the side of the firepit.

Uki tugged at it, but it was stuck tight. Worse, his right arm was stretched outwards, leaving his body wide open. Valkus stepped closer, into striking distance, and drew a long, curved dagger from his belt. He raised it up and all Uki could do was stare at the shining tip. That, and the eyes of the mayor that were now mixed with the stare of Valkus, glowing red pinpoints of hatred at the centre of his pupils.

'Uki! Your other spears!'

A voice echoed down from the rafters. For one second Uki thought it might be the ghost of his mother, until he remembered Jori was up there. She must have woken just in time to see the battle, to see him die . . .

Your other spears. Of course! He had more in the

sheath at his back. If he could reach them in time . . .

Valkus's dagger began to fall, the curved edge heading for the base of Uki's neck. He could see its path like an inevitable, unstoppable line.

Using every last scrap of speed and strength in his body, Uki began to move. His only chance, slim as a whisker, was that Iffrit's power would make him fast enough.

Uki's left paw reached up behind his head, grasping for a spear haft. He had less than a heartbeat to grab it and strike. Half a blink to save his life, to save everyone . . .

Please, he prayed. *Please* . . .

Chapter Seventeen

The Knife and the Spear

The long, curved dagger. Silver steel, flashing orange in the firelight.

It seems to hang there, frozen. Everything has stopped: swirls of smoke from the fire, the blade plunging towards him, even his own heartbeat.

Uki thought this in the space between seconds. Time had slowed to a sticky crawl somehow. Each breath seemed to last a lifetime. Was this another of Iffrit's gifts? Or was it just what happened when you were about to die?

Stop wondering about that, you stupid rabbit. You've been given a chance. Use it!

Uki's dark voice was right for once. He focused on the blade, seeing there was no way to avoid it. But there was hope: if he moved just a few centimetres to the right . . .

Time snapped back into speed, and Valkus's blade came down, slicing into Uki's flesh.

Not his neck, which would have killed him, but his shoulder. That tiny movement, the width of his paw, had saved his life.

It still hurt, though. A burning shock of pain that made him scream. He turned it into a yell of rage, as his reaching fingers finally connected with a spear haft.

While Valkus's dagger was still stuck in his shoulder, Uki brought the spear up and over in a stabbing motion of his own. He smacked the tip of the crystal right in between the eyes of the mayor, as hard as he could.

Even with Uki's boosted strength, the blunt crystal was barely sharp enough to break the mayor's skin. But that didn't matter. As soon as it was close enough, the crystal began to do its job, sucking out the spirit form of Valkus like an oversized mosquito drinking blood.

Uki heard the echo of a scream and felt a surge of heat and rage. It flooded the tip of his spear and flowed down his arm, filling his body completely.

For a horrible instant, he knew what it was like to *be* Valkus. To want to fight and kill and destroy for no other reason than the twisted pleasure of it. It made him want to snatch the mayor's sword and attack the two stunned guards, and then rush out of the longhouse to battle anything else that moved. It made him want to scream and burn and kill. It was pure, primal anger from some ancient memory of being a frightened animal. Something his body had forgotten and buried with better instincts of peace and kindness.

And then the power of Iffrit took over.

Uki could actually *see* the calming orange glow as it washed out from his head, down over his body. When it reached the crystal, it seemed to soak in, like water poured on dry sand. Uki felt the change almost instantly. It was as if a door had been locked shut, a flame had been blown out. Every last scrap of Valkus's fury was gone. The most potent and important of all the powers Iffrit had been given, Uki now realised, was to be able to bind these creatures inside their prisons, cutting off the spells they cast on the outside world.

Valkus was sealed inside the crystal, which was now glowing scarlet. All the anger and hate was now channelled into strength. Uki felt his own power, which had been slowly ebbing, come bubbling back, twice, three times greater than before.

He stood for a moment, gasping, just as the longhouse door burst open and a crowd of guards rushed in, weapons drawn.

The mayor, free of Valkus now, slumped to the floor. The guards stood, frozen in place by the sight of their leader apparently knocked out by a small, black-and-white furred rabbit with a glowing spear. More than that, the overpowering feeling of rage and battle lust that had filled them for days had suddenly vanished. It was like they had woken from some terrible blood-soaked nightmare, and were back to their ordinary rabbit selves. They blinked and shook their heads, not sure what was real or dream any more. One or two actually staggered, leaning against each other for support.

'Wh— Where am I? Who am I?' Mayor Renard looked up from the floor, staring at Uki with puzzled eyes.

Uki slotted his unused spear back in his harness, then reached up to his shoulder where the dagger still jutted, and pulled it out with a sharp tug. He let it clatter to the floor, wincing as he felt his body begin to stitch the wound back together.

'Don't just stand there! Run!' Jori hissed down at him from her perch on the windowsill. Uki looked up at her and shrugged. He could probably charge through the guards and knock them all to the floor, but there was a chance one of them might still be angry enough to jab him with something sharp, and he'd had quite enough of that for one evening. He was, he discovered, sick to his back teeth of fighting and running and being scared.

Instead he calmly unscrewed the crystal from the end of his other spear and slotted it into his harness buckle, next to Gaunch's. There was a little crackle of lightning as the captured spirits came close together.

Uki dropped the empty spear shaft to the floor and wandered over to one of the feasting tables. It was solid oak, over a hundred years old, and a good four metres long. He grabbed it with two paws and hoisted it into the air like it was a piece of kindling. There were gasps from the guards, and some of them rubbed their eyes, unable to believe what they were seeing.

Jori was leaning over the windowsill now, yelling at him. 'What under earth are you doing? Stop rearranging the furniture and get out of there!'

Uki walked until he was just beneath her and then propped the table up against the wall, making a ramp. With a final backward glance at the guards, he began to climb up it to the window that Jori was hanging from.

'Hey … um … stop?' said one of the guards, although he didn't sound very convincing. The others just stared at him.

Their attention was drawn away a second later by the mayor, who had managed to sit himself up. 'Help me,' he groaned.

While the guards rushed to pick up their confused leader, Uki hopped up to the window and then kicked the table end away. As it crashed to the floor, he clambered out on to the roof, next to Jori.

'What are you playing at?' she said. 'They could have captured you easily!'

'Can't you feel it?' Uki replied. 'Valkus is gone. The spell he held over all these rabbits has disappeared. They're all dizzy, confused. I expect they can't even remember what they've been doing.'

'What about the mayor?' Jori looked back through the window to where the guards were carrying Renard out of the hall, backs straining under his considerable weight.

'It'll be like Nurg's brother, I should think,' said Uki. 'He won't know where or who he is for a while. Then he might come back to himself.'

Jori stared for a moment at the new crystal in Uki's buckle. Its glowing red light throbbed and surged, and she imagined the furious Valkus in there, battering helplessly at the walls. 'We'd better go,' she said. 'Whatever's confusing all the guards might not last long.'

Uki started to help her walk along the rooftop, but then found it was easier just to pick her up. Jori was so exhausted, she couldn't even object. He hopped back up to the walkway, and then over the fence in a bound, landing on the steep side of the mound.

'Capturing Valkus gave you more power, I see,' Jori said as they skidded their way down the slope.

Uki nodded. 'Yes. But we still have to get through that lot.'

Setting Jori down, he pointed to the fortress gateway. There were crowds of rabbits milling around, most with empty buckets hanging from their paws. Buildings smouldered around them as they scratched their heads, wondering what they were doing out of bed in the middle of the night, and why everything was black and crispy.

As they watched, some kind of commotion started. The dazed rabbits were being shoved aside as something large pushed its way through the crowd.

Uki held his breath. The way the night was going, it was bound to be something awful like Necripha or Venic come to attack them again.

Instead, he was pleasantly surprised to see Mooka

the jerboa hopping towards them with Kree on his back, waving.

'You did it!' she shouted. 'I knew you had! The fighting suddenly stopped and Mooka wasn't going crazy any more! I knew you'd beaten Valkus. I rode straight here to find you . . .'

Uki hurried over, handing Jori up to her. 'We did do it,' he said. 'But we had better not stand around here for too long. The guards could come to their senses at any moment, and there's the others to worry about.'

'You mean Venic and those rabbits that captured you?' Kree helped Jori to sit on the saddle in front of her, wrapping the bigger rabbit in her little arms. 'I haven't seen any sign of them, but you're right. We should get as far away from the city as we can before dawn.'

With Uki leading them, they headed out of the fortress gates, turning south and making for Syn's main entrance. The streets were still filled with smoke but were now eerily silent. Small crowds of rabbits stood here and there, that familiar look of bewilderment in their eyes.

They were almost at the gate itself when a hulking dark shape stepped out of the shadows, blocking their path. Uki recognised the figure of Balto, Necripha's henchman, in his black hood and robes.

'*Pok ha boc!*' cursed Kree. 'Why is nothing ever easy?'

Balto took a step towards them, breaking through the wisps of smoke like a slinking serpent through long grass. Something glinted in his paws – a dagger in each, curved and deadly. Uki scanned the buildings all around for Necripha herself, and caught a glimpse of a second hooded figure inside a burnt doorway, keeping back out of danger.

'Do you think you can take him, Uki?' Jori asked. 'I still can't even hold a blade. I took too much potion before . . .'

'Maybe,' said Uki. The strength of the spirits still bubbled through his blood, but Balto was at least three times the size of him. And then there was Necripha. Who knew what she was planning to do while Balto was attacking them?

'Climb up here with us,' said Kree. 'Mooka can charge through him.'

‘Will he be able to take all our weight?’ Uki asked.

‘Neek!’

Taking that for an answer, Uki hopped up behind Kree and the three of them clung together. ‘Hai! Hai! Mooka!’ she yelled and kicked at his flanks. Just as in the challenge on the plains, Mooka leapt forwards, leaving the ground like a speeding sparrowhawk.

He reached Balto in seconds, barging past the startled rabbit, who didn’t even have time to raise his daggers. Just for good measure, Uki gave him a kick as they passed. He put all of his boosted strength behind it and watched over his shoulder as Balto flew through the air and into the window of a shop.

The hulking henchman burst straight through the shutters and disappeared from sight. Judging by the cascading, smashing sound, it was a pottery shop. Uki hoped there would be lots of sharp clay shards involved.

Even more satisfying than the crashing and tinkling was the cry of frustration from Necripha. Uki thought he saw her step into the road and glare after them. There was a flash of those three, red eyes . . . and then they were gone around the corner, flying through the streets to the gate.

*

They found the gate open, with scores of rabbits wandering aimlessly around the fields and farmland. Judging by their packs and bundles, they had been fleeing the fires and the fighting. Now that their minds had suddenly cleared, they were lost and dazed, like startled sheep, like freshly woken sleepwalkers.

Mooka kept up his gallop until they had left the cities well behind. He took them up the road, on until they reached the crest of a hill, where they all clambered down and flopped into the long grass at the roadside. The air was clear of smoke here, fresh and sweet. To the east, the sky was beginning to lighten as dawn crept across the plains.

'At last,' said Kree, with a happy sigh. 'Open air. No buildings squashing you in on every side.'

'And no evil rabbits trying to kill us,' Uki added.

'For now,' said Jori. They all sat in silence for a while as Mooka nibbled at the grass seeds and flowers around them. Their paws were shaking, their bodies exhausted. What a night of endless running, fighting and terror it had been.

'So,' said Kree, breaking the silence. 'What do we do now? Where do we go?'

All eyes turned to Uki, who chewed his lip for a moment.

'What happened at the match,' he began, 'when I left you behind . . . It was wrong and I'm sorry. But I did it because I was scared of you all getting hurt. This thing I'm doing . . . it's not a "quest" like in the stories. It's real and it's dangerous. I don't have any right to ask you to come along, and you don't *have* to. It's not like you're my family and I can just expect you to do things for me.' Uki stopped and rubbed his face. He was tired. *So* tired, and finding the right words to say was difficult at the best of times.

'What I mean is . . . *I* have to go on and find the other spirits now. It will be hard and frightening. Maybe even worse than capturing Valkus was. But I have to finish what I started, even with Necripha and the Endwatch trying to stop me.

'I would love it if you two came with me. But I will understand if you don't want to. The spirits are out there and I will find them. You both have lives and problems of your own. If something happened to you because of me . . . I would never forgive myself.'

Silence fell again and Uki closed his eyes, hoping against hope that his new friends would want to stay with him and dreading it too, a little. Would it be better to have them by his side always, or to never see them again yet know they were safe?

In the end, it was Jori who spoke first.

'Pretty much everything you just said was completely wrong.' She laughed. 'Except for the parts about it being hard and dangerous.'

'What do you mean?' Uki asked.

'Well, first of all, this *is* our task now, as much as it is yours. Am I right, Kree?'

'By Mooka's invisible tail, yes!'

'Secondly, you *do* have the right to ask us because – and here is where you were the most wrong of all – we *are* family now.'

'Really?' Uki found tears beginning to pool in his eyes. 'Family?'

'Of course!' Kree shouted, giving him one of her bone-crushing hugs.

'Of course,' Jori agreed. 'We've all lost or escaped or been cast out by our real families. But we have each other. We take care of each other, and worry about each other and protect each other. Isn't that what a family is?'

'And after everything we went through last night,' added Kree, 'we trust each other with our lives. *That's* what makes a family. Trust and love.'

'Thank you,' Uki whispered. Trust and love. Two things he didn't think he'd have from any other rabbit than his mother. He'd never even considered that a family doesn't have to be related to you.

Through the tiredness and tears, he smiled. A great big smile that seemed to stretch out all over his body, filling him up completely.

'And now all the talking's over,' said Jori. 'Does anyone mind if we find somewhere to sleep? I think I might actually die of exhaustion in a minute.'

With much groaning and stretching, they picked themselves up and looked for a quiet copse of trees to sleep the day away in. The Endwatch might be hunting them, Clan Septys might be hunting them, there were two more spirits still to find … but all those were problems for another morning.

I might have mixed-up fur and eyes, Uki thought. *I might be an outcast. But like Mother said, I have a good heart and kind thoughts. And now I have true friends to go with them.*

And for once, his dark voice could say nothing to disagree.

Chapter Eighteen

Endwatch Tower

The bard finishes his tale and there is a long moment of silence. From the corner of his eye, Rue watches Jori as she stares into the firepit, reliving memories from long ago that have suddenly had a storyteller's life breathed into them.

Finally she speaks. 'Bravo, Pook. Bravo.'

The bard smiles, as though this praise is as good as any standing ovation.

'Was that really what happened?' Rue asks. 'I mean, my master wasn't actually there, not like with Podkin's story . . .'

'Yes,' says Jori. 'How did you make such a good account? You knew things that I didn't.'

'Ah,' says the bard. 'The story came from Yarrow, *my* master. And he spoke at length with you and Uki and Kree, if you remember. I think he might even have travelled Hulstland, searching out all the other characters, before he stitched the story together. He taught it to me when I started my training with him. It was the first tale I learnt.'

'And now you're passing it on, too,' says Jori, with a smile. 'How sweet.'

'Yes, yes, enough of that,' says the bard. 'Shall we try and get some sleep? I'm guessing it's a long walk to this tower tomorrow, and you and I are not young rabbits any longer.'

Jori laughs again and begins to shovel soil back into the firepit, putting out the flames. For a moment Rue considers asking her where Uki and Kree are now, why she isn't with them. But then he thinks better of it. She isn't the bard, after all, and – nice as she seems – she is still a trained fighter. The worst the bard can do when he gets annoyed is to clonk Rue on the head with his staff. No, that question will keep for another day.

The darkness of the forest comes flooding in, and Rue shivers. It takes a moment for his eyes to adjust to the dark. When they do, he sees Jori reaching one of her scarred paws out to him. 'Here, little one. We have to put the fire out, in case the light is seen. But if you sleep on top of the pit, it will keep you warm.'

She helps him spread his cloak over the patch of earth where the firepit had been. Just as she said, there is welcome heat spreading up through the ground. Rue snuggles into it, while the bard makes himself comfortable nearby and quickly begins to snore. Rue's eyes are already beginning to close too. The last thing he sees is Jori, sitting against one of the white-barked trees. Her fingers tap gently against the flask on her belt as she stares out into the forest.

He has a feeling it will be a long while before she joins them in sleeping.

*

They wake at first light and break camp. Little is said as they all slept poorly. Rue's dreams were full of sneaking forest creatures and monsters buried underneath the ground in ancient prisons. The bard must have been worrying about what he will find at the tower. He keeps staring off into the distance and tugging his beard. Things he does when something is on his mind.

When everything has been stowed in their packs, they take an apple and some cornbread with them for breakfast, munching them on the way. Rue carries the sparrow cage in both paws, trying not to shake the little bird about too much. It cheeps and flutters, peeping out at him with its bright, brown eyes.

Out of the forest they walk, and begin to follow its edge, up towards the foothills of the Arukh mountains.

It is bleak countryside. On their right is a stretch of brambly, knotted ground and behind that, the tangled trees of Icebark. On their left, the hills begin to rise. Tufts of grass sprout here and there amongst knobbly lumps of granite. There are gorse bushes and heather scattered about, breaking up the greyness with their yellow-and-purple flowers. Behind them, the mountain peaks block out the horizon. They stare down on them like silent giants, their snowy heads hidden by wisps of mist and cloud.

Not much grows here and there is no sign of rabbit life, except for a faint path that traces the forest edge.

They walk in silence for most of the day, each of them flicking nervous glances towards the mountains, half expecting a screaming party of Arukh braves to charge down from them. But there are no signs of life except for the odd eagle, tiny dots spiralling lazily in the distance.

It is an hour or so after midday that they see it. A black smudge on a misty hilltop: the remains of the Endwatch tower. They stand for a moment, staring at it suspiciously.

'You have the youngest eyes, Rue,' says the bard. 'Any signs of life? Wood smoke? Movement?'

Rue squints at it until his eyes water. As far as he can see it's nothing but a jumble of blackened stone.

Just in case, they move closer to the treeline, using the bramble bushes as cover. It makes the going slow. The tower doesn't seem to get any bigger, and Rue begins to think they'll never reach it.

At one point, they startle a group of crows. Fat, flapping things with feathers black as midnight.

They burst into the sky in a thunderstorm of caws, making all three of the rabbits jump.

'Well, that's given us away,' says the bard. He mumbles a curse under his breath.

'What were they doing here?' Rue asks. His little heart is hammering against the walls of his chest.

Jori bends to the ground and holds up a withered carrot top, a hunk of dried orange flesh still clinging to the stalk. 'Someone made camp here,' she says. 'There's other bits of food, signs of a fire. And the ground is trampled.'

'Can you tell who? When?' The bard asks.

Jori shakes her head. 'I don't have Kree's tracking skills. It was a fortnight or more ago at least.'

'Probably just those woods rabbits,' says the bard.

'Let's hope so,' says Jori.

*

They reach the tower soon after. Hiding in the bushes, Rue peers out at it, his ears trembling.

Some places seem to have their own character he has noticed, and the character of this one is not good. Cold, desolate, unwelcoming. If it were a rabbit, it would be an evil old hermit living alone in a cave, waiting to jump on innocent passers-by and eat them.

Made of stocky granite blocks, it juts up from the hillside, three or four storeys high. There are bare, empty windows at the top, and a crudely carved eye stares out above each one. If it had a roof, it has now burnt away and crumbled, just like the other buildings that once surrounded it.

Rue can see that there used to be quite a settlement here, one that was thoroughly put to the torch. Only jumbles of stone remain to mark walls and doorways. Here and there are pieces of roof framework, reduced to blackened ribs by fire. He shudders at the thought of rabbits that would choose to live here, that and the image of the three-eyed Necripha stalking between the huts and houses with her evil red glare.

'What do you think?' whispers the bard. 'Is anyone there?'

Jori watches for a long time before she shakes her head. 'If they ever were here, they're not now. I can't see or hear anything moving. It doesn't look like anyone's been here since it burnt down.'

'You did a good job of destroying it,' says the bard. 'There's almost nothing left.'

Jori flicks her tattered ears. 'Quite. I can't see what anyone would want here. Unless we missed something.'

'Shall we go in?' asks the bard.

Jori nods. 'We should see if there are any traces. A quick scout, and then we can get away as soon as possible.'

Nobody wants to be here, Rue thinks, relieved it's not just him. In its cage, the little sparrow cheeps, as if agreeing with him.

Holding their breath, they dash across the open ground to the tower. Rue has convinced himself an arrow or a spear will come flying down on to his head, but nothing happens. Keeping close together, they tiptoe around the tower edge until they come to a doorway.

A dark, open rectangle in the black stone, it stands amongst a toppled heap of rubble and timbers. The door itself has burnt away, leaving nothing but charred hinges. To Rue's horror, there are signs the rubble has been cleared, leaving the way open. There are footsteps in the soot and dust.

'Someone *has* been here,' says the bard, through gritted teeth.

'And recently, too,' adds Jori. She bends and points to the prints, still clear and untouched by wind or rain.

'It could be just travellers,' says the bard. 'Passing woods rabbits looking for shelter. Children daring each other to go in the haunted tower . . .'

Jori draws her sword, making Rue's eyes bulge. It looks sharp enough to cut through sunlight. 'Stay behind me,' she says.

And they all step inside.

*

The air is different in the tower. Damp, freezing, full of the ghostly scent of old fire and mildew. Even with the light from the open doorway, it is hard to see anything. Their feet scuff amongst the dirt and ash on the stone floor.

'Hold on a minute,' says Jori. She unslings her pack and roots in it. Rue hears the rasp of flint and metal followed by a flash of light. A few seconds later, Jori holds up a candle. She lights two more with its flame and hands them out.

Holding his flickering candle in one paw and the

sparrow's cage in the other, Rue looks around the room. He sees piles of rubble against the walls, covered with the pale tendrils of weeds and vines. There are empty torch sconces here and there. A broken table, pieces of smashed, burnt pottery. The silent reminders that rabbits once lived here – eating, talking, drinking.

'Look!' Jori's voice echoes around the empty room, breaking the ghostly silence. Rue hurries over to the bard, presses as close to him as he can, and feels the old rabbit wrap a protective arm around him. They hold up their candles and peer over to where Jori stands, pointing.

She is by a staircase leading upwards, the door at the top choked shut with bricks and wood. In front of her a trapdoor stands open, its depths an even deeper black than the inky darkness they are standing in.

'We never knew this was here,' she says. 'We *did* miss something.'

'What's down there?' asks the bard, his voice wobbling slightly.

'Looks like some kind of library,' says Jori. 'I can see piles of scrolls and books. They're all thrown across the floor, like someone's ransacked the place.'

‘A secret library,’ whispers the bard. ‘All the knowledge of the Endwatch.’

Rue hopes that they don’t have to go down there, secret knowledge or not. He looks back towards the entrance, longing for daylight and open air . . . and spots something on the wall.

‘What’s that?’ he says, holding up his candle.

The bard lifts his too, lighting up the wall in flickering orange. Somebody *has* been at the books and scrolls, it seems. Pages and scraps of parchment have been stuck to the stone with blobs of candlewax. Some have been circled in charcoal, as if marking them out as important.

The bard hurries over and begins to read, his eyes darting and lips moving as he translates and deciphers all the different runes and languages. Rue recognises one or two pieces of ogham, but there are many more types of writing. Pictograms and symbols, flowing script and scratches. To him they just look like senseless inky scribbles.

‘Prophecies,’ mutters the bard. ‘These are all pieces of prophecies.’

‘About what?’ Jori asks, coming over to stare.

'I'm not sure yet,' says the bard. 'This one is in Old Gott, from hundreds of years ago. These are Thriantan, even older, and this one is from *The Gormalechnicon* by Rabdul Bunhazred. I've met him, you know.'

'Why are some of them marked?' Rue asks. 'Are they important?'

'Let me see,' says the bard. 'This one says:

'Neath thorny mound, by swamp
and grass,
The legend rests 'til evil's passed.'

'Some kind of riddle,' Jori says. 'But it must be important. They came all the way up here and tore through the library to find it.'

'Here's another circled one,' says the bard.

'Bane of the iron god: hoarder of Gifts,
Hidden by thorned wood, while
Watchers exist.'

'There's a candle down there,' says Rue, spotting

a cluster of items on a broken chair. 'They must have left it here.'

Jori goes over, rifling through pieces of charcoal, a chunk of flint, an empty clay bottle. Her fingers pinch at the abandoned candle's wick, and then she jumps back, raising her sword.

'It's still warm!' she cries. 'They're here! They're here!'

As soon as the words leave her mouth, there is a grinding, crunching noise from outside. Stone blocks and rubble from the pile by the doorway come crashing down, blocking the entrance, cutting off the daylight, sealing them inside.

'We're trapped!' Rue shouts, making the sparrow flutter madly in its cage.

Jori dashes to the blocked doorway, where a small gap at the top still remains. She jumps back a second later as an arrow pings off the stonework. 'Whiskers! That nearly took out my eye!'

'Did you see how many?' the bard asks. 'Are they Endwatch?'

'There's at least five,' Jori says. 'Black, hooded cloaks. It looks like the Watch.'

'Clarion curse them!' The bard slaps his paw against the wall, dislodging a sheet of parchment.

'I can see two leaving,' says Jori. She has crept to the hole again and is peering out, trying not to let herself be seen. 'The others have gone into the ruined buildings for cover. Damn it!'

She jerks back as another arrow pings from the rubble.

'Hold your fire!' she shouts out. 'We're just travellers, looking for shelter! We mean you no harm!'

The sound of laughter echoes back to them. 'Nice try! We know who you are, dusk wraith. And the bard with you must be part of your stupid Foxguard. You can stay in there and starve, or step out and be shot. Either way, you're all dead.'

'Nixha take them!' says Jori. 'How did they find out about the guard?'

The bard doesn't answer. He is staring at the piece of parchment in his paw. His ears are trembling and his fingers shake. He looks terrified.

'What is it?' Rue asks, hardly daring to find out if something could be worse than getting trapped in a scary tower by armed villains. 'What does it say?'

The bard licks his lips. He looks at Jori and Rue with wide, startled eyes. 'It's another piece of prophecy,' he says, then reads aloud:

'Twelve Gifts, One Ear: a hero grand.
The razor's back blocks seeker's hand.'

'But what does it mean?' Rue asks, his eyes brimming with tears. 'Why are you so frightened?'

'I understand it now,' says the bard. 'I know why they came here.'

'Why?' Jori moves next to Rue and takes his paw. Both of them hold their breath.

'They've found out,' says the bard. 'They've found out the very thing we've always dreaded. The one thing we wanted to keep from them.'

The bard closes his eyes, scrunching the parchment in his clenched fist.

'They know where Podkin is. They know he's hiding in Thornwood, and they've gone to kill him.'

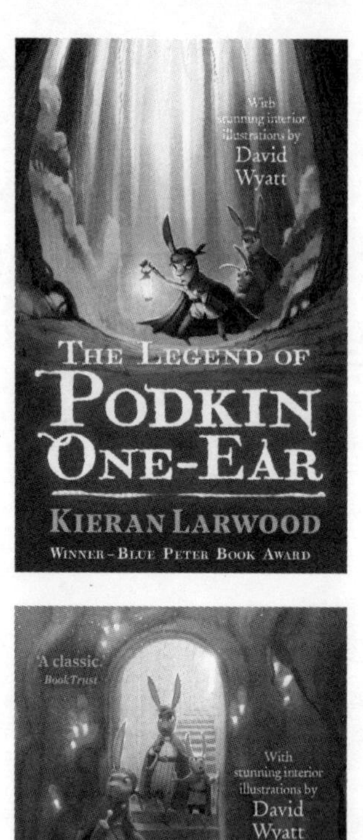
With stunning interior illustrations by
David Wyatt
THE LEGEND OF
PODKIN ONE-EAR
KIERAN LARWOOD
WINNER – BLUE PETER BOOK AWARD
'A classic.' Book Trust
With stunning interior illustrations by
David Wyatt
THE GIFT OF
DARK HOLLOW
KIERAN LARWOOD
WINNER – BLUE PETER BOOK AWARD

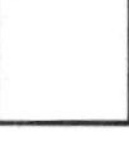

'World-class... five stars.' Lovereading4kids
David Wyatt
THE
BEASTS
OF
GRIMHEART
KIERAN LARWOOD
WINNER – BLUE PETER BOOK AWARD

Have you read the other exciting adventures in the Five Realms series?

A thick white blanket covers the wide slopes of the band of hills known as the Razorback Downs . . .

Podkin is the son of a warrior chieftain. He knows that one day it will be up to him to lead his warren and guard it in times of danger. But for now, he's quite happy to laze around annoying his older sister, Paz, and playing with his baby brother, Pook. Then Podkin's home is brutally attacked, and the young rabbits are forced to flee. The terrifying Gorm are on the rampage, and no one and nowhere is safe. With danger all around them, Podkin must protect his family, uncover his destiny, and attempt to defeat the most horrifying enemy rabbitkind has ever known.

Coming in September 2020

Uki, Jori and Kree's quest continues as they confront the third evil spirit, Charice, who is spreading disease across the Fenlands.